Escape to the

Helga Jensen is an award-winning British/Danish best selling author and journalist. Helga holds a BA Hons in English Literature and Creative Writing, along with a Creative Writing MA from Bath Spa University. She is currently working on a PhD.

Also by Helga Jensen

HELGA JENSEN

Escape *to the* French Riviera

hera

First published in the United Kingdom in 2025 by

Hera Books
Unit 9 (Canelo), 5th Floor
Cargo Works, 1–2 Hatfields
London SE1 9PG
United Kingdom

A CIP catalogue record for this book is available from the British Library.

Print ISBN 978 1 80436 931 9
Ebook ISBN 978 1 80436 934 0

Look for more great books at www.herabooks.com

Printed and bound in Great Britain by Clays Ltd, Elcograf S.p.A.

I

To the captain of my heart

Chapter One

The sound of the halyards clanking in the distance distracts me as the wind brews up in the marina. Normally, the repetitive chime would relax me, but today, it's like some kind of earworm that I can't get out of my head.

I stare at the blank page on my laptop, trying to ignore the outside noise as I wait for inspiration to come. But all I can hear is clink, clink, clink, and as much as I force myself to focus, no words come into my head. Zero, zilch, nada.

Oh, come on, brain. I want to write this book. Why is my head not on the same page? Like literally.

My creative writing tutor, Annie, said that I have talent, and I actually believed her. Now I am starting to think she might only have been saying that to get me to attend each week. The praise she gave me in the evening classes that I joined recently filled me with confidence. I thought I could make something of myself for once. I felt as though I could finally be more than that woman who had been made redundant from the local pet food store, or Michael's ex-wife and Poppy and Jasmine's mam. I could be the person I dreamed of being when I was young and had ambition. A woman who wasn't told by the careers officer that I couldn't be a novelist like I aspired to be but that there was a Youth Training Scheme at the local fashion retailer where I could earn £19 a week instead.

I duly applied and was reminded how fortunate I was to do the same amount of work as everyone else for a lot less pay, but at least I was being trained for a career in retail. A thirty-year career that ended in redundancy at the same time I found out about Michael's two-year affair. Eighteen months ago, I discovered I was to be made redundant in more ways than one.

With a redundancy package, a divorce settlement and a devastatingly unexpected new start, I found myself bewildered, single and shocked. How on earth was I supposed to suddenly adjust to life without the job I could do in my sleep and the husband I thought I knew so well? It took time. After nine months of feeling like a zombie, I had an epiphany. It was almost like a sign when the local community centre advertised creative writing sessions with a best-selling author. I felt as though this was my chance to be who I wanted to be all those years ago. Could I finally be a novelist and write that book? As I slowly came to terms with my new routines, I knew this was exactly what I needed.

Of course, it was nerve-racking the first time I walked into that class. All my confidence had evaporated after losing my husband and my job within three months of each other. Despite that, I was excited and went out and bought a beautiful new notebook before my initial class. I was so eager to learn.

However, even though I left home early, an unexpected road diversion held me up. I was the last one to arrive, and the whole room turned to glare as I walked in. With only one seat left for me in a crowded room, my nerves got the better of me. I wanted to walk back out and pretend I had a phone call to make as everyone stared at the latecomer. But before I could make any excuses, someone pulled a chair out for me and shuffled up the table with a smile. Then our tutor, Annie, put us at ease, and I remembered how much I wanted this. It was going to be okay.

The class was full of fellow introverts who were similarly terrified about sharing their work but within six weeks, we trusted each other and had built a bond. By the end of term drinks, Annie pulled me to one side to tell me she thought my work had promise. Her words made every endorphin in my body explode. I relished those words for weeks. I even wrote them down on a sticky note and stuck it on the side of my laptop screen.

'There's no reason you can't be published,' she told me over her gin and tonic. 'You just have to write that book. If you don't get those words down, well, you'll never be published. Just keep writing, it's that simple.'

I repeated the words to myself in the mirror every day for a month, but now, left to my own devices with the blank page, I am not feeling nearly as confident. Although the sticky note is crumpled and losing its stickiness, I keep it safe and remind myself of those words.

You have promise.

But, while I try to focus on the words and the laptop, sitting alone in my living room, I get a flashback to the moment I found out about Michael and his lady friend. The flashbacks won't go away, although they're not happening as often as they used to. I only had an Instagram account so that I could follow cat people, so I was shocked to find a message in my inbox from someone who had clearly made up a fake account. But there, waiting for me, was a picture of my husband's prized Porsche on someone's driveway. I recognised the house as it was only

3

around the corner from our family home. So, one night, I drove past to snoop. The house had fabulous hanging baskets outside, so I immediately assumed a woman lived there. Then I saw her walk out and look straight at me. She looked as though she had seen a ghost. Stereotypically, she was younger than me by about ten years. I got out of the car and asked her if she knew my husband, Michael. She informed me that she knew him as Mickey and not Michael. Was he lying about his name, or simply trying to sound more her age? I wasn't sure what he was trying to do, and I suppose it didn't really matter. The fact was that this affair had been going on for a lot longer than I would ever have guessed. I kicked myself for not seeing the signs, but perhaps Michael was a better liar than he was a husband. The woman said she was sorry that she didn't realise he was married and had only found out recently. He had lied to both of us.

The discovery that my perfect family life was a sham was the hardest thing I have ever dealt with. How could I not have known? There were days when I was as angry with myself as I was with Michael. Was I not enough for my husband? On a good day I realised that actually he wasn't good enough for me. But it wasn't always that easy to remember, and some days the tears and devastation over the loss of the future I had imagined in our old age were too much to deal with.

I closed my Instagram account and disappeared out of sight to try and pick up the pieces. But, despite my determination to become the person I wish I could be, when I get one of these flashbacks, my confidence flounders, and I think to myself that perhaps the time has come to stop living the dream. I have no inspiration to write the love story I want to, and the redundancy and divorce payout won't last forever either.

Perhaps it's time to get myself a 'proper' job as Michael keeps telling me. It probably is, but if he says that writing is only a hobby one more time, then I might put one of my cacti somewhere that the sun doesn't shine the next time he comes over on some spurious excuse for a visit. If you can't have a dream, then there's no hope in life.

He has always dissuaded me from my love of writing. I tried to write a short story once when the girls were born and I was on maternity leave. I read it excitedly to Michael, but he had no interest in it whatsoever. He suggested I enjoy the time off with the girls and that it wasn't the right time to take up a new hobby. Secretly, though, I kept a little journal in my bedside drawer. Sometimes, when everyone was asleep and I woke up in the night overthinking about the girls' problems in school, or whether they'd do well in exams, I would make notes in there. I used to read back what I'd written in those days, but I've stopped that now. It feels sad to look back at a time when we had so many plans as a family. So now I try to simply look forward. The only problem is that although I finally have the time and there's nobody to stop me writing, I struggle to write the love story I have always wanted to when I've no romance in my life. Some days I wonder if I shouldn't turn my hand to horror stories. I could probably relate far better to those right now.

Dating has certainly changed since Michael and I got together in the early Nineties. Carol, one of my best friends, tells me that it can quickly become a horror story if you're not careful, and the thought of a date with some stranger terrifies me.

Also, I don't even know how people manage to find dates unless they want their photos plastered all over an app. This doesn't appeal to me at all. Perhaps I need to write an old-fashioned love story where people bump into each other and fall in love. Although that doesn't seem to happen nowadays. But I know if I were ever to consider dating again, it would have to be with someone charming and romantic. I'd want to get to know them and take things nice and slowly. Proper courting stuff. Do people even do that any more?

As I try to stop my mind diverting to the scary methods of modern-day dating, I stare at the laptop, accepting that I am not going to get any writing done this morning. It's useless even trying, so I decide to ring my other best friend, Soraya, for a chat.

'Lucy, what good timing. I was just talking to Andrew about France.'

'Oh, right.'

I love Soraya, but she is determined that we are all going on an expensive holiday for her fiftieth. It's alright for Soraya and her rich husband, Andrew, but I am a single mother with writer's block and a dwindling redundancy package. As much as I would love a dream holiday with my best friend, I cannot possibly afford such a frivolity. Of course, I wish I could live the high life with her and help celebrate her birthday, but the mention of this trip is starting to stress me out.

'So, yeah… Monaco, Antibes, Cannes, where shall we go? Andrew's got a client with an apartment in Cannes or Monaco we should be able to use. Any preference? I'm leaning towards a weekend in Monaco at the moment, I must admit.'

How on earth do you tell your best friend that you can't go, but you also don't want to let her down or sound like a miserly mate? The pressure is on, and I think of ways I can get out of it without explaining the truth. I've never been one to just come out with it and always try to please people by sugar coating things.

'Oh, I don't know. I'm so sorry, but I think you'll have to count me out. It doesn't look like I'll be able to make it. I set myself a deadline to write this book, before I have to start looking for work again, you know...'

'Ooh, I didn't realise you'd started the book. I'm so thrilled for you. Do you know, I remember you saying you wanted to be a famous author when you grew up, the very first time we met.'

'Oh, did I? I suppose it's all I ever wanted since I was little. Maybe this is my chance. I've started writing today.'

My eyes turn to look at the blank page. Technically, I have started. After all, I've opened a new document and called it 'The book I want to write'. Isn't it the thought that counts? If only the words would flow as easily as the title came to me.

'Well, you can bring your laptop with you to France. You can write from anywhere. You've got to be at my fiftieth. It wouldn't be the same without you. How can I celebrate if you're not with me?'

This makes me feel even worse and is another reason why I keep skirting around the truth.

Soraya has told me time and time again that I must be on our girls' trip. I know how much she wants me there. We have been best friends since primary school when a horrible boy in our class broke her pencil before a spelling test, and I stepped in to offer her one of my scented ones. I am ashamed to admit that before that incident, I had been

7

a bit envious of Soraya when she first turned up at our school. She was so perfect, so pretty and confident. But, when I got to know her, I discovered that she was the most beautiful human on the inside too. Our lives might have turned out differently, but she has never let the wealth she built with her husband go to her head. The only problem is that she likes to go to places that I can't afford. Like a weekend in Monaco for her birthday. What is wrong with Minehead?

I take a deep breath and finally admit what is holding me back from the offer of this fantastic girls' holiday. I would hate for Soraya to think that I don't want to celebrate with her.

'Look, you know you're my best friend in the world, but I… I'm sorry, I just don't have the money for a weekend in Monaco.'

'You don't need money! Andrew's paying for the three of us to go on a girls' holiday, and one of his clients will put us up.'

Carol is the other invited guest. It's always been the three of us, ever since Soraya joined me and Carol's little friendship circle that day of the pencil incident. I wonder if Carol's aware that Andrew is providing us with such a generous opportunity.

'Goodness, that's very kind of him, but I can't take such a lavish gift. It's going to cost a fortune.'

'Listen, it's my birthday, and that's my pressie. It's what I want more than anything else. Just to spend time with you two.'

–

After Soraya has insisted that she won't take no for an answer, I ring Carol to see what she thinks of it all.

'Of course we're going. Andrew can well afford it. You wouldn't seriously say no to a free holiday in Monaco, would you? Soraya wants us all to be together and celebrate. That's her pressie.'

'I know, but I feel terrible having someone else paying for it.'

I am a proud person and don't feel comfortable taking anything from Soraya and Andrew, no matter how genuinely kind they are.

'Stop being silly. How could you not celebrate with Soraya when that's her birthday wish?'

'I know.'

'Well, there we go then. The financial aspect is what it is… Forget about it. We'll have the best time ever. Anyway, it might be a good chance for you to do some networking. There could be a publisher there for your book, and it'll be turned into a movie. These places are full of big shots. Ha, you never know.'

'That's hilarious. I love your optimism, but even if I bumped into the best publisher in the world, I haven't even started the book yet.'

'Well, bring your laptop with you. You never know when inspiration may strike. You can't miss this chance for us to have a girls' trip. I mean, we couldn't celebrate your fortieth because Stella got sick, remember?'

I think back to my fond memories of Stella, my beautiful nineteen-year-old Siamese cat who sadly died the day I signed the divorce papers. They always say bad things come in threes.

'Yeah, when she had all those fur balls.'

'Come on, it's time to have some fun. We'll have the best holiday ever. I promise,' says Carol.

I love my two best friends, and it would be wonderful to have a weekend away with them, but when I check my bank account for spending money, I realise that more than anything, I need to think about a new career. Could this trip give me the inspiration I need to do that? One thing I do know is that staring at these four walls in my flat at Swansea Marina certainly isn't helping right now.

I picture myself floating around the French Riviera with the sun beating down on my skin, dressed in a kaftan, meeting film directors. Even if I am far too old and sensible to believe this could actually happen, my imagination enjoys the daydream for a moment. A weekend with my two best friends celebrating another milestone in our lives is just what I need. I mean, what could possibly go wrong?

Chapter Two

Despite being a fifty-year-old mother, I have never managed to assert any authority over Jasmine and Poppy, no matter how hard I try. If they ask me for money, they get it. If they insist I pick them up from somewhere late at night, I go. The problem with wanting to keep my daughters safe and happy is that sometimes I feel like I have created monsters.

Before they both came back from uni for the Easter break, I couldn't wait to have them home. Now, as they throw their clothes all over the living room and dirty the kitchen with their pans from boiling penne pasta for breakfast, my nerves are a little frayed. Clearly, my peri-menopausal hormones are clashing with their youthful oestrogen levels and I am struggling to stay calm. It makes me realise how much I need a holiday.

Having them home creating chaos means I was kidding myself if I thought I'd have any chance of starting the first chapter of my book. Although, to be fair, maybe that isn't all on them. Right now, I will take any excuse not to start writing. My creativity is still being held back no matter how hard I try to concentrate. However, there is no way I am getting anything done with the noise levels these two are making and so I decide to use them being here to my advantage. I ask the girls about dating to see if they can provide me with any inspiration for my novel.

'Well, a friend of mine did meet this gorgeous guy on a dating app,' says Poppy.

'Okay, and did they have a happy ever after?' I ask.

'Oh no, he kept bailing on her, writing her messages over and over saying he was just off to his sister's birthday party. It was obvs an excuse. I mean, how many birthdays can one person have in three weeks?'

'What if he had a few sisters and they were all born in the same week?' I ask.

'Oh, Mam. You're so gullible.'

'I'm not gullible.'

'Yes, you are. Remember when you believed that April Fools about towels being banned on the beach, and you started a petition to stop the council from allowing the ban?'

'All right. Well, I thought it was ludicrous, which is why I wanted to start a petition. Anyway, that was a long time ago, and I didn't remember it was the first of April. You know what I'm like with dates,' I sigh.

This is pointless. What if all men are cheats? Is there anyone decent out there any more? Should I really be trying to write a romance?

'Jasmine, can you come up with something better for me?'

Jasmine hasn't been listening to a word as she is too busy on her TikTok account. She looks at me as if I have just landed from the moon.

'Huh?'

'I'm trying to write a book and need some inspiration. Any ideas about boy stuff?'

'Boy stuff?'

'Yeah. Boy stuff.'

'I'm not in junior school, Mam. No. Sorry, no ideas.'

'Okay, well, I'll just have to go on my girlie trip and get some inspiration then.'

'You're not going to that health spa we always wanted to go to, are you, Mam? Please don't go without taking us. It'd be lovely to have mam and daughter spa time, don't you think?' says Poppy.

'That would be lovely, my darling girl, but, no, I promise I'd never go there without you. We're thinking Monaco, possibly.'

The mention of this is enough for Jasmine to put her phone down.

'Monaco?' She looks at me in disbelief. 'Monaco?' she repeats.

'Yes, that's right. Soraya's fiftieth. I've been invited along, and it's all paid for.'

'Can I come?' says Poppy.

'What do you want to hang around fifty-year-olds on holiday for? Oh, my gawd, I can't even imagine. Ew,' says Jasmine.

'That's very rude, Jasmine. Besides, we wouldn't want you cramping our style, thank you,' I say.

'When are you going, Mam?' asks Poppy.

'Around May bank holiday.'

'Oh no. You can't go then. I was planning on coming back for the bank holiday,' says Jasmine.

I can't help but think that if I was here then she would probably decide to spend the long weekend with her friends at the last minute, and I'd be left alone.

If Jasmine doesn't want me to go, then this might just make me want to head off even more. Just like her dad, she is always wanting things her way. She is definitely a daddy's girl.

'It's just something we're talking about.'

'Oh right, you know we'll miss you if you go away. And Dad will.'

'Dad? Why should he miss me? He's busy with his own stuff.'

I don't say that stuff is mostly Jess, the latest woman he met a few months ago. Although I am beginning to wonder how that relationship is going. Lately, he's been popping over with any excuse. Just the other week, he came over on the pretence he wanted to borrow a screw-driver.

I am beginning to get the feeling that Michael regrets his former choices as he is trying to make conversation with me over anything. If he can't get hold of Poppy when he knows she is in a lecture, he even messages me to see if I have heard from her. He has been acting very strange lately.

'I think he misses you, Mam,' says Poppy, confirming my suspicions.

'Well, he should've thought of that a long time ago.' I throw down the tea towel that I am holding as I realise I have unconsciously scrunched it into a ball.

I am still hurt that he did this after all the years we had together. I would never trust him again, no matter how much he misses me. Leopards never change their spots, and I get the feeling that it wouldn't be long before he reinvents himself and gets himself another new convertible and abbreviated name. He'll probably want to be known as 'M' if this goes on much longer.

'Oh and, Mam… Did I see a photo of you in a new top on Facebook? That pink one?' says Jasmine.

'Yes, bargain it was.'

'Can I borrow it tonight? We want to go to that new bar that opened in the Mumbles.'

I have only worn it once, but I suppose it wasn't expensive, and Jasmine knows I never say no to anything.

'Okay, but please don't spill red wine down it or it'll never come out.'

'I won't. Oh, and could you drop us and then pick us up around midnight?'

I had hoped I could watch TV with a glass of wine tonight, but making sure the girls are home safe is my priority, and they know it.

'Of course I will, my little munchkin.'

'Thanks, Mam.'

A few hours later, after I have dropped Jasmine and Poppy off at the trendy new bar that someone told them about, I park up and walk along the pier before heading home. As I feel the breeze on my face and look at the views across the Gower that I remember as a child, I think about how much I have always loved coming here. I suppose it has always been my happy place since the days my parents would take me to the arcade before stopping for an ice cream. It's hard to believe my parents are no longer here, and now my little girls are on nights out drinking shots. Time goes so fast. It seems like only the other day I was here with my parents, building sandcastles; then I got married, then along came Poppy and Jasmine and now it is me walking alone here. It's not what I ever imagined. It feels like my life has gone round full circle, only this time without my mam and dad. What a shame things can't stay the same.

I kick at a pebble and wish I could get an ice cream to cheer myself up. Sadly, the ice cream kiosk has already closed. The kiosk is a landmark. I have so many memories whenever I see it. It is where Michael proposed to me all those years ago. We were sharing a vanilla cone when he looked at me and said, 'Shall we get married, then?' and that was my romantic proposal. I didn't mind though. It was the natural thing to do. Our friends were getting married, some had even started having kids. It was what happened in our neighbourhood. Most settled down at this age. It felt as though it was now or never. I was twenty-five and thought we were ready to live the rest of our lives together. Of course, I was wrong. With hind-sight, he wasn't ready to spend the rest of his life with anyone. Perhaps he will always think the grass is greener somewhere else. Who knows what goes through that head of his.

With no partner and no ice cream, I head back home with The Big Apple kiosk behind me.

At home, knowing that I'll have to return to pick the girls up soon, I flick through the TV channels but can't concentrate on anything. I give up in the end and message Soraya to see what she's up to.

> Just checking out the apartments. So, we can definitely stay in Franco's place in Cannes or Gianni's in Monaco. Which do you think?

Two photos of the sights of Cannes and Monaco follow. I look at the bright lights that sparkle out from the marina views of both properties. I can imagine the impressive yachts bobbing up and down with millionaires on board swigging their champagne. Both places look equally glamorous and tempting. It would be impossible to work out which one is the nicest. Although the nearest apartment to a supermarket would be handy to make sure I don't have to spend too much. I certainly won't be able to dine in fancy restaurants like the people on the yachts probably do.

> They both look pretty amazing to me.

> We're checking flights and transport arrangements and will let you know. We'll just go with whichever's easier.

> Sounds great.

I zoom in for a closer inspection of the photos to see if I can get a close-up of the little blobs that are in fact people on the yachts. I can't help but wonder what they look like, what they are wearing and what sort of jobs they do. Do they even work if they are sat on a yacht all day?

The one thing that's certain is they are both stunning resorts. How could anyone ever choose between them? I zoom in as far as possible on my phone and realise I should probably think about buying bifocals with any money I have left before worrying about cash for the holiday, but why bother when you can so easily zoom into things? Mind you, I found myself picking up a magazine recently and trying to zoom in on an article with my hands to have a better look. Unfortunately, Jasmine caught me and gave me a look of sheer disgust. I can still see her face. I am at that stage of my life where I am embarrassing to my own child.

They are never embarrassed by their godmother. Soraya is always cool in their eyes – and mine too, I suppose. She even has the most amazing connections, if the offer of this free accommodation is anything to go by. I daren't show the girls these photos of the resorts, or they will want to tag along despite me being such an uncool person to hang around with.

For now, though, I am putting my dreams of the French Riviera aside, returning to dependable mam mode in time to collect them from their night out.

Pulling up outside the bar, I see they are already waiting. I feel terrible that I must be a few minutes late after dreaming about the holiday for so long. Anything could have happened to my poor mites out on the street at this time of night.

'So sorry I'm late, girls.'

'It's alright. There was a fight, so we came out early,' says Poppy.

'Oh no. Are you okay?'

'Yeah. We're fine,' slurs Jasmine.

The two girls slump in the back of the car, leaning on each other, already almost snoozing. How much have they had to drink?

Despite their inebriation, I smile as I look at the two sisters, snuggling up close like two peas in a pod. But then, as usual, my hormones begin to rage.

'What happened to my top, Jasmine?'

This quickly wakes Jasmine from her doze.

'It's alright, it's not what it looks like.'

'What is it then?'

'Grenadine. This woman had a cocktail. I was standing in the wrong place at the wrong time. It was an accident. Sorry, Mam. It'll come out. At least it's not red wine, hey?'

I try hard to control myself from screaming and take a deep breath. I remind myself that the girls are safe after another night out on the town with who knows what dangers lurking. The main thing is they are okay. Their drinks weren't spiked, nobody dragged them somewhere only a mother's imagination could conjure up and they are in the car coming home with me. But, still, as I look at my brand-new top, I can see that this is one stain that isn't going anywhere.

I grip the steering wheel and force myself to meditate. Well, when I say meditate, what I mean is that I remind myself that I love my girls, and they are only here for five more days. I have wine on demand, and there is always that family pack of Minstrels I bought for myself. I can get through this visit without a menopausal breakdown.

As we stop at the traffic lights near the marina, I look in the mirror at the two of them, who are now both fast asleep. It reminds me of how they used to sleep in the car when they were small after we had taken them on a long day out to Longleat or some adventure park. Here they are once again, looking like my two angels, and despite their little annoyances, I wouldn't swap them for the world.

Chapter Three

Once the girls return to uni, the plans begin full force for our trip. Soraya has decided on Monaco, and Gianni has happily agreed to let us stay there for the weekend. She says we will use the apartment as a base and maybe his chauffeur can drive us to the surrounding areas if we want to explore further. Apparently, Gianni's driver is happy to pick us up from the airport at the very least. Soraya has suggested he might even be the man of my dreams. I have told her not to dare try fixing me up. I remind her that I am there to have a good time and enjoy her birthday. Whilst I might want to write about romance, that is the last thing on my mind for my own life. And there is certainly no chance of an affair with a chauffeur called Paulo just because he drives a big fancy car belonging to Gianni.

Carol and Soraya have excitedly bought beautiful new clothes for the trip, while I have tried numerous times to soak the stain out of my pink top, but to no avail. I was hoping there might be a sale in Primark before we went, but as our departure date beckons, I realise that I will just have to make do with what I have. It's been years since I had a summer holiday, and half my clothes are too tight. I throw everything out of my wardrobe and have a sort-out. I look at all the clothes I kept thinking would fit me again one day. Looking at a size ten pair of jeans, I realise there is no hope of that. I wish I could wave a magic wand and squeeze into my favourite white denim skirt. It used to look lovely with a tan. I examine the seams in the hope that a dressmaker might be able to make it three sizes bigger, but there's not that much material spare.

At Easter, I swap chocolate eggs for boiled ones, and the day before our flight to Nice comes around, the waistband on the larger of my summer skirts is just about manageable.

As part of my mission to get back out into the world, I decide it is time to announce to the creative writing WhatsApp group that was formed in the pub on the last night of the course that I am going to write my book. Despite us all getting along well, the group, which is in an archive on my phone, has been very quiet lately. Perhaps I am not the only one who lost inspiration once the course ended. I decide that my news might hopefully motivate them.

> Hi, everyone! How's your writing going? Anyone have any writing news? I wanted to let you all know that I'm starting the book I talked about. Wish me luck! X

Now it's official. I have announced that I am doing it. I press send and immediately start to get cold feet. Oh well, if the worst comes to the worst and I am a complete failure, I guess all I have to do is leave the group and hope I never bump into any of them anywhere ever again. I watch as the notification shows that five of the group have read my message. They haven't responded! Couldn't someone at least give me a thumbs up?

My confidence takes a bashing again. Am I making a mistake? I think of Michael standing there in those yellow chinos that looked far too young for him and the new haircut he got with the shaved sides as he stood and ridiculed my dream of writing when I casually mentioned I was doing a course. Why would anyone be interested in my writing news? We were all strangers, but I thought we had bonded; obviously not. Should I listen to Michael? Does anyone really care if I write this book or not? Probably not, but I know in my heart that I care. As I doubt myself, I also worry about the thought of my holiday tomorrow. I was never made for a posh break in Monaco.

To calm down all the doubts, I open a bottle of wine that was on special offer at the supermarket and scroll through other people's social media posts.

After two glasses, my creative crisis shifts a little, and I tell myself that I am not giving up. It also helps that Christian, a lovely young chap on the course, has messaged to say that he wishes me luck and that he has decided to give up on his writing for now. I am sad to hear this. He says he has a new job collecting trolleys in the supermarket, and he's doing a lot of extra shifts, but he hopes one day he will have the time to fulfil his dream.

I think how this redundancy has given me the gift of time to write, and I must make the most of it.

By morning, one of the lovely ladies, Judy, has written a message saying that she can't wait to hear more about my book and she's happy to be a beta reader if I need another pair of eyes to look over it. My faith has been restored, and I write back to her thanking her for being so kind.

I smile to myself as I pack my laptop in my hand luggage and confidently stride out of the flat for Andrew to collect me downstairs. He is already waiting in his

Bentley 4X4, and Soraya and Carol are giddy with excitement as Soraya opens a bottle of champagne for our journey even before we reach the traffic lights to get out of Swansea.

'Got to start as we mean to go on. Come on, girls,' says Soraya handing me a plastic glass. I am almost afraid to take it in case I spill anything on the beautiful cream leather seats. But Soraya pushes it towards me as we go over a speed hump, and I grip the glass for dear life.

'Cheers, my loves. This is to the best girls' holiday ever,' says Soraya.

'Cheers. Thank you so much for inviting us, and thank you, Andrew, for paying. It's so generous of you.'

'It's alright. Only the best for my Soraya and her mates,' he says.

I swoon as I look at the two of them. Maybe my novel should be about these two. That would definitely give the readers a nice happy ending. Twenty-five years together and he still treats her like a princess. They must be a match made in heaven as despite working with each other every single day, they still get on like a house on fire. I wonder if Soraya would mind me writing their love story? I'd probably have to change the bit about how they met in a kebab shop after a night out at the Top Rank. It wasn't exactly the most romantic of meet-cutes when he took a bite of her kebab at three a.m.

I turn to Carol as she starts hiccupping.

'It's a bit early for champagne,' she says to me.

'Nonsense. They drink champagne in France from the moment they get up,' says Soraya.

'Do they?' Carol asks me.

'Umm, I don't think so.'

Carol rolls her eyes, and I laugh in the back while Soraya places her hand on Andrew's knee.

'Ooh, I'm so excited. A couple more hours and we'll be in a beautiful apartment in the sunshine,' says Soraya.

'Sounds bliss,' says Carol.

I think of the pile of dirty bowls the girls left behind and the state of the spare room when they last left for uni. This break sounds like heaven. Apparently, Gianni's apartment comes with a housekeeper too.

I have lost count of the number of glasses of champagne we have gone through by the time we say goodbye to Andrew and board our flight to Nice. With a delay to our afternoon flight, which we spent at the airport bar, I am not surprised that Soraya and Carol doze in their seats when we finally take off. Meanwhile, I watch the clouds go by as the sun starts to shine on the horizon. I tried to stay a bit sensible as I thought I might be able to work on the plane. However, when I open my laptop to start my new book in the peace and quiet, despite all the excitement of a holiday, no words will come out. I begin to worry that it will always be like this. Maybe there won't be any new book updates from me to the group after all.

I lean back onto my headrest and think about the break we are about to have. My tummy does somersaults with the combination of nerves and excitement. If anywhere is going to inspire me to write, this must be it.

Sipping on the last drip of my inflight glass of wine, I imagine myself by the pool, having fun with my besties and coming home from the holiday of a lifetime with not only a tan but the start of a dream too.

Chapter Four

Getting from the airport to Gianni's apartment is straight-forward as Soraya spots the driver as soon as we walk out of arrivals. She recognises him from a photo she's seen and says that's the uniform he wears, which is a smart grey suit. He also has a big sign with an address in Monaco that we can't miss, so we follow her lead. He takes us to the car park and off to a waiting Mercedes. I take in the aroma of a new car as Soraya sits in the front, while Carol and I jump in the back.

We make our way out of the airport past palm trees, their fronds waving at us in the gentle breeze. The delay to our flight has meant we have arrived later than expected, but it's still warm, even though it's early evening. According to Soraya, the region is experiencing higher than normal temperatures for this time of year. I'm happy to hear it; I have been looking forward to the sunshine, and the last thing I wanted was the drizzle we had back home. I watch as convertible cars zoom past us with their roofs down, their sophisticated-looking drivers speeding off onto the highway.

Carol nudges me as we pass a Ferrari.

'Look at the cars around here. I wonder if that driver's famous,' says Carol.

'I wouldn't be surprised. Although I bet he's the owner of some big yacht conglomerate, or the CEO of a private Swiss bank,' I say.

'I'm sure I saw Michael J. Fox once when I was leaving an airport in Toronto. This big limo pulled up beside us, and I could have sworn it was him in the back,' says Soraya.

She turns around to look at us for dramatic effect.

'That's amazing. You forget celebs have to go places and aren't only on movie sets,' laughs Carol.

A beautiful silver vintage Mercedes passes us, and I can't help thinking how much my ex-husband Michael would love this place. Shame he spoilt everything between us. There was a time I would have been excitedly recalling everything back to him whenever I was somewhere without him. Now he's just an annoying stranger in a loud shirt who keeps coming around asking for a screwdriver. It's strange how you can love someone so much, then they break your heart, and one day you feel nothing for them.

'Look at this tunnel, girls. It's like the one in Newport,' says Soraya.

As we go through a tunnel under a mountain, we all laugh at the comparison.

'Umm, I think it's a bit bigger than that one and more mountainous around here,' I say.

Before long, we pass a toll, and Paulo hands over a couple of euros. Carol can't help compare this with the former toll for the bridge into Wales, when it was known as the Severn Bridge.

'You can take the girl out of Wales, but you can't take Wales out of the girl,' I tease.

After driving on a highway, we watch as the signs for Monaco show that we are getting closer. Finally, the sea comes into view and is illuminated under the sunset. I catch my breath at the sight. With pretty buildings perched in an arch around the bay, the sea glistens under the pink-tinged sky. I have never seen such a beautiful sunset.

'Wow, look!'

Carol leans over me to look out of my side of the window.

'Oh, that's the most gorgeous view ever. What a beautiful place! We're going to love it here.'

As the road begins to narrow, the area becomes more built up. Eventually we pull up outside a plush apartment block and drive down to a basement where there is parking. Paulo leads us upstairs, where security watches us.

'Bonsoir,' says the security man sitting behind a large desk. I can't help but admire the beautiful flower arrangement to the side of him which is filled with birds of paradise. They are the perfect exotic flower for this marble-filled lobby. It's certainly not the kind of place you'd see a few limp carnations. Everything here signifies elegance, from the large white vase to the portraits of posh people that hang on the walls. Meanwhile, the white marble floor sparkles like a diamond of the highest clarity. This is going to be some pad, if the entrance is anything to go by.

Paulo says something in French to us, and we head off in a private lift.

'It's posh here, innit?' says Carol.

I wink at her. 'Shh. We have to pretend we're used to this sort of thing.'

Gianni's Monaco apartment is absolutely stunning. The hallway has navy wooden panelling, and the most enormous crystal chandelier greets us as we open the door. Hanging on the panelling are artworks that look as though they cost millions. I wouldn't be surprised if there was a Van Gogh hidden amongst the collection.

The only problem is that we seem to be missing the housekeeper. Paulo hands over the key as the three of us sneeze simultaneously. We look around, unable to tell what is beneath the white sheets that are covering most of the furniture.

'How long has Gianni been away?' I ask Soraya.

'Oh, I don't know. He's always somewhere. He spends most of his time in Dubai. Maybe he hasn't been back for a while. Perhaps he gave the staff some time off. At least Paulo is here.'

Paulo hasn't been much help, but I am just glad he was at the airport waiting for us. Our French isn't good enough to converse with him, and when we mention the name Paulo, he just keeps saying *d'accord*. At least I know there won't be any risk of me regretfully snogging the chauffeur on this trip.

'It's fine. We can clean this place up. At least the jacuzzi isn't neglected,' says Carol, looking towards the floor-to-ceiling windows that lead out onto the huge balcony.

'What a shame the apartment hasn't been cleaned. I'm allergic to dust mites,' says Soraya. Her eyes are already going a little red, although I can't decide whether this is the effect of the dust mites or the champagne hangover kicking in.

'Let's get some fresh air,' I say.

Since Paulo has already left us to our own devices, we open the large glass patio doors that give us views over Monaco. Yachts are moored for the night in the marina below and buildings crowd around with a dramatic backdrop of a rocky outcrop. Flags on board some of the boats, bearing the Monaco livery, sway gently in the light wind. I'm not surprised they call this the playground of the rich and famous.

'Well, this is stunning. You know me, I'm never speechless, but I have no words,' says Carol.

'Yeah, I know. It's so gorgeous, isn't it? Ooh, look! Down there… Is that where they do the Grand Prix? Are those the roads you see on the telly?' I ask.

Michael was always watching the Monaco Grand Prix when it was on, and the view is very recognisable, although thinking of him while I am here is annoying me.

'Amazing, isn't it? I knew it would be fabulous. I'm just sorry that the housekeeper seems to be missing. I thought it would be spick and span. Oh, well, at least the temperature of the jacuzzi is perfect,' says Soraya, as she dips her hand into the jacuzzi.

We soon come to the conclusion that Gianni must have special chemicals in there to keep it clean since the housekeeper is nowhere to be seen. Unless Paulo takes care of the jacuzzi and the driving.

'It's a waste of electricity, though. Leaving that on when nobody's here. Imagine the bills this Gianni guy gets,' says Carol.

'I don't think he's bothered about his bills if he can leave a place like this empty for months on end,' I say.

As the lights of Monaco twinkle below us, I can't get over how close we are to the centre. This place must have cost millions. A view like this would command zillions alone, without the grandeur of the apartment.

'You know, I might sleep out here tonight. Stop me sneezing,' says Soraya.

'You can't sleep on the balcony.'

'Well, those sunbeds look comfy.'

'Don't be silly. I'll clean up inside, after all, it's your birthday trip. You stay outside and enjoy the views. We'll pull off all the dust sheets and arrange everything. It can be a thank you for giving us a free holiday,' I say.

'Yeah, I'll help you. Let the birthday girl relax out here and we'll sort it all out,' agrees Carol.

'Aww, are you sure? It's just my eyes will be puffy for days.'

'Of course. Now put your feet up on one of those sun loungers.'

Soraya sits down and makes herself comfortable on one of the oversized rattan wicker beds.

With Soraya relaxing, we pull off the dust sheets in the living room to find Louis XVI cream sofas hiding underneath.

'Wow, this furniture looks expensive. We'd better not put our feet up on this,' says Carol.

'Yes indeed,' I say, marvelling at how the chandelier lights reflect on the Louis XVI marble coffee table as I remove the next dust sheet.

'You wouldn't want to put your tea down on this without a coaster,' I say.

'I could really do with a cuppa now, couldn't you? I've got a bit of a headache coming on,' says Carol.

Although Paulo left us with the key for this place, he hasn't left us with much else.

'At least I brought tea bags with us. Although I'm not sure there'll be any milk here. Let's check the fridge,' I say.

We move to the open-plan kitchen where I find that the fridge is completely empty.

'He hasn't had that fridge on for ages,' says Carol.

'No. Soraya said that he's definitely been in Dubai for a good few months. I'll switch it on now and in the morning when it's not so dark, we'll walk down and try to find a supermarket.'

'Yeah. Thank goodness I took that bottle of water off the flight. I'm parched. Come on. Shall we check out the bedrooms next?' says Carol.

We venture into a corridor to try the various doors. I never knew apartments could be so big. The first door is locked. I start to worry that all of them will be and we can't access the bedrooms, but thankfully, the next door leads us into what must be the master bedroom. Carol barges in before I can get close.

'Oh my god. No way! You've got to come and see this,' says Carol.

'It's nothing scary, is it?'

'Come and see.'

I peep my head around a door that leads off from the master bedroom, with no idea what I am about to find.

'Goodness, how the other half live, hey?' I gasp at the walk-in wardrobe that looks like something from a Hollywood A-lister's mansion. It feels bigger than the whole flat I own back home.

Once we have calmed down on the excitement, we pass through a sliding door in this Tardis-like room and find ourselves in a yoga studio. A yoga studio off a bedroom!

'I reckon if this place was for sale, it wouldn't even have the price on. It would be one of those "price on application" places,' says Carol.

'Yeah, you're right there. I suppose we should give Soraya this room, but I don't think even she brought enough clothes to fill this wardrobe up.'

We check out the next set of doors, which lead us into two further spacious bedrooms with en suites. Carol and

I agree which rooms we'll take between us, and luckily, there's no squabbling, as every room is equally fantastic, with sweeping curtains and over-sized beds.

Carol tries the locked door again as we pass it on the way back into the lounge.

'I wonder what's in there then?' she says.

'Come on, it's none of our business. Perhaps it's a study that Gianni wants to keep private.'

By the time we finish removing all the dust sheets from each room, the place looks like a show home, and we get Soraya back inside.

'You two are the best. Thank you. I would have helped if it wasn't for my allergies. I promise.'

'Don't think about it. Now, I just wish we could all have a cuppa. But that will have to wait until morning as there's no milk,' says Carol.

'Right, okay. Well, how about the first one up in the morning goes out to buy the milk?' I suggest.

'Sounds like a good idea. I'll set my alarm. I owe you both after you've sorted all of this,' says Soraya.

'Let's see in the morning. I don't know about you two, but I'm shattered,' I say.

'Yeah. We definitely need a good night's sleep because tomorrow the partying in Monaco begins,' says Soraya.

'Night night, my loves. Sweet dreams,' says Carol.

I sink into my gloriously comfortable, ornately carved bed, which has just had a change of sheets thanks to a pile of folded up laundry we found in the utility room.

Ah, this is the life, I think. If I don't have inspiration for a story after being here, then I never will.

I close my eyes and think about all the things we will be doing over the next few days. I feel like a kid in a sweet shop. Will we bump into movie stars? Could I really run into a publisher or literary agent? With the thought of all the potential possibilities running through my mind, not to mention the sunbathing, cocktails and fun with Soraya and Carol, it takes me forever to get to sleep. Although I am pretty sure that by the time I drift off, I have a huge grin on my face.

Chapter Five

Waking up dehydrated, I search for my water bottle to find there is only the teeniest drop left. I hold the bottle over my tongue and shake it for any drip I can get out of it. I really need tea this second.

Even though Soraya promised she would be first up, I tiptoe into the living room in case anyone is still sleeping, and I wake them with my banging about. However, there is no sign of either of them. For a moment, I wonder if perhaps Soraya has already gone to the supermarket, but I notice her handbag is in exactly the same place as she left it last night. There doesn't appear to be any movement from either her or Carol.

In case I am mistaken, I open the fridge door with a glimmer of hope. I keep my fingers crossed that a pint of semi-skimmed milk has miraculously appeared on a shelf overnight. Alas, just as I had feared, the fridge is as empty as the last time I looked.

I don't want to wait any longer for Soraya to get up, whenever that might be, so decide to get some milk myself. Quickly brushing through my hair and throwing on the first loose-fitting summer dress that I find in my suitcase, I grab the front door key from the console by the door and rush out.

The sun is already shining brightly, and I squint my eyes as I realise in my haste to get milk that I forgot to grab my sunglasses. I also realise that while people dash to the supermarket back home wearing whatever is closest to hand, here, everyone is super elegant. Their outfits look as though they were planned months in advance, although I suspect this isn't true and they just happen to be casually put together at this early hour. How they can look this amazing before nine a.m. beats me. Whatever it is, I wish I knew their secret.

Ladies walk past me showing off their teeny waists in white jeans, with Chanel loafers finishing off the look. I almost want to curl up and hide myself. At least now I know I need to make more of an effort when I come back out later. I knew it would be glamorous here, but this place is *trop chic*. I stop for a moment as I see a shop selling designer clothes for dogs. The contrast between this and the pet food store I worked in is quite astonishing. We used to have a special food bank area for pet owners who struggled to afford food. I can't imagine how much the navy and white sailor suit costume, complete with its coordinating hat, must cost. It seems it isn't only the humans who lead an affluent life here. When I die, I want to come back as a pet in this place. I'm pretty sure they have a much better wardrobe than mine if this store is anything to go by.

Since I am dressed less stylishly than the local pet population, I try to stay invisible, keeping my head down as I continue my search for the nearest supermarket. I never look my best before three cuppas as it is, let alone somewhere so glam.

Finally, something resembling a corner store comes into view. A posh one, though, of course. I make a note of my surroundings so that I can remember where I am and so that we can all come down together later and fill the fridge properly. I am quite partial to French cheese and that is definitely on the shopping list for later. For now, though, milk is my priority.

Walking through the automatic door feels like a mirage in a desert at this point. I am so in need of caffeine. By the time I get to the milk fridge, I could hug it. Looking at the labels, I realise I have no idea which is semi-skimmed, but, at this point, I will take anything, even the organic, skimmed milk of a camel that has been crossed with a llama. Fortunately, though, I do find something that has a picture of a cow on it and head in the direction of the till. With the milk in my hand, I end up making a detour and look for a basket to hold everything since I get carried away when I spot some huge croissants that the girls will appreciate. I also throw in a family-sized bar of chocolate for us to share later. Finally, I pick up a small bottle of water on the way to the cashier to keep me going until I get back to the apartment and get the kettle on.

I notice a distinguished-looking man in navy shorts and a smart polo T-shirt who reaches the till at the same time as me. I am grateful that he politely lets me go ahead of him. I assume he's a local, coming in for his freshly baked morning baguette and has all morning to kill before taking his spaniel for a walk.

When my items are rung through, I could kiss the cashier with relief. I finally have my milk. But then she tells me how much I owe, and I realise that it wasn't only my sunglasses I forgot back at the apartment.

'Fifteen euro, s'il vous plait.'

I feel in the baggy pockets of my sundress in the hope that I have a twenty euro note in there, but I know what the answer is.

'Oh my, I've… umm… forgotten my purse. Oh no, I've never done anything like this before.'

I hear someone tutting and assume it's the man behind me. Now I feel terrible that he let me go ahead. The cashier repeats the price, not listening to a word I have said. I feel my skin flush as a whole queue of annoyed people stare at me.

'Look, I'll put the basket back. But is there any chance I can take the milk and bring the money later?' Stupid question, but I know Mavis in the Londis around the corner from me would always feel sorry for someone who had left their purse at home.

The thought of walking back up the hill to the apartment block empty-handed is too much to bear. Soraya and Carol will be wanting their cuppa too. It's already getting hot out there and I am getting more and more dehydrated. However, the lady's face says it all. There is no getting around her. This is not a local corner store in Wales.

'You have no money, then put back.'

'Oh, no, I'm so desperate for a cuppa.'

I have no choice but to pick up the items and turn around, until the man behind me speaks.

'Put 'em back down. I'll pay. We can't have a Brit not having her morning cuppa, now, can we?'

His broad Manchester accent is such a welcome sound and I quickly realise that he is definitely not French.

'I promise to pay you back,' I smile.

'Don't worry about it. My treat, mate. Just pay it forward and do a good deed for someone else one day.'

His eyes crinkle as he smiles at me, and he is like some kind of Mancunian saviour in the middle of Monaco.

'Cheers. Look, I'll put everything else back, but if you could get the milk for me, I'd really appreciate it. Thank you so much. I can't tell you how desperate I am for that caffeine hit.'

He offers to pay for the whole basket, but I tell him there is no need. The milk will be sufficient, that's the most urgent item. In the end, we compromise, and I take the bottle of water too, as I can see the queue behind me is now stretching around the corner.

I take my goods and thank the Mancunian saviour once again.

Happily walking up the hill, taking a big swig of water, I smile as I think how kind the man was and how his eyes crinkled as he grinned. It might have been horrifying to stand there with no money, but what a lovely man to bump into and at just the right moment. Thank goodness for fellow Brits abroad!

By the time I open the door to the apartment, Soraya and Carol are up and about.

'I was just going to go down to the shops. So sorry I slept in,' says Soraya as she sees me carrying the milk.

I can't help noticing how magnificent Soraya looks, even at this time in the morning, as her long dark curls swing loosely over her flowing pink kaftan.

'It's fine. It was a long day yesterday, and you drank quite a bit of the champers. You needed a lie-in. You wouldn't believe what happened though.'

I tell them both about the man in the supermarket, and we all thank our lucky stars that I managed to bring home the milk.

We root through the cupboards and find a couple of fancy mugs with some kind of crest design on them and take our drinks outside to the balcony. The heat hits me once again. It's going to be a warm day for sure.

The view from last night is clearer in the daylight, and I can see the yachts in more detail. The flags now barely move as the wind has died down, although the smell of Soraya's fancy moisturiser still manages to waft across to me in the slight breeze.

'I think this is the nicest cup of tea I've ever had,' I say, taking a big sip.

'Is that because a hunk from Manchester bought you the milk, or because you were desperate for a cuppa?' teases Carol.

'He was just a nice, normal guy who helped a fellow Brit in need. That's all. It's the best cup of tea ever because I was desperate for caffeine. Well, and these mugs are gorgeous.'

'Do you think Gianni would notice if I took one home?' asks Carol.

'Don't you dare,' says Soraya, glaring at her.

'You're lucky Dave isn't here. He'd have the lot.'

Carol had met Dave on a dodgy dating site after her divorce. I just seem to be surrounded by stories of men like Dave.

'Has he ever tried to get in touch again after you caught him stealing your undies?' asks Soraya.

'No. I made sure I blocked him from everything. Weirdo. I'm done with dating.'

'Oh, me too. I am so not interested.'

'I know I'm so lucky with Andrew. We have our moments, of course, but he's an amazing, hard-working, decent man.'

The three of us lift our cups in a salute to Andrew.

'To men like the amazing Andrew who spoil their wives and let us tag along.'

We finish off our drinks, and Carol offers to make us another cup. As I wait for her to come back out, I look at the views of the Monaco marina in the daylight. It looks different from last night as I watch everyone hurry about.

'Look at all those boats. Stunning.'

'I know. I thought there were nice boats in Swansea Marina, but this is something else,' says Soraya.

Andrew mentioned in the car on the way to the airport that Port Hercules is one of the bigger marinas in Monaco and it is obvious from the size of some of the boats.

'Look at that one over there...' Soraya points to what must be the largest yacht in the marina.

'What you reckon? Must be around one hundred and twenty metres, maybe more,' she says.

'Don't know. I've never been very good with measurements. It just looks enormous to me. It must be one of those superyacht things. I wonder who owns it?' I say.

'Some of them are chartered out, Andrew told me. Like those boats on *Below Deck* on TV.'

'Oh, Poppy and Jasmine love that. I watch it for the food. Those chefs are amazing. I liked Chef Ben. Imagine having someone like that cooking for you.'

'That reminds me. Where shall we eat tonight?' says Soraya.

'I've no clue what's around here.'

'What's that now?' says Carol, returning with our drinks.

'We're just talking about where to go tonight.'

'Don't ask me, babes. Did Andrew recommend anywhere?'

'Well, there's a yacht club. We could see if we can get in there. That'd be nice, wouldn't it? It might be members only, though.'

Carol and I look at each other as we both wonder how much the food there might set us back.

'I doubt they'd let non-members in. Why don't we go for a walk and scope out some places?' says Carol.

'Sounds like a plan,' I agree.

By the time we come to ourselves after more mugs of tea, I make sure I am better equipped for leaving the apartment for a wander. I put on my sunglasses and a panama hat I borrowed from Carol.

The three of us set off like we are something out of *Thelma & Louise* with an extra hanger-on.

No sooner have we turned the corner from the apartment when a woman on a Vespa with a small dog in the basket at the front passes us.

'Did you see that little fluff ball?' says Soraya.

'What a life,' says Carol.

It reminds me of the dog clothing store I passed, and I excitedly tell them how I'll have to show it to them. We seem to be on a different road down to the centre this time, and instead, we pass expensive boutiques for humans. Soraya *oohs* and *aahs* over every shop window.

'It's a good job I'm starving, or I'd have the credit card out,' she says.

We chat and laugh as we walk down to the marina, where we finally see the yachts from a closer angle.

'These boats are huge, aren't they?' says Carol.

'That's what I was saying to Soraya earlier.'

When we pass a souvenir shop, Carol can't resist stopping. She insists she wants to buy a magnet saying

'Monaco', claiming it will look posh on her fridge at home. However, Soraya has other ideas.

'There's no rush. We can come back here anytime. Isn't anyone else hungry? We missed dinner last night after that delay. I can't believe you're not both complaining you're starving. Do you realise it's almost lunchtime?'

'Yeah, I'm ravenous, but it's the excitement of looking around that's keeping me going,' says Carol.

As we leave the souvenir shop, the smell of seafood grilled over charcoal wafts over to us and my mouth starts watering. The three of us look at the welcoming bistro by the marina, where the aroma is coming from. I suppose I can afford one nice meal here, but from tomorrow, I shall be on an economy drive. Although I realise we haven't even had Soraya's birthday meal yet!

Before I can think of the hefty price tag, a waiter ushers us to a table that overlooks the boats. I honestly thought they might shove us at the back if we weren't glamorous enough, but it must be Soraya who swung it.

The young waiter passes us the menus, and I am grateful that Jasmine isn't here. She would be swooning all over him.

'This looks nice, doesn't it? I might have half a lobster. Oh, they've got champagne too. Shall we get some to share?' asks Soraya.

Carol's eyes widen in panic as she looks at me. It is one thing having a bite to eat, but lobster and champagne will wipe out the budget for the week, if not the year.

Soraya looks at us as she awaits our response and then pulls out her purse.

'Andrew's credit card. I've got free rein. He's insisted we enjoy ourselves.'

It doesn't sit comfortably with me, but Soraya is grinning and calls the waiter over to order us a bottle of fizz.

'This is far too generous. But after this, you must let me get some bits in the supermarket,' I say.

'Aww, is that so you can go back and see your knight in shining armour, or should I say, knight in shorts and T-shirt?' teases Carol.

'No. Will you give up about him, please? He felt sorry for me, that's all.'

I turn to the waiter, who pours our champagne into proper glasses and not flutes like I have at home. Despite the restaurant being full of glamorous couples and ladies who lunch, it feels as though he is giving us his undivided attention. What a gorgeous place for our first lunch.

'This is really incredible, Soraya. It's a great way to celebrate your birthday,' I say.

'I know – but wait until tomorrow night! Andrew booked us somewhere he says we'll love. I can't remember the name now.'

As we all gaze out at the yachts, I can't believe I am sat here drinking champagne after the horrendous time I have had with the loss of my job, Michael's midlife crisis and then losing my sweet cat, Stella.

I take a sip of my bubbly to enjoy the moment, and I almost choke. The bubbles shoot out of my nose, and I start to cough as I hear a male voice.

'Well, hello! All right there?'

Soraya and Carol sit with their mouths wide open.

I feel Carol's sharp nudge in my ribs. They are both looking up at the man who is towering above us.

I take a swig of the water that is thankfully on the table beside the champagne and try to stop myself from choking further.

'Hello,' I wheeze out through my breaths.

'Didn't think I'd see you again this soon,' he says.

'No. Well, I did hear Monaco is quite a small place.'

'It is indeed,' says my knight in shorts and T-shirt.

'Are you going to introduce us to your friend then?' says Carol.

I look at my two friends with their cheesy grins and it takes me right back to secondary school. If I could get away with kicking them both under the table like I used to, then I would.

'This is the kind gentleman who helped me this morning when I went out for the milk.'

'Yeah, we guessed that. We've heard all about you. In fact, we were just talking about you.'

I shake my head at Carol, willing her to please shut up. If she continues, I am going to tell everyone here how her ex stole her knickers and put them on eBay!

'Pleased to meet you. I'm Elias,' he says to the three of us.

'Sorry, I didn't introduce myself to you this morning. I'm Lucy. This is Soraya and Carol.'

'What a delight to meet you all,' he says.

'Anyway, look. I have my purse with me now. Please, let me give you the money I owe you from this morning. I can't thank you enough for that.'

'No. As I said, pay it forward. Help someone else in their moment of need.'

'If you're sure. Okay. I promise I'll do that.'

'Well, I'd better leave you ladies to enjoy your champagne.'

'Oh, no, we're eating.' I don't want him thinking I am here to drink all day.

'Well, I'd better leave you to enjoy your lunch then, ladies. I'm sure I'll bump into you again around here.' Elias looks into my eyes and smiles.

'Ooh, I'm sure we will see you again,' giggles Carol. A pang of jealousy hits me. Does Carol fancy him? I thought she said she wasn't looking for anyone. Oh well, no man is worth fighting with your friends over. If she likes him, she can have him. Anyway, I am not here for romance. I am here to celebrate my friend and hopefully get some writing inspiration.

'See you around then, Elias.' I smile, and by the time I look around, he is nowhere to be seen.

'Now he is some catch,' says Carol.

Chapter Six

'Well, you're a dark horse. You didn't tell us quite how gorgeous your saviour was,' says Soraya, as she tucks into the lobster that has arrived on the table.

'I didn't notice, to be honest. I didn't get a good look at him this morning. I was too flustered, and I hadn't had my tea.'

'You're fibbing. I can tell. How can you not notice someone like that? Did you see that face? That body, that... everything. I wonder what he's doing here?' says Carol.

'He's probably on holiday with his wife – and before you ask where she is, she is probably just resting back at their accommodation,' I say.

'I didn't notice a wedding ring,' says Carol.

'Trust you to look,' laughs Soraya.

'Well, if Lucy isn't interested, then I definitely am.'

'Will you behave, both of you. Just because he was kind to me this morning doesn't mean he's some sort of eligible bachelor hanging around Monaco looking for someone like me.'

'Someone like you? What on earth does that mean?' asks Soraya.

'I don't know. I'm in my fifties, unemployed, with a bum that's never been so wobbly and thighs that seem to expand just by looking at a custard slice.'

'Come on now. That's no way to talk about your beautiful body. You have strong legs that carry you, and young girls pay good money for a booty like yours nowadays,' says Carol.

'She's right. You're gorgeous, and you need to know it. I bet he couldn't believe he bumped into such a beauty first thing in the morning like that,' says Soraya.

'Right. Let's change the subject. Enough about my bum and the Mysterious Mancunian of Monaco.'

'Ooh, I quite like the sound of that. "The Mysterious Mancunian of Monaco"! Sounds a bit like *The Count of Monte Cristo*, don't you think Soraya.'

Carol and Soraya both laugh at my expense. I begin to wish I hadn't bumped into him now. I'll never hear the end of it.

'I'm sure we won't see him again. We're not here that long, and he'll be off on some day trip with his wife to *Cap d'Antibes*, or somewhere like that,' I say in my best Welsh/French accent.

'Yeah, but what if he's a single man looking for love in Monaco,' says Carol.

'Look. Let's just enjoy a girlie trip. No men allowed. I'm not looking for any relationship whatsoever, even if he is gorgeous,' I say.

I lift my champagne glass up and repeat my mantra for this trip.

'No men allowed!' I remind Carol once again.

She scowls at me, but we somehow manage to agree on the pact.

'Now, if he were a movie director with a million-pound budget to get the book I haven't even written into Hollywood, I might bend the rules. Not in a funny way, you understand. Just, I mean… Oh no, that sounds awful, doesn't it? Look, let's change the subject. How's the lobster?'

'Simply scrumptious,' says Soraya.

'Yeah, so is the trout,' says Carol.

'The food is fabulous here. This was definitely the right choice,' I say.

After a long boozy lunch, we head for a wander around the shops, which, on reflection, probably wasn't the best idea if I am to stick to my strict holiday budget.

We walk past palm trees against the backdrop of high-rise apartment blocks and window-shop for the most part, almost bumping into each other as we admire the displays.

Soraya impulsively decides that we should go to the casino tonight and needs a fancy new frock, so we stop at one of the ubiquitous boutiques selling designer clothes. Despite having brought plenty of clothes with her, she insists she needs something new. I grimace as I think about what I will be wearing. I hope the dress code isn't too lavish, or I won't be allowed in.

Carol and I sit around waiting on the deep purple velvet sofa in the posh boutique as Soraya tries on a few dresses. We give our opinions, and when she comes out in the most beautiful black dress with diamante around the neckline, both Carol and I agree that this is the one for her. Soraya looks absolutely stunning. I can't believe she will be fifty tomorrow. Neither can I believe how quickly we have all hit our half-century. When we were in school, we all wanted to be the eldest. But when I was the first to celebrate this milestone birthday, I quickly went to wishing I was the youngest.

After hitting the shops and with Soraya's dress safely wrapped in a fancy bag, we head back to the apartment to get ready for tonight. If we are going to a world-famous casino, it's going to take hours. At least there are so many bathrooms in the property that we won't have to fight over whose turn it is.

Excitedly, we prepare for our glamorous evening, which takes me back to our teenage years. We blast out an Eighties radio station that Carol has managed to find on the state-of-the-art stereo in the living room, and it is just like being back in 1989 before the disco in our local church hall. Except now we sit around in Velcro curlers getting ready, instead of those bendy rag things we used to put in our hair and use normal hairspray instead of something that would make our hair abnormally rock hard for weeks.

By the time we are ready, I begin to feel as though I can mingle with the best of them and walk into the casino with my head held high. However, when we approach the casino and I am faced with columns and chandeliers so grand they would only be fit for the most extravagant of palaces, my imposter syndrome kicks in, and I am forced to realise that I am not part of the jet set whatsoever. I may have thought the long black and gold dress that I bought a few years back would be ideal when I was getting ready, but now I realise it just looks dated as I look at the elegant women playing blackjack in the latest collections. The material suddenly feels inferior: thin and cheap compared to these women in their fine silks that are probably made from the cocoons of rare types of silkworms that I haven't even heard of. I am a polyester girl walking among this cashmere society. As for the men, they are equally swanky, and a group of them in tuxedos and bow ties cheers as they win on the roulette. Carol looks over, and I tell her to behave as the croupiers rake the chips back in and prepare to start a new game.

'Oh, look at those guys on the roulette table,' says Soraya.

'Yeah, don't worry. I already noticed. Actually, I've always fancied a go at proper roulette. I bought a little set in Argos once for when the boys turned eighteen, but it wasn't quite the same as playing in a casino. I think we lost half the chips,' says Carol. That sounds typical of Carol; she's always the most disorganised out of the three of us.

Both Carol and Soraya are eager to play on the roulette. However, the thought of losing even the slightest bit of money scares me. Buying a scratch card seems like a luxury nowadays. I insist that I will stand next to my friends and watch as they place their bets.

'Oh, go on. Have one go,' says Carol.

'What's your lucky number?' says Soraya.

'No, I can't.'

'It's almost my birthday. I can do whatever I want. Give me a number, and I'll put a bet on for you.'

I tell her there is no way I am accepting anything more from her than I have already taken. Her generosity knows no bounds.

Soraya looks at the croupier and then at me.

'Come on. Quick, she's starting. Number?'

'Seven then.'

'Black or red?'

'Umm, red.'

Soraya manages to place the bet just in time, and we watch as the wheel spins. It rumbles along the lower numbers, the higher numbers, and everything in between. Then we watch closely as the roulette wheel begins to slow down.

'Come on. It's got to be twenty-three,' shouts Carol. But slowly the wheel passes her number and stops. It takes a moment to register, and it is only because Carol and Soraya are grabbing me and trying to high five me that it all computes. I watch as the croupier hands over a load of chips to me.

'You won, my dear. It's yours,' says Soraya.

'No. I'm not taking it. It's your money. You paid for the bet.'

'Stop it. When you are a massive bestselling author, you can treat me. But you can buy us a drink, and that won't be cheap,' says Soraya. Then she points towards the cashier's glass compartment for me to exchange my chips for the real stuff.

'No arguing. Just go and cash your chips in, will you.'

I give Soraya a stern look and shake my head. She is generous to a fault.

Trying not to drop any chips, I slide them through the window to the cashier. He takes them efficiently and then grabs a wad of euros.

I watch in disbelief as the man counts out five hundred. I will definitely be treating Soraya to a bottle of champagne here for that, and I'll save the rest for a little extra spending money.

I almost bump into the man waiting behind me as I turn around.

I am still wearing the biggest grin on my face when I hear a distinctly recognisable voice.

'It must be your lucky day.'

Umm, it is now, I think as I look at him dressed up in his suave black tie and tuxedo. He is quite the sight for sore eyes. If Carol thought he looked good in shorts, then she hasn't seen anything yet. The sophisticated version of the Mystery Mancunian of Monaco is even more pleasing to the eye.

But before I respond with anything I might regret, I remind myself that it was me who made up the *no men* rule. There is no romance happening on this trip. Besides, he is off on that imaginary trip to Antibes with his wife tomorrow. So, I try to stop my thoughts from running away with me as he stares into my eyes, awaiting a response.

'Well, hello. Fancy bumping into you here,' I say.

'We were only just saying how small Monaco is, weren't we? Beautiful casino, isn't it?' says Elias.

I look around for a wife behind him, but all I see are two couples nearby.

'Oh, it's lovely here. So, umm, are you here with your friends... Or...?'

'No, it's just me.'

'Ah, a holiday alone then. It's nice to have time on your own sometimes.'

I feel flummoxed and don't know what to say as I look at him standing there in front of me. This vision of godliness is making me tongue-tied!

'I'm here with work, actually. I'm a skipper on a yacht.'

He is smiling that gorgeous grin again, and as our eyes meet, there is some kind of sparkly connection. I tell myself I mustn't look into his eyes, so I avert my gaze to his black tie, which is tied so perfectly around his neck. All I can think of is how enticing it would be to pull it off. Oh god, I don't know where to look that is not going to give me palpitations!

'Yeah, so I'm just hanging around waiting to deliver the boat to wherever my boss wants me.'

Ah, so does this mean his wife is waiting for him back in Manchester?

'Might head towards Andalusia next, I'm not really sure,' he adds.

'Gosh, that's some life then.'

'Yeah, it can get a bit lonely sometimes, though. That's why it's nice to meet a fellow Brit.'

Nice to meet *me*, or just because I'm a fellow Brit? I try not to analyse his words and tell myself to focus on the conversation. *Do not look at his eyes, his bow tie, or any part of him that is attractive.* I look down at his perfectly polished shoes.

'Hmm. I can't ever imagine it would be lonely when you have a yacht at your disposal, but I suppose it could be.'

'Well, it's not mine. As I say, I'm just the poor skipper. Luckily, my boss is a very good person.'

'Right. Cool.'

Cool? *Cool?* I haven't used that word since the Eighties. What am I saying? The girls would scold me for being full-on cringe if they heard me.

'So, how long you here for?' he asks.

'We leave the day after tomorrow.'

'Can I be direct and ask you something?'

'Umm. Okay.'

My heart is beating so fast now that I have to cough to get over the fact that I have just had the hugest palpitation!

'This is incredibly forward of me, but if you're leaving soon, I don't suppose you fancy going for dinner tomorrow?'

I don't know if it's the lights of the casino, but I swear he is blushing, and so I feel terrible for turning down his offer.

'Ah, I can't. I'm so sorry. It's my best friend's big birthday tomorrow. This is a girls' holiday. That's why we're here. Then we leave the following day, as I said. I'm really sorry.'

'No, of course. I totally understand. Well, it's been lovely meeting you.'

'You too, Elias.'

'You remembered my name?'

'Of course I did.'

We smile at each other, and a warm, tingly feeling comes over me. I tell myself to ignore it. That will just be the reminder that I need to increase my HRT.

'Well, bye, Lucy. As I said, lovely meeting you.' He remembered my name too!

I watch as Elias walks away for the second time today. Only this time, I know there's no chance of seeing him as he will probably set sail before our paths can cross again. If things had only been different then I might well have been persuaded to join Elias for dinner. What bad timing.

Chapter Seven

Over a bottle of the cheapest fizz available in the bar at the casino, Carol quizzes me about Elias.

'You looked like you were having a good conversation there.'

'Not really.'

'Well, you both looked pretty engrossed from where we were standing, didn't they, Soraya?'

'Yeah, you did look pretty captivated.'

'He just said he was a skipper on a yacht, that's all.'

'He has a yacht?' says Carol. Her eyes widen in excitement.

'No, he sails a yacht for his boss. They're off to Andalusia next, I think.'

'Does he have room for us?' says Carol.

'I dunno. I didn't ask him.' I shrug my shoulders and remind Carol that we aren't even allowed to talk about men on this trip.

'Oh, you're too slow for your own good. You've just found out that the Mystery Mancunian of Monaco is sailing around on a yacht, and you didn't even ask him if he could show your friends around. Some friend you are.'

I roll my eyes at Carol.

'Look, we're here for a girls' holiday.'

'Yes, but us girls love yachts, don't we, Soraya?'

'Yeah, I do love a nice yacht.'

'Right, I'm off to find him. I'm going to ask him,' says Carol.

'You can't do that!'

People sat behind us turn to look at me as I seem to get everyone's attention except Carol's.

'Look, there he is. He's still here.'

I am horrified as Carol jumps up and heads off in Elias's direction.

'Oh my god. Soraya, do something to stop her.'

'You know what Carol's like when she's on a mission, nobody can stop her.'

'Oh, don't I just know that.'

This is just like the time we were in school, and I confessed I had a crush on Shaun who sat next to me. I still can't forgive her for passing him a note telling him I loved him. It wasn't reciprocated, and I never dared look his way again. Forty years later, I still avoid him in the supermarket. Why does Carol always have to be so in your face?

Soraya laughs, but the only thing I am doing is scowling.

I watch in disbelief as Carol approaches Elias, then says something in his ear and walks back with him. She looks like the cat that got the cream.

The champagne has already tinged my cheeks pink, and they are fast becoming a glowing scarlet.

Carol never really cares what people think of her, and so she breaks my stunned silence.

'Lucy was just telling us you're a skipper on a yacht?'

'I am, for my sins.'

'Well, I was just saying, she could have asked if it's possible to have a nosy. Did you know she's an author?

Maybe she could write something about the yacht in her book?'

I grimace at Carol.

'I'm not an author. Not yet, anyway. I want to be one but…'

'An author, hey? How very interesting. Of course. Anything for a fellow Brit. I suppose I'll have to clear it with my boss first though.'

'Oh, yes. We wouldn't want to get you into any trouble.'

'I'm sure it'll be fine, but I'll check. Lucy, shall I take your phone number so I can confirm? Would tomorrow morning be okay if I can work something out?'

'That would be spiffing,' says Soraya.

Spiffing? I mouth at her. Soraya shakes her head at me, looking as shocked as I am about the choice of vocabulary that has left her mouth.

'Well then, it's a date… I mean… It's a…yeah. Anyway, Lucy, if you would be so kind as to give me your number, I'll message you in the morning and confirm.'

'It's O797…' says Carol before I can even respond.

'Perfect. I've got your number stored safely. I'm calling it a night now. Enjoy yourselves. Have a good evening, ladies.'

'Have a good evening, ladies,' repeats Carol in his accent as soon as he is out of earshot.

'You don't meet many guys with manners like that, do you?'

'No, fair play to him,' says Soraya.

The bottle of champagne is almost empty, and despite our win, we don't have that much money to splash on drinks. I suggest to Carol and Soraya that we go back to the apartment for a nightcap. Thankfully, we managed to pick up some bits from the supermarket on the way back from lunch, and there is a rather lovely-looking French wine waiting for us in the fridge that would make a suitable nightcap.

Back at the apartment and sitting outside on the balcony, we look down at the yachts below.

'What sort of boat do you think Elias drives?' says Carol.

'It's not a Porsche. I don't think you *drive* a boat, Carol,' says Soraya.

'I think she means sails,' I say.

'Yeah, whatever. But what sort of size do you think it is?'

'Well, I suppose it's got to be pretty big if you need to hire someone to sail it.'

'I'd definitely say it's a pretty big one,' winks Carol.

'I think it's time for someone's bed,' I say.

'Oh, I do hope he messages you first thing, though. It would be good if we could have a nosy straight after breakfast, wouldn't it?' says Soraya.

'Let's see what happens. Hey, I've just realised it's midnight. Happy birthday, Soraya,' I say.

Carol and I hand Soraya her birthday gifts.

Carol gives her a tiara which says 'Fifty' and comes in a pack with a pink sash, which Soraya happily puts on.

'It suits you. I always said you were a bit of a princess,' I tease her.

I take some photos of her on my phone and then Soraya opens the other gift from Carol. It is a bottle of Anaïs Anaïs perfume, which was Soraya's favourite in her late teens.

'Oh my god. I loved this. What a thoughtful gift,' she says. Then Soraya tears open the packaging and sprays it all over herself as if it were a can of Impulse.

'Oh, it reminds me of being in Barnums and when I met Andrew in the kebab shop. Oh – and the three of us falling out of that pub down the Mumbles. It also reminds me of my lovely mam too. She used to have a bottle on her dressing table, and I was always nicking it.' Soraya laughs.

We all remember going to Soraya's mother's house. She was glamorous, just like Soraya. She always had her nails painted and her long dark hair neatly pinned up.

'Wow, so many memories this brings back. This is incredible, Carol. It's like memories in a bottle. Thank you.'

Amid the cloud of Anaïs Anaïs that still lingers pleasantly in the air, I give her my gift and hope Soraya likes it just as much as Carol's.

'Sorry, but what do you get the woman who has everything?' I apologise in advance in case Soraya is disappointed as I hand over an album full of photos of the three of us, spanning our primary school years until now.

'Ooh, what is it?'

I feel nervous as I wait for her reaction as she tears at the wrapping paper. Fortunately, her face lights up as she opens the album.

She strokes her hand over the gold embossing on the leather cover.

'*To my best friend, Soraya,*' she reads out loud. Then she flicks inside at the photos.

'Wow. This is the best present ever. And the perfume, of course.'

'Oh my god, is that us on the first day of secondary there? Look at my perm. Can't believe my mam let me have a perm at the age of eleven. No wonder my hair's like straw now,' says Carol, looking over Soraya's shoulder.

We all laugh as we huddle together, looking over the photos that bring back so many memories of all the things we have got up to together over the years. Luckily, I managed to find photos of our first holiday abroad when we went to Ibiza at seventeen; a photo of Soraya standing in front of her first car, which was a very rusty Ford Fiesta that was scrapped on its first MOT, and when Carol and I were bridesmaids at her and Andrew's wedding. All the stages we have gone through together are in the album.

'This is the most incredible gift imaginable. It's making me emotional,' says Soraya.

'I'm so glad you like it.'

'I absolutely adore it. I'll treasure it forever.'

'Aww, well, I've left a little space at the back so that we can get a photo from this trip too. I managed to get a nice one of us at the casino last night, but maybe we can get one on the yacht, if Elias calls.'

As much as I try to pretend that I couldn't care less if he calls, I feel a wave of excitement at the thought.

Chapter Eight

By the time I open my eyes and look at my phone in the morning, there is a message already waiting from Elias.

> Good morning, hope you had a nice sleep. If you give me your address, I can pick you up when you're ready. It might be easier if I take you to the marina so you find it okay. Boss says he's happy for you to look around!

Since I'm in the middle bedroom, I shout through the walls at both Carol and Soraya.

'Girls, Elias says we can see the boat. What time shall I ask him to pick us up?'

A sleepy-sounding Soraya suggests ten a.m., and we all agree. After all, she's the birthday girl.

I message Elias to arrange the time, and he comes straight back. I give him our address so that he can pick us up. We quickly shower, get ready to meet him and pack up our swimming stuff for the pool we plan on going to later. For luck, we all steal a squirt of Soraya's Anaïs Anaïs before we leave and walk out smelling of the Eighties. It isn't wasted on Elias.

'What a lovely scent. Reminds me of something. I can't put my finger on it.'

'Your mother?' laughs Carol.

'Blinking heck. I was racking my brains. How on earth did you work that one out? You're bang on,' he says. I can't help but be impressed that I have come across a man in Monaco who is familiar with our favourite perfume of the Eighties.

We all laugh, and I explain how it used to be Soraya's favourite perfume. Then we climb into Elias's convertible hire car. As we head towards the main marina, which the apartment overlooks, we expect him to stop. However, he quickly drives past, and my stomach starts to flip. I realise we don't know who this man is or where he is taking us.

Nervously, I ask where we are heading.

'Oh, did you think the boat would be in that marina? Sorry, that's for the bigger boys. My boss isn't that big a hotshot. *Lady Jane* is moored in another marina. It's not too far away.'

'Lady Jane. Is that your boss's wife?' asks Soraya.

Elias looks at her in the mirror and gives a noncommittal smile.

'What music do you ladies like? I've got a playlist on here somewhere. Scroll through.' I take Elias's phone and look through his music selection.

'ELO? Genesis? 10CC! Goodness, I've not heard of any of these for years.'

Carol and Soraya groan, so I continue flicking through until I find a Take That song.

'Yay, that's more like it,' says Carol.

Soraya reaches her arms out through the open roof and waves them around.

'Woohoo. Take That. The birthday girl says bring it on.'

As she waves her arms in the air, I think how lucky it is that she is saving her birthday tiara for this evening, or she may well have lost it in the breeze by now. I desperately hang onto my panama hat as Elias navigates the bends and chicanes of Monaco in the little soft-top Fiat as we sing along to Take That. The breeze picks up further as we go around a corner, and Carol's vintage silk scarf slips from her head. I watch in the mirror as she holds onto it for dear life. She is very proud of that headscarf, which used to belong to her mother.

A wave of happiness washes over me as I sing along to Take That and enjoy this moment of freedom. Here, in this car, it is back to being me and my friends, like the old days before those adult commitments, divorce and household bills all came along. It feels like being fifteen again, before life gave me a few lemons. I am so thrilled we bumped into Elias last night and we get to spend Soraya's birthday like this. I'm also looking forward to what I might find on board the yacht, not to mention the research for my book. Maybe I should include a handsome skipper on a yacht in my romcom.

I lose track of time and enjoy the feeling of the sun on my skin until finally a harbour comes into view.

'Almost there,' says Elias.

The marina is smaller than the main one at Port Hercules, although it's still impressive as it sits at the foot of the Rock of Monaco. It's sheltered by the rock and surrounding buildings and is a delightful, cosy cove. Whilst the boats are smaller here than at the main marina, they are definitely not small by any stretch of the imagination.

'Wow, look at that one,' says Carol.

'That belongs to a sultan,' says Elias knowledgably.

'A sultan? Is he single?' laughs Carol.

'I'm sorry to disappoint you, but I think he has a few wives.'

'Oh, that's a shame. What about that boat over there? Who owns that?' She points at a beautiful, sleek silver yacht that looks like a bullet.

'I don't know. Think it came in last night.'

'I like that. I think that's my favourite one,' she says.

Carol is like an inquisitive child in the back and can't stop asking questions as Elias parks up.

'So, do you get to meet everyone in the marina?' asks Soraya.

'No. You get to chat sometimes, and there are some staff that are quite friendly. The owners tend to keep themselves to themselves, though. But, yeah, I get to meet other captains and deckhands and things. You know how it is when you all work in the same industry,' says Elias.

'Yeah, because it's just like that when you're a hairdresser,' says Carol sarcastically.

Elias smiles politely and strides ahead.

We walk along the moorings and past some of the most beautiful yachts I have ever seen. I particularly enjoy looking at the stern of the boats with their names and colourful flags that swing in the breeze. The yachts are registered to so many different glamorous places, including Barbados, Antigua, Dubai, and Corsica; they come from all over. Then I spot one with a British flag that is registered to the UK. I look at the name, and it is *Lady Jane*. I think it must be one of my favourite boats here. Some of them seem too ostentatious and probably have helicopter pads and goodness knows what on them.

However, *Lady Jane* is just perfect. She's big and beautiful but not too much. If I was a squillionaire, like some of these people, and I wanted a yacht, this is just the type of thing I would go for. It looks more intimate than the others, and you wouldn't need an army of staff either.

'Right then. Are we ready to see *Lady Jane*?' asks Elias.

'Absolutely,' says Soraya.

'How funny. I was thinking that this is my favourite boat here, and it's the one you work on,' I say.

'How many floors has it got?' says Carol, looking at *Lady Jane* in wonder.

'Just so you know, we call them decks, and there are only three on here – unlike some of the ones around us,' says Elias.

'Yeah, Carol. You should know they're called decks,' Soraya teases her.

Elias's lesson in yachting terms doesn't deter her and she rushes straight after Elias to walk over a small gangplank to get on board. Soraya and I follow behind her and giggle at how excited Carol has become.

'Do you mind taking your shoes off? Sadly, that's boat etiquette – not my rules,' says Elias as he removes his deck shoes.

We place all our shoes in a pile and make our way to the main deck. Beyond two sliding glass doors is a lounge area with huge comfy sofas and a bar area.

'Wow. Imagine being sat here, sailing the Med with the man of your dreams,' says Carol.

'This is beautiful. Do you mind if I take some photos to show my husband?' says Soraya.

'No, be my guest,' says Elias.

'Can you imagine Andrew seeing this? It's just his kind of thing. What a lucky lady Jane is to have a yacht like this named after her.'

'Maybe her husband bought it for her,' says Carol.

'Umm, and why can't she buy her own yacht? She doesn't need a man to buy her a yacht. It's obvious there is a woman of style and class behind this somewhere. I bet she doesn't need any man behind her,' I argue.

'Fair enough. You're right. She does need a hot captain, though,' says Carol.

'Yeah, but that's only so she can relax and not have to worry about driving. It's hard enough to park in the supermarket sometimes. Imagine trying to park one of these up in its mooring,' I say.

'Are you saying women are bad drivers?' laughs Elias.

'No, I'm definitely not saying that. I'm just saying men sometimes have their uses. I've never been much of a parallel parker, that's all. But Soraya here, she can do it in her sleep.'

'Yeah, I admit, I am pretty good when it comes to parallel parking.'

'Oh well, I'll have to give you a go at the controls then. We can have a parking challenge,' says Elias.

'Oh yeah. Challenged accepted,' says Soraya.

'Come on. I'll take you all onto the bridge.'

We follow Elias like he is the Pied Piper and look around in awe at the artwork that hangs around the lounge area. The bright colours of the landscapes perfectly complement the neutral palette of the furniture. Cream sofas plumped up with cushions look inviting and a lot more comfortable than the cheap sofa I picked up to furnish my flat. I notice the hardback books about yachts that appear to have been carefully chosen to adorn the coffee table. It seems they've thought of everything.

The boat gently bobs about in its mooring as the three of us spot a sculpture of a panther with a diamond necklace.

'I can't make my mind up about that. Bit chavvy perhaps?' whispers Soraya, as she eyes up the panther.

'I don't know. I wouldn't waste that necklace on a sculpture though. I'd rather wear it than leave it gathering dust like that,' I say.

'What if it's real diamonds?' says Carol.

'It can't be, surely?'

'It could be. If so, then Lady Jane and her husband are seriously loaded,' says Carol.

'I think you'd have to be pretty loaded for the boat alone, without the furniture,' I say. By the look of the glossy walnut woodwork and the cream and blue carpeted spiral staircase leading downstairs, clearly no expense has been spared. Elias then gives us a sneaky peek into the galley, which is a lot more basic than the rest of the boat, although it still has the best of everything, including a high-tech coffee machine and Smeg fridge.

Meanwhile, stepping onto the bridge reminds me of a spaceship. There are so many screens, knobs and buttons that I don't know how Elias is so familiar with them.

'I wouldn't know where to begin. You must be very smart,' I say.

'No, not really. It's easy when you get used to it all. I was a Boy Scout, it helps.'

He pushes a button, and the engines roar in the water below us.

'Woah. This thing must be fast,' says Carol.

'I can bore you with all the facts and figures if you like?'

'No, it's okay. I went on a date once with a guy who didn't stop talking about his Vauxhall Astra and how fast it could go. He told me five times how many miles per gallon he got out of "her". It was one of the worst dates ever.'

'Oh, I'd better stay quiet then.' Elias laughs.

As Carol flirts with Elias and they get on like a house on fire, I get a burst of jealousy. I feel like reminding her that it was me who met him first. I try to tell myself that would be so petty; besides, I am purely here for inspiration for my book, and I need to make a note of everything I see.

Feeling a bit left out, I turn away from them and look over to the boats to the side of us. A couple board their splendid silver yacht and quickly disappear inside the huge glass doors. With them gone, I turn to watch a deckhand scrub the decks of a neighbouring yacht with a brush as he gets it ready for the owner, no doubt. There are so many people to watch here. The contrast between the yacht owners and deckhands doesn't go unnoticed. I am definitely in the deckhand category with all the cleaning and picking up I do after the girls.

'You okay?' asks Elias, noticing that I have gone quiet.

'Yeah, I'm fine. Just watching that guy over there. Looks like quite a hard job.'

'Yeah, that's why I insist people remove their shoes on here. That and the white carpets, which aren't very forgiving.'

Elias puts his hand on my shoulder, and I feel his gentle grip. I try to remember how long it has been since I felt a man's hand anywhere near me. It would have been in the days before Michael became Mickey and wore the Hawaiian shirts. I turn around to look at Elias. He has such lovely, long, dark eye lashes, kind eyes and a square jaw that somehow makes him look like the perfect captain. He seems powerful and calm under pressure. Like Popeye, only much better looking.

'Shall I show you the cabins,' asks Elias.

'Umm, yes. I'd love to see them,' I say. I clear my throat and let out a little cough at the thought of going down into a cabin with him.

Elias leads us down some polished oak stairs until we reach the lower deck with two doors in front of us. The first door leads us to the master bedroom. As Elias swings the door open, the three of us let out a gasp.

'Oh my god. I've never seen anything so perfect,' says Carol.

'There's definitely more wardrobe space than I have at home,' I say as I look at the dark wood-panelled fitted wardrobes that line one of the walls. The gloss on them is outstanding. I'm sure you could see your reflection in them.

'It's amazing, isn't it?' says Soraya.

'Wow, it really is,' I say.

It is as much as I can do to not throw myself on the round double bed with its pale blue silk sheets; it is so inviting. However, I try to keep some level of decorum. Besides, someone might spot me lying there through the large round porthole, which has a fantastic view of the marina.

'Look at all this wardrobe space,' says Carol. I cringe slightly as she opens one of the floor-to-ceiling wardrobes. She's so nosy!

'Although if I was staying on here, all I'd need are a couple of bikinis and some sun cream,' she says.

'Look at all those pillows and cushions,' I say, trying to distract her from going through the rest of the storage. The bed is one of those where you'd have to spend five minutes removing all the cushions before you could climb in.

Elias looks at me and smiles.

'It's very comfortable in here.'

'Do you get to sleep in here? Don't you have to stay in some kind of staff quarters?' I ask.

'Oh, the owner's very kind… And generous. I can stay in here if I want to.'

Carol looks at Soraya, and then they both look at me. *Affair with Lady Jane?* mouths Carol.

'Well, it must be incredible to wake up somewhere like this,' I say.

'It's not a bad place to wake up at all,' says Elias.

For some reason, as he looks at me and says this, I become all flustered, so I remind the girls that we wanted to hit the pool before lunchtime, or we might get burnt in the midday sun.

'We don't want to look like lobsters tonight,' I tell them.

'No, we did say that. Well, thank you so much. This has been a brilliant birthday treat. Thank you again, Elias,' says Soraya.

'Oh, definitely. It's been awesome. Thank you, Elias.'

'You're very welcome. Nice to have the company. Now, let me drop you back into Monaco.'

The drive seems faster coming back into the principality, and we soon recognise where we are.

Elias drops us off at a hotel we've found that will allow us to use the pool as day visitors, and we head off with our suntan lotion.

We wave goodbye to Elias as he drives off, and I can't stop myself from looking back three times until he is finally out of sight.

'Well, he's a bit of alright, isn't he?' says Carol.

'He certainly is. And a lovely man too,' says Soraya.

'I hope we'll see him again. Can't you arrange something?' says Carol.

I start to get annoyed and don't even understand why. Carol has been my best friend forever, but suddenly, I feel so irritated with her. We are here for a girls' holiday. How many times does she have to be told?

'No, I can't arrange anything. Now will you stop going on about Elias?'

'Ooh, touched a nerve, have we?' she says.

'No. I couldn't care less about him. It was just embarrassing seeing you all doe-eyed every time he said anything.'

'She fancies him,' says Carol to Soraya.

'Don't be so childish. You're not twelve.'

'She does fancy him. It's obvious,' says Soraya.

'I don't fancy him. I don't like him and I'll never see him again anyway. Look…' I get my phone out from my woven beach bag and delete Elias's messages along with his number.

'There. Now I don't even know how to contact him. He'll be off to Andalusia, or wherever he's going by this time tomorrow, and he'll sail off into the sunset with his rich boss.'

Carol and Soraya look a bit shocked as they spread out on their sunbeds near the pool bar, with a nearby palm tree for shade. I am hoping the loud music coming from the bar will deter any further conversation.

I kick my legs around as I huff and puff on my yellow and white stripy towelled sunbed. I can't get myself comfortable, and I begin to regret having my little tantrum. I have just met the most gorgeous captain of a yacht, and even if there is no romance, he could have provided some great inspiration for my book. The truth is that Carol has hit a nerve; I'm never this narky.

I wriggle about, turn away from my friends and grab a crime novel out of my bag. Who needs romance when you can read about gritty murders? But, as I calm down, I realise I shouldn't have deleted all record of Elias from my phone. After all, I have a book to write, and I need inspiration. Elias was wonderful inspiration. Half an hour later, I can take no more.

I turn to Carol and Soraya.

'Does anyone know how you retrieve a deleted phone number?'

Chapter Nine

Since none of us are handy with finding deleted things from phones, I decide to do some work in the sunshine. I rummage around for my notebook to start planning a plot I can write about.

Maybe this is where I have gone wrong. Until now, I haven't really planned out my book. Instead, I tried to write different things, and nothing worked out. Yes, that is what it will be. However, ten minutes later, my mind keeps drifting off to why I deleted Elias's number.

I throw the notebook back in my bag. I'm not going to be able to write anything and I'm not going to be bumping into Elias again.

Agitated and fidgety, I look around at the Monaco jet set posing around the pool and wonder how much time they've spent in the gym and how many biscuits they must have sacrificed to get bodies like this. I would think it must be a full-time job. Even the best genes couldn't give the toned triceps these women have. I self-consciously suck my tummy in as one of the women walks past me in a gold bikini. I would look like one of those round toffee pennies that you find in a box of Quality Street if I tried wearing something like that. Thank goodness for plain black swimsuits with tummy control.

A few hours later, once we are all rested, have had a good swim and can take no more of the fierce sun, we walk back up the hill towards our apartment. The walk feels harder than usual after a few hours in the sun, but after a quick siesta, we get ready for Soraya's big birthday dinner, still feeling the effects of the UV rays.

'Does my nose look burnt?' says Carol.

'I've got a fab new concealer. Try some,' says Soraya, as she kindly avoids telling her the truth. Someone is going to have a peeling nose for the next few weeks.

'I think I burnt my shoulders,' says Soraya.

'Yup, I've burnt my inner thighs,' I admit.

'How on earth did you burn there?' says Carol.

I don't admit that I was lying on the sunbed in a very strange position so that all the gravity went in the right direction and made my cellulite look less visible. Soraya will only tell me off for not loving my body. It's easy for her to say.

'Dunno, it's weird,' I say.

Tonight, Soraya is wearing a stunning red strapless dress that shows her figure off beautifully and perfectly complements her dark hair. She looks sensational. In fact, when Carol puts the special birthday tiara on her, you'd be forgiven for thinking Soraya was a beauty pageant contestant. Although, Soraya would undoubtedly have an issue with that, since she doesn't feel that people should be judged on their appearance and thinks beauty pageants are unnecessary in this day and age.

As we have a glass of the French wine from the fridge, we hear a beep.

'Ah, there's the taxi,' says Soraya. We thought perhaps we would have Paulo at our disposal, although that would be very generous of Gianni, who is already kindly lending us this amazing flat, but there has been no sign of him since he dropped us off that night. I suppose Gianni must have given him the rest of the weekend off.

Through the twinkling streetlights of Monaco, we head to the restaurant in Nice that Andrew has arranged for our special evening. We make our way along the hairpin bends on the corniche roads, gasping at the ocean and the steep drop below us. The taxi driver takes the bends sharply with a terrifying confidence. At every turn, I pray there are no cyclists who could be knocked over by us.

'What a view,' says Soraya, looking down at the huge drop below.

'It's like a movie, isn't it? You can just imagine someone like Audrey Hepburn in a vintage sporty convertible driving along these roads with her headscarf staying perfectly on her head. Unlike me in Elias's car this morning,' laughs Carol.

Did she have to remind me of Elias again? I get angry with myself for thinking how I might have to look for a phone shop to see if someone can help me restore my deleted messages.

We pass through Cap d'Ail, where little sailing boats and yachts are scattered around the sea like confetti. Then we arrive at Eze-sur-Mer with its white sandy beaches and medieval architecture. I wish we had time to stop here, but the taxi driver carries on through the seaside resort of Beaulieu-sur-Mer and onto Villefranche-sur-Mer. Finally, we are welcomed into Nice with its palm tree-lined promenade. Since it's a bustling Saturday night, mopeds whizz past us, alongside Ferraris and small French cars.

When the taxi pulls up outside our restaurant, I can't get over the views. The waterfront restaurant balances on a rocky promontory that is lit up from beneath. There are diving boards at the side of the bar for the more audacious. I watch as someone dives off into the sea below. I think I will be sticking with the eating and drinking.

A waitress leads us to a table on a large balcony that is laid out with bright yellow sunflowers and perfectly co-ordinated pale blue plates. The twinkly lights hanging above us reflect onto the silverware, and our table teeters on the edge of the Mediterranean beneath us. It is absolutely perfect.

'Well, you certainly know how to celebrate a birthday,' I say, looking around at the views over Nice. Andrew knows his stuff when it comes to picking venues for a special bash.

We are perusing the menu, trying to decide between sea bass, octopus or cod fillet, when the waitress comes back with a fancy champagne bucket.

She removes the white napkin from the side and wipes at a bottle of very expensive-looking champagne.

'I don't remember you ordering any drinks yet?' I say to Soraya.

'Isn't that the stuff celebs drink?' says Carol, looking at the bottle.

'Excuse me, we haven't ordered anything. I think it might be the wrong table,' says Soraya.

'No, no. It's the right table,' the waitress assures us.

We all look a bit baffled and then conclude that Andrew must have bought it for us all as a surprise.

'Bless him. How amazing is he?' I say.

Soraya takes a photo of the three of us with the back-drop of Nice and the champagne glasses in our hands and sends it to Andrew, thanking him for the surprise.

It is only when Soraya is biting down on her octopus that Andrew answers her thank-you message. She almost chokes and starts coughing as she reads it.

'Andrew says he hasn't sent any champagne. He's confused now, saying it must be some mistake.'

We make eyes at each other and then look at the half-empty bottle. This is the really good stuff, and there is no way I could afford to even contribute to it. As the waitress walks past, Soraya stops her.

'I'm sorry, but was the champagne already paid for, or has it been charged to our bill? I think there's been a mistake.'

'It's paid for, madame.'

'Umm, by who?'

'Ah, he wanted it to remain a surprise for you.'

Carol and Soraya both stare at me.

'Elias!' says Carol.

'What? Why Elias?'

'Well, it must be. Who else would it be? He's the only person apart from Andrew who knew we were coming here tonight. I told him when you two were looking in the galley. He asked me where we were going for dinner tonight. He said he'd been here.'

'Oh, Carol! Maybe you shouldn't have told him,' I say.

'Of course I should have. I was asking him what it was like. Then you two came back upstairs, and that was the end of the conversation. Well, now, I don't know about you, but I really want to meet Elias again. Maybe we should try and find his boat tomorrow to say thank you,' says Carol, her nose getting redder by the minute with the combination of sun and alcohol.

'I've no idea where it was. Do you?' says Soraya.

'Nope. I could never find it again. I was too busy singing along to Take That to watch where we were going, and now I don't even know his number. Oh no. I feel bad now. I wish I could thank him.'

'Well, if I know anything, it's that a man does not spend that much on champagne for someone and then disappear. He'll be wanting something.' Soraya waves her champagne glass in the air as if she is giving me a lecture.

'And if *I* know anything, it's that free champagne tastes even nicer than when you pay for it yourself,' laughs Carol, taking a sip.

As we sit back, I can't help feeling a glimmer of hope that Elias will be in touch. I also feel slightly smug that, for once, it is I who has brought something glamorous to the table and not Soraya. I may not have met the miraculous director who can turn my unwritten book into a movie, but I have met the Mysterious Mancunian of Monaco who has treated us to the finest champagne, something I never thought he could have afforded, if I am honest. Although, the terrible thought occurs to me that he could have put it on his expense card and Lady Jane and her husband will have to pick up the tab. If that is the case, then I would be horrified.

'Actually, sorry to say this, but do you think Elias could be some fraudster who is trying to woo us all?' says Soraya.

'Well, I wasn't expecting that one,' says Carol.

'Do you think?' I ask.

'No, it's silly. It's just this champagne is so expensive. I mean, it's a lot to pay for something with no motive. No, I'm being silly and paranoid. He's a lovely guy. Forget I said that,' says Soraya.

What is his motive? As my mind goes into overdrive, I regret not having my handy notebook with me. So many ideas are running through my head for the book, although most of them would involve some sort of crime. I am so confused that I am glad when our conversation changes course, and the three of us laugh about some of the adventures we have had over the years.

'Remember when Soraya's waters broke in the middle of the C&A closing-down sale,' says Carol.

'Meanwhile, people were nearly trampling over us to get to the bargain underwear. Then you nearly slipped in the amniotic fluid, and I had to rush and get help. We were a right bunch,' I say.

'We've been through everything together, us three. Births, deaths, marriages and divorce,' says Carol.

'That's what makes us the Three Musketeers. Nothing will ever come between us. Through thick and thin, we are besties forever,' says Soraya.

We raise our end-of-the-night cocktails and make a toast.

'Through thick and thin.'

'I was thinking I'd use this photo for the last pic in the album. What do you reckon?' says Soraya, holding her phone up for us to see.

We all agree that tonight's photo with our champagne glasses and the view of Nice will be the perfect one to end on.

'Next thing, it'll be your sixtieth,' says Carol.

'Oh, don't. Time doesn't stand still for any woman, does it.'

I think about our next milestone birthdays. What will we be doing? Will we all go away and celebrate together, or will Carol have met someone who will whisk her away from us by the time I turn sixty? Maybe I will be even more of a penniless wannabe author than I am now and have given up on my dream. If Michael hadn't strayed, I wonder how different things would have been. The divorce was the hardest thing I have ever been through in my life. Harder even than my parents dying in a way, because I lost *everything*. I lost the little family unit that I thought we were. I lost my home. I lost the life I thought I had and the future I had imagined. I grieved for all those things we would never get to do. Michael and I would now never be one of those couples celebrating a ruby wedding anniversary with our grandchildren around us. Everything had changed forever. But, sat here in Monaco, I recognise that change isn't always a bad thing. I'd much prefer to be on my own than stay with a philanderer. I have far too much self-respect to ever stay with someone like that. Because of his choices, I can now live my life as I want to. It is my time, and Monaco is a pretty wonderful place to start living my best life and fulfil my dream career. Finally, I am excited about what the future has in store instead of being fearful.

The waitress interrupts my thoughts when she asks if we want more drinks. Since we have to get back to Monaco, we decide to have the last nightcap at home again, like last night.

We are heading back in the direction of the apartment, and dozing in the taxi, when Soraya reads a message that Andrew has just sent.

'Oh, girls. I know who sent the champers.'

I thought we already knew who had sent the champers. We have all worked out that it was my handsome yacht skipper. But then my heart skips a beat as I register what Soraya is saying.

'Aww, that's so sweet. It was a present from Gianni. He gave Andrew the restaurant recommendation, you see, so Gianni arranged the champagne.'

I cringe to myself as I sit in the back of the taxi, feeling like such a fool. Why on earth would a skipper on a yacht that I have just met be sending us a bottle of the most expensive champagne in the middle of an upmarket restaurant? I must have been completely deluded to even consider it. Although, on a positive note, this means that at least Elias isn't trying to swindle us by luring us into investing in some kind of cryptocurrency scam, or some lie about needing to borrow money for a spurious operation in the States.

But, still, I feel incredibly disappointed, having built up all sorts of scenarios in my head. I desperately try to smile and hide my chagrined face from my best friends. I am grateful that the back of the taxi is so dark.

Chapter Ten

For our last day in Monaco, Soraya decides we should do something cultural, rather than more shopping, champagne and casinos. I am quite impressed by her decision and wonder if she is becoming more sophisticated in her older years.

With a bit of a sore head after the combination of the finest champagne, cocktails and French wine, we set off early for our last day of sightseeing. We start off with the Prince's Palace of Monaco to try and catch the changing of the guards. We had hoped we could go inside the palace. Carol loves nosing around people's homes, but sadly, we are here too early in the season. So, we can only look at it from the outside. We admire the palace from under the shade of the trees that protect us from the sun, which is already glaring down on us. It is going to be a hot one today, and I am glad we got the sunbathing out of the way yesterday.

I look up at one of the palace balconies where pretty lavender-coloured flowers cascade down. If it wasn't for the turrets and cannons, I'd have thought it was a beautiful mansion in the centre of Monaco. The three of us look up to the windows, desperately hoping to spot someone of importance. Sadly, it seems there is no sign of any royalty today.

Crowds of tourists line up outside the palace as the time approaches for the changing of the guards. The guards stand tall and upright in their pristine uniforms, and they strut about as we watch them from the Palace Square.

'It's like Buckingham Palace really, isn't it?' says Carol.

'Only warmer. Don't know how those guards stand around in uniform all day in this heat,' says Soraya, wiping away a bead of sweat from her face.

As soon as they finish handing over to the new guards on duty, the crowds disperse, and we consider where we should go next. I'm hoping it's somewhere air-conditioned.

'Do you think we should have a look at the Grand Prix track?' says Carol.

'Don't know. I'm not that bothered myself, but I suppose I could get some photos for Andrew. How about we head there next, then?'

We walk around Monaco, and all agree these are the views we have seen on the Grand Prix.

'You know, I think this is it. It's just a normal road. I'll take a pic for Andrew, and then let's move on.'

Next on the itinerary is the white stone Roman-Byzantine cathedral in the old town of Monaco. Soraya reads up on it before we arrive and tells us that this is where Princess Grace and her husband Prince Rainier are buried.

'Did you know this is where they married back in the Fifties?' she tells us, clearly relishing her role as tour guide. This impresses Carol and me immensely.

It's so fortunate that the church is open to visitors, unlike the palace at this time of year. We pass the pews, walk along the aisle, and then towards the altar with its tall white candles on silver candlesticks. I imagine Grace Kelly in the beautiful wedding dress she wore as she walked along here and into the arms of her prince.

'I can't believe we are walking down the same aisle as Grace Kelly. This is seriously cool,' says Carol.

'Unbelievable, isn't it?'

It surprises me that the cathedral is quite small – nowhere near as big as I would have imagined for somewhere a prince and princess would get married. However, it is classy and quite modern, although some parts of the cathedral have obviously been renovated, such as the pipe organ that is visible way up high on a balcony.

'I'll have to show you the photos in my guidebook of that when it's lit up,' says Soraya pointing at the organ. 'It's all blue and quite the sight.'

'Goodness, yes. That is some organ,' I say.

'And I bet I know someone who has a fabulous organ too,' says Carol, looking at me. She starts laughing so hard that someone shushes her.

'Oh my god. Carol!'

'Can't take her anywhere,' says Soraya, stifling a giggle.

'Well, I'm only saying what Lucy is really thinking.'

'No, I'm not. I wasn't even thinking of Elias.'

'Well, if you weren't thinking of Elias, then why do you think I'm talking about *him*?'

'I don't know what you're on about, but I'm getting peckish. Anyone else?'

'Do you know, I wouldn't mind going back to that place we ate on the first day for an early dinner. Shall we go there?' says Soraya.

'Well, I suppose it is our last day and sometimes it's better to stick with what you know,' says Carol.

Even though the prices there make my eyes water, I still have some of the casino win left, so we all agree to finish the holiday off in style.

The waiter shows us to a table at the front, and we move our chairs to make sure we have some shade under the big umbrellas.

'I love this place. We'll have to come back again,' says Carol.

'Yeah. Next time, maybe we can stay in Nice and come for longer. We haven't seen half of what's around us. I'd have loved to stop at that place we passed… What was it called, Eze, or something? It was so quaint with all those old medieval buildings, and the sea was so clear there,' says Soraya.

'Oh, yeah. That looked gorgeous. I suppose it would've been nice to have a hire car, really. Shame Paulo buggered off,' says Carol.

'Perhaps he isn't paid enough to take us around,' I suggest.

'Well, Gianni is very generous. I don't know what happened. I suppose we'll just have to arrange a taxi to get to the airport.'

'Yeah, that's fair enough,' I agree.

'So, have you managed to get any inspiration for your book now?' asks Carol.

'Well, a little, but I could have done with a bit more time. I don't want to go back now, do you?'

'I could stay here forever,' says Carol.

'Oh, me too. But, to be fair, you haven't had much chance to think about things when we've all been partying together and shopping. You know what you should do?' says Soraya.

'What? I'll take anything you suggest because I really want to write this book. I've done nothing so far.'

'Right. In that case, why don't I see if you can stay on? I am sure Gianni wouldn't mind. In fact, he'd probably prefer someone to be here, since his housekeeper seems to be away. He's not due back for another couple of weeks. It would make no difference.'

'Goodness, I can't do that. He doesn't even know me.'

'I know him, and he's a lovely guy. He won't mind, I promise. You'll be doing him a favour. Like house-sitting. He may even pay you for it. I'll ask Andrew to give him a ring now.'

'You can't! He's done enough for us already.'

'He won't mind. I told you… He's so generous, he's a great guy. I'm messaging Andrew now. He'll sort it out. Just you wait. You'll be helping him as a house-sitter. I mean, I wouldn't want to leave a home like that empty, would you?'

'No, I agree. Anything could happen. House-sitting, eh? Hmm.' Now Soraya puts it that way, house-sitting a lavish apartment in Monaco sounds like it could be too good an opportunity to miss.

'Yeah, you can sit on the balcony in the morning with that gorgeous fresh orange juice we get from the supermarket, a warm croissant, laptop open and write your book,' says Soraya.

'Well, see what he says. He might not like the idea of a house-sitter.'

'Oh, he will.'

By the time we have finished our early dinner, I find myself hoping that Gianni agrees.

I don't want to count my chickens, though, and as we head along the front and take in the last of the views of

86

Monaco, I try to lock the beautiful images in my head. Some of the shops are starting to close, and when we turn the corner, I hear a voice I would recognise anywhere.

'Just for one, thanks,' he's saying.

'Oh my god, look. It's Elias!' shouts Carol.

'Sshhh,' I say.

I want to turn the other way as I see Elias grabbing a stool at the bar around the corner from our favourite restaurant.

'Let's say hello,' says Carol.

'Let's not.'

'Oh, come on. Don't be miserable,' says Soraya.

The two of them barge up to Elias's bar stool before I can say anything. But just before they reach him, he looks around and spots me, and if I am not mistaken, his eyes light up as though he has seen an old friend.

He immediately jumps off his bar stool to greet the three of us and kisses our cheeks in an informal French way. I try to ignore my goosebumps.

'Well, how nice to see you all again,' he says.

'You too. It's our last day. We're making the most of it. We thought we'd go for a quick walk before heading back to pack and all that stuff,' says Carol.

'Your last day already? Time flies.' Elias looks at Soraya and smiles. 'I trust you had a wonderful birthday.'

'Oh yes, I did, thank you.'

'It was so funny as this bottle of champagne turned up and we thought you had—'

I look at Carol and give her the eyes that tell her not to dare continue.

'I had what?' he asks.

'No. Nothing. We had a lovely evening. It was great. Yeah.'

87

'Yes, so, anyway, we're back to the rain tomorrow. Do you know, it hasn't stopped raining at home since last September?' I say.

'Yeah, the wettest year on record apparently,' says Soraya.

There is nothing like talking about the UK weather to get someone to change the subject. The four of us talk about what a miserable winter we had, and then the conversation turns to us leaving early in the morning.

'I was just telling Lucy she should stay on a while and see if she can get some inspiration for the book she's trying to write. So far, she's done nothing.'

'Oh dear. Too busy partying around this playground, perhaps,' says Elias, with a teasing smile.

'Yeah, definitely. That's why I've told her she needs to stay on. The apartment we've got is vacant for ages. It's not a problem. Don't you agree, Elias?' says Soraya.

'I think that sounds like a great idea. If you stay on, maybe I could take you on a day trip somewhere on the boat. If the wind in your hair and the sea air don't give you inspiration, then I don't know what will. How about it? I could take you somewhere tomorrow if you like?'

'What about your boss?'

'Oh, yeah. I'll check, but I think the Andalusia trip is a bit delayed. It shouldn't be a problem.'

'I've asked Andrew to see if it's okay with Gianni, who lent us the flat, which it will be, and you, Mrs, are getting your flight changed. What have you got to rush home for?'

'Well, Poppy and Jasmine. They'll be wanting me back in case they need something.'

'Tough. They're old enough to manage. This is your time now. How often does an offer like this come along?

They'll still be whinging at you when you get back,' says Soraya.

'Yeah, I love them to bits, but they do take me for granted sometimes.'

'Grown-up kids can do that. I know the feeling well. Sounds like someone needs to change their flight,' says Elias.

Carol, Soraya and Elias stare at me. I have never been a spur-of-the-moment type of person. I have to meticulously plan any holiday, and even a trip in the car must be carefully prepared by checking my tyres and ensuring I have my warning triangle in the boot. I never say yes to anything immediately. I have to mull things over. I can't believe I have been so easily swayed.

'If Gianni agrees, then, yes, I'd love to. Thank you, Soraya.'

'I think I still have your number, so shall I message you later and see what's happening?' says Elias.

'Yeah, sure. That sounds great.'

The bartender puts down an ice-cold beer in front of Elias, and it feels like the right time to move along.

We say our goodbyes and make our way further along the street.

'Can you believe we bumped into him? That was meant to be, definitely. I might get the tarot cards out when I get back. Have a look if he comes up,' says Carol.

'Don't you dare. I don't believe in all of that. Stop it.'

'Well, they're usually right.'

'No, they're not. Remember when you were convinced Steven was the one because your tarot cards told you so? Only one date you went on, and you couldn't stand each other.'

'Well, most of the time they're right. Maybe I didn't shuffle the cards properly. Anyway, that was a long time ago. So, where are we off to next?' says Carol.

'I don't know about you, but I'm exhausted after all the sightseeing. How about we pick up a final bottle of that nice French wine and watch the world go by from Gianni's balcony?' says Soraya.

'Do you know what? I must be getting old, but that sounds amazing,' I say.

We pop into the supermarket and head back to the comfort of our apartment, where we open another bottle of French wine, kick our shoes off and lounge around on the balcony, putting the world to rights.

The evening is every bit as wonderful as being in the casino, looking at the palaces, or exploring the yacht, because what is important is the friendship we share, no matter what we are doing.

Chapter Eleven

Gianni agrees that I can stay, but I decide not to tell Poppy and Jasmine that I am here for a while longer until it is too late to change my mind. I am glad I haven't said anything yet, as when Soraya and Carol leave for the airport, I begin to get cold feet.

'Would I have time to quickly pack up and come with you?' I beg.

'No. It's for your own good. We know you'll come back home with that best-seller worked out. Now, make the most of this lovely apartment and enjoy yourself. It's only for two weeks, and you'll soon be home and complaining about the rain again,' says Soraya.

'Yeah, very true. You're amazing. Thank you for arranging such an opportunity for me.'

'You deserve it after everything you've gone through with Michael. Oh, and before I leave…' Soraya hands me her turquoise kaftan that I have always loved so much.

'Here. I know there's a washing machine, but you might need some extra clothes. Take this, it might come in handy.'

I look at the delicate beads and the silver sequins that embellish the neckline.

'I can't take this. It's far too beautiful. You know it's my favourite on you.'

'You can. Please. I won't be needing it in Swansea. Have you seen the weather forecast next week?'

'You are just too kind. I promise to look after it.'

I hug Soraya and Carol goodbye and then wave as I watch their taxi drive away. As soon as I close the door, the apartment feels bigger than ever. Here by myself, I seem to be rattling around. Although, it doesn't stop me moving my things into the master bedroom. I couldn't resist the four-poster bed with the white lace curtains.

Eventually, I decide I am ready to give Poppy and Jasmine a call to explain about my extended holiday. I know they will already be up, as they have lectures on a Monday morning, and so I ring our group chat.

'Are you on your way back, Mam?' asks Poppy.

Jasmine talks over her as she tells me to grab perfume and some make-up in duty-free for her.

'Woah, woah. Right…' I have to take a big gulp. I can't believe I am so apprehensive about telling my own kids I am staying on.

'The thing is… You know how I have this book I want to write. Well, I've decided to stay on in Monaco for some ideas for it and…'

'Are you serious? How long you staying on for?'

'Just a couple of weeks. There's this guy who sails a yacht, and he's offered to take me out on it. So, you know, that should give me plenty of material to think about for the book…'

'You've met a guy who sails a yacht. He's not a drug dealer or some kind of scammer, is he?' says Jasmine.

'Don't be silly, he's from Manchester. He's a decent sort of chap.'

'Oh. My. God. Mam's met a scammer from Manchester and she's going off on a boat with him. I'm calling the police,' says Poppy dramatically.

'Calm down. Don't be so silly.'

'Well, how did you meet him?'

'He kindly gave me some money, actually.'

'What? He gave you money? Bingo. There you go then. He's a fraudster, obvs. Nobody gives someone money when they first meet.'

'It was a few euros!'

'Exactly, you see. These guys, they know what they're doing. He pays you a couple of euros, he gets a hundred thousand out of you.'

'Come on, Jasmine. Where on earth do you think I'd find money like that to give anyone?'

'It's on TV all the time, Mam. They get ways around you, and the next thing you know, you're remortgaging your house. No wonder he's sailing around Monaco in a yacht. What poor woman paid for that? Some child's mother will have been scammed because of that little shit. Heartbreaking.'

'Oi, mind your language. He's not a little shit. He's a lovely kind chap from Manchester, and I'm sure there's been no scamming anyone's mam.'

'Are you for real? I'm telling Dad, and if necessary, he'll come out there and drag you back and bring you to your senses.'

'I don't want your dad knowing anything about this. It's none of his business.'

'Well, I'm telling him. We have to protect you,' says Poppy.

'Do *not* tell your father. It's nothing to do with him or anyone else.'

'Yes, it is if you're about to be scammed and he could do anything to you if you don't give him what he wants. Oh my god, Mam, what have you got yourself into?' says Jasmine.

'He's done nothing wrong. Don't be so dramatic. Have you been watching those Netflix shows again?'

'This is how it starts, Mam. I'm telling you now. This is only the beginning. He'll have your flat in the marina next. You'll be waving goodbye to it as he takes everything,' says Jasmine.

'Oh, you are a silly billy. He's not after any money. He's got a decent job. He works for rich people and…'

'Yeah, yeah, yeah. Heard it all before. Scammer material right there,' says Jasmine.

'Oh, there's no talking to you two when you're like this. Let's just agree to disagree.'

'This is deffo how they start. Loan you a bit of money and then take ten times that from you… Only the other day I was watching this story, right? And this woman met a man she thought was a high-ranking general in the US army and then…'

'Look, I'm not stupid. I know all those stories. Besides, those types of scammers don't even exist in real life. Those are someone hiding behind a screen. I've met this chap in real life. Believe me, I promise… It's nothing like that. I'm sorry I told you now.'

'No, I'm glad you did tell us. We need to know these things so we can protect you. She's getting older now, isn't she, Poppy? She might get some kind of dementia and sign everything over to him next,' says Jasmine.

'Will you two stop!'

My menopausal rage starts to rise up again with the two of them. Oh, they know how to push my buttons.

'Well, it's only the truth, Mam,' says Poppy.

'Right, that's it. I'm going now because I'm off on the yacht. I'll message you both later.'

'What? You're not serious,' says Jasmine.

'Yes, very serious. Bye girls, speak later.'

The truth is that Elias hasn't even messaged me yet, so there are no firm arrangements, but they provoked me so much I didn't want to tell them that.

I put the phone down and search in the fridge for the nice bits I picked up in the supermarket. I start off with Soraya's suggestion of a fresh orange juice and a huge croissant that I warm under the grill.

Out on the balcony, as the sun shines down on me, I tell myself that everything will be fine. At least I don't have to put up with the dramatic moments from the girls when I am away. I'll keep my contact with them to a minimum for a few days. This is me time. I am going to have an inspirational holiday, and I am finally going to get some words down on that blank page of mine.

I watch the people down below who look like ants walking about the marina. I wonder where they are all going. Are they all just millionaires from birth, or do any of them work hard to scrape by?

I have just pulled out my trusty notebook to start work when my phone bleeps.

My heart misses a beat as I realise it's Elias asking if he can collect me at eleven a.m. to take me to the yacht. His offer comes as a welcome distraction to plotting ideas. So, I rush off to wash my hair, even though it will no doubt be wrecked by the sea breeze. I must try around three different shades of lipstick before I am finally ready to meet Elias, even though I tell myself this is a research trip and it really doesn't matter what I look like. Still, I twiddle my long, mousy hair around until I have the perfect curls that peep out from under my borrowed panama hat, which will hopefully protect my hair from frizzing up in the breeze.

'That'll do,' I say to my reflection in the huge floor-to-ceiling mirror of the master bedroom.

When I hear the beep of a horn outside, I jump and try to calm my breathing as I open the door to see Elias's little Fiat.

'Good morning, Lucy,' says Elias as I jump into the passenger seat.

'Morning.' I smile at Elias as he gives me one of his charming broody looks that make him so handsome in a craggy, masculine sort of way.

'Music?' he asks.

'Yes, please. Whatever.' It feels awkward without Soraya and Carol. It was much less intimidating when there was a gang of us, and I could rely on Carol to come out with something if there was ever a moment of silence.

'How about a bit of Oasis? Good old Manchester band.'

'Yes, that'd be fabulous.'

To the sound of *Wonderwall*, we drive down the now-familiar hill and weave through the streets of Monaco as we head back towards the marina where *Lady Jane* is docked.

'So, what did you do in Manchester anyway? Not many yachts there?' I ask as we get stuck at some traffic lights.

Elias laughs and asks me to guess.

'Oh no. I hate things like this. I've no idea.'

'I'll give you three guesses and then I'll tell you,' he smiles.

I look at his hands on the steering wheel, which indicate he has possibly done some kind of manual work.

'A plumber.'

'Haha. No, but being a plumber does involve water and I suppose you could say my previous job did too.'

'Well, I was going to say an electrician next, but that wouldn't involve water.'

'Is that your second guess?'

'No. Let me try again. Umm, a lifeguard.'

Although, somehow, I can't imagine him strutting up and down at the local swimming baths in his Speedos, but you never know.

'No, I can see why you'd think that. I am a good swimmer, though. You have one last guess.'

'Oh gosh, I really have no clue now, so I'm just going to say you built swimming pools for rich people.'

'Ha. Now, I wouldn't have minded doing something like that. I'm quite good with my hands. I'd imagine laying all those mosaic pieces could be therapeutic if you're patient enough. But no. Do you give up?'

'Yup. No idea.'

'Okay, but did I mention there was a booby prize if you didn't guess?'

'Yikes. No.'

Elias laughs. 'You can have another guess if you like. Otherwise, the booby prize might involve me inviting you out for dinner.'

I don't tell him how nice that sounds.

'Oh no, well, that sounds terrible. I definitely need another guess in that case.' We both laugh as we tease each other, and I try to think of any other occupation I can.

'You were a dentist.'

'Did you get that completely wrong so you win the booby prize?'

I feel a tingle all over as I look at him.

'Hmm, maybe.'

We both have big grins.

'So, it looks like I'm taking you for dinner then.'

'Well, if you must.'

I sit back in my seat and think about how nice dinner will be with him. Maybe I'll wear Soraya's kaftan.

'Umm, anyway, so what was it that you did in Manchester?'

'I was a window cleaner. See, that's why I said about the water. Went through tons of it.'

'Oh, wow. That one hadn't crossed my mind. No wonder the windows are sparkling on the yacht.'

'Oh, yeah. Don't get me started on the best way to get your windows sparkling. My dad was a window cleaner before me, and then I took over from him. Family business since 1963.'

'But now you're a yacht skipper. What about the family business?'

'It's a long story… One I'll tell you another time.'

Elias pulls the car into the marina car park and pulls up the handbrake. He looks quite serious.

'Yeah. I will tell you… Maybe one day, if the time is right.'

'Sure.' The Mysterious Mancunian of Manchester has just become a whole lot more mysterious. Jasmine and Poppy's words spring into my head. *This is how it starts, Mam. I'm telling you now. This is only the beginning.* I try to ignore their little voices as I spot *Lady Jane*.

'Anyway, here we are. *Lady Jane* awaits.'

We walk to the yacht, and Elias leads me onto the bridge. He does some safety checks, running around the boat like a headless chicken while I sit on the seat beside the captain's chair. It is like I am second in command,

and I momentarily feel a sense of importance until Elias returns to start up the engines.

The engines roar with power, and once again, the water bubbles beneath us. The rope tied to the marina has been hauled in, and we are off.

'I'll be a bit busy for a few minutes, just while I steer us out of here. But we can sit back a bit once we hit the open sea, okay?'

'Yes, of course. I'll sit here quietly and try not to distract you.'

I feel like a queen as I sit on the yacht as people watch us leave our mooring. For a moment, I am Lady Jane, and for once, I experience what it must be like to have such luxury at your fingertips. I just wish my clothes were a bit fancier and I wasn't wearing an old jumpsuit I bought in Swansea market. How the other half live. Despite my fashion crisis, I think I am beginning to feel inspired. I go to grab my notebook from my bag to make some notes as we set sail, and I notice that I have a message on my phone.

A message from Michael flashes up in large print on the screen.

> The girls just told me you're going on a boat trip with some scammer. What the hell is wrong with you? You have no idea who he is. Get off that boat now. Anything could happen to you!!!

How *dare* he tell me what to do. He is allowed to go on any midlife crisis he wants and even change his name to make himself sound younger. But god forbid I go sailing with a very pleasant skipper. Why is it that my family all think I don't deserve my own happy life? So selfish, the lot of them.

I roll my eyes under my oversized sunglasses. *Oh, Michael, I'm going to have words with you when I get back. Very strong ones.*

'Everything alright?' asks Elias.

Instinctively, I touch his arm.

'Oh, yes, fine. Hopefully, we won't have phone reception where we're going.' I try to smile and swiftly switch my phone off, throwing it back into my bag.

But as I head further out into the open sea, completely alone with Elias, as much as a part of me is delighted and enjoying every moment, I realise that we are heading into choppy waters. The truth is that Jasmine, Poppy and Michael are right: I don't know the slightest thing about Elias. He could be anyone, but the problem is I am starting to enjoy his company. I am just going to have to go with my instinct on this one.

Chapter Twelve

After we have sailed for half an hour, Elias suggests we anchor up. I look over to the beautiful bay nearby and agree it is the perfect spot. I have no idea where we are, but it is certainly stunning, with crystal-clear sea and shoals of colourful fish swimming around us.

As we gently sway in the water, I relax on the deck and lie on a sunbed decorated with the yacht's insignia of gold and blue whilst I wait for Elias to get us some drinks. I thought perhaps if we lay on the sunbeds for a while, we might be able to have a chat, and I'd get my chance to find out more about him. However, Elias suggests we dive off the boat since this is the perfect place for a swim. Fortunately, I packed my swimwear, assuming that swimming might be involved today.

Once I finish my soft drink, I change in the small bathroom with gold-plated taps. I must adjust my sarong twenty times before I have the confidence to walk back out.

As I approach Elias, he smiles, and the look on his face tells me that he likes what he sees. Shyly, I avert my eyes from him and focus on the ground.

'Is that a batik sarong?'

His question takes me aback. How on earth does Elias know about batik sarongs? Was it the sarong that he liked the look of when I walked out? There was me getting ideas!

'Umm, yeah. Soraya picked it up on a stall in Indonesia on one of her wonderful trips.'

'Very clever how they do batik with the hot wax. Have you ever seen it being done?'

'Umm, no.'

As Elias talks about wax, I self-consciously cross my legs as I think about how my bikini wax might need redoing and start cringing. Thankfully, though, Elias seems nervous and starts rambling, delaying our swim. From talk of the art of batik, he tells me about the time he realised he needed glasses.

'So, there was this woman walking down the street with a hamster. Now, I had a hamster when I was a kid, so I had to say something. I stopped her and went to pet its head, and she shouted at me to get off her chocolate muffin. It was a bloody muffin and not a hamster! Of course, I offered to pay for a new muffin after I'd had my hand all over it. The next thing I did was book an optician's appointment.'

We laugh together, and I soon forget about my bikini line and, indeed, anything else.

'Anyway, what am I going on about? Let's have that swim.'

'As long as you can see where you're going,' I tease.

'Oh, don't worry, I've got my contacts in, and I can see you very clearly.' I notice his cheeks go red as he says it. Maybe it was better when I thought he was short-sighted!

Hesitantly, I remove my sarong, worried about exposing my wobbly bits and anything else. I hear Soraya's voice in my head telling me to be confident and love myself, wobbly bits and all. Elias lifts his arms up to remove his T-shirt, and I try not to stare at those muscles underneath a long scar on his chest. I am glad Carol isn't here now. I may have had to push her overboard to cool her down a bit.

When we get to the diving board, I insist that Elias dives off first. I don't want him seeing me with my bottom wobbling everywhere as I belly-flop into the sea. Instead, I watch him as he flies through the air in the perfect dive. Then he disappears beneath the sea and pops his head up as though he is some great shark looking for prey. Let's just hope I'm not his target.

I take a deep breath and jump off the back of the boat, closing my eyes until I feel the water smash against my body. It is refreshing and invigorating. This must be how those women who do that cold water swimming stuff feel, only chillier, obviously. I have never seen the appeal until now. But as I bounce up from the water, I feel regenerated, confident, and as though I am living my best life.

I smooth my hair with my hand in a way that makes me feel as though I am Bo Derek in that famous movie scene and smile at Elias as I tread water. Then he does something strange with his hand, in a sort of wave around my shoulders, and then he says, 'Sorry, your top, umm, it's…'

I look down and die. One boob is hanging right out, and I didn't even notice. Was I too busy trying to create the perfect pose that I didn't feel anything was wrong? I scramble so hard at the strap of my swimsuit to cover my modesty that I manage to scratch my skin.

'Oh my god. I'm sorry. This blasted swimsuit. I'm mortified.'

'Hey, you're amongst friends. Forget it. I just wanted you to know, that's all. I mean, gosh, people around here go topless all the time. Nothing to be ashamed of.'

Nothing to be ashamed of! I am dying and can never look this man in the eye ever again. I dive down under the water so that I can regain some composure, holding onto the strap as I bob back up. Elias is still there, looking at me, and the embarrassment has not ceased in the slightest.

'Fancy a race?' he says.

I'll do anything not to look at him right now, even a competitive swim.

'I'm not that good a swimmer, but I'll try.'

'I'll give you a head start then,' smiles Elias.

I don't think I have ever swum so fast in my life. I was never a great swimmer, but suddenly, I have a strength and determination that I didn't know I had. However, Elias quickly catches up with me, and we reach our agreed winning post, with him easily beating me.

'I've an unfair advantage. Not a lot of people know this, but I was in the National County Team Championships a very long time ago. I should have slowed down.'

'No, it's fine. I don't need any special treatment.'

Catching our breath, we tread water for a while, and then Elias floats up on his back. I follow his lead, and we float together, looking up at the bright blue sky with the shoreline in the distance. Everything is serene and perfect out here. I feel so free and at peace with life. I can't ever remember feeling this relaxed.

When we finally start getting tired out on the water, Elias suggests we go back on board for a glass of wine.

I hadn't planned on having a drink at lunchtime, but after my mortal embarrassment with boob-gate, I could probably do with one. How could I be so unlucky?

Back on the yacht, I wrap up in one of the large beach towels that Elias hands me as I step on board. I wrap it around me like a cloak to protect myself in case I exhibit any further body parts. Then I go into the shower room to rinse off and change.

By the time I come back upstairs, an ice-cold glass of Chablis is on the table waiting for me.

'I thought we could sail out a little further while you relax with your wine. I want to show you something really special,' says Elias.

'Yeah, sure.'

I quickly take a sip of wine, making sure it tastes okay. I am always cautious when a guy pours a drink; it comes from worrying about the girls when they are out so much. It is ingrained in my head. However, it tastes like Chablis, and I relax a little as my hunch tells me that Elias isn't a scammer who is going to take me out into the ocean and rob me of any assets. I mean, he could have drowned me just now if he wanted to, surely? He can also probably tell by my clothes that I don't have any assets to scam.

The wind blows stronger, and the boat rocks slightly more vigorously as we move further away from the bay. Then, I finally hear the engines slow down.

'I've got to turn the engines off here, okay?'

'Yeah, whatever you need to do.'

Elias rushes over with a pair of binoculars and tells me to look starboard. I get confused with his yachting language and look to the left.

'Sorry, that means the right,' says Elias gently.

'Oh, yes. Of course.' Why do sailors have to make up this confusing terminology? I wish they would just say left and right.

I try to zoom in with the binoculars, but I just make everything blurrier.

'I can't see anything.'

'Here, give them to me.'

Elias looks out to sea and then plays with the focus until he gets it right.

'Now, you have to look this way.'

Elias stands behind me as he guides me where to look. He holds his hands around my waist as he directs my body in the right direction. I desperately try not to let him notice how my body is responding to the touch of his hands.

'Oh my gosh, I can see it! I can see it! Is it a dolphin?'

'It is indeed. I think it's a common dolphin. If you're lucky, you might spot a bottlenose or striped dolphin too. It's a protected area for mammals along here. The Pelagos Sanctuary.'

'Wow. How wonderful. We get dolphins in Wales. Although every time I've gone out on a trip to see them, the weather hasn't been the best. Now I can see why you enjoy sailing out here so much. To just be with nature like this. Do you see sharks and whales too?'

'I've seen a sperm whale once or twice, yeah.'

'Amazing.'

Elias's enthusiasm is delightful as he talks of the wildlife he's seen on his yachting adventures.

'I used to get excited when I saw a hedgehog in the garden in my old house. I've never seen anything like this unless it was on a David Attenborough programme,' I explain.

Elias laughs and then offers me another glass of wine. Still smarting from my shoulder strap incident, I agree, before we start heading back towards Monaco.

'So, what will you do for the rest of the day?' asks Elias.

'You know what? After this adventure, I think I might be able to start writing that book.'

'That's great news! You see… You can't beat a bit of sailing to brush the cobwebs off.'

'So it seems. Who knows, I might even have to think of a way I can add a magical dolphin into my story. Although I had planned on having a cat in there somewhere in memory of my beauty Stella who died.'

'Oh, bless her. How old was Stella?'

'She was a week off her twentieth birthday. To be honest, I'd love another cat one day. The timing just isn't right now with the apartment I live in. I'd like a cat to have a garden, you know.'

'Yes, of course. Well, let's hope you can share your life with another cat one day.'

'Yes, maybe. I dream of writing my book with a little furball brushing up against my leg as I type. Then forcing me to stop work as she demands I feed her.' I laugh.

'I do understand. It's not the same without a cat in the house,' says Elias.

'So, you're a cat lover?'

'Oh, yes, we always had cats when I was growing up and until recently,' says Elias.

'That's wonderful. They really are family, aren't they?'

'Totally. Even when they're gallivanting about, just knowing their cat bowl is there and they will come back in when they're ready is a nice feeling.'

'You make it sound like having teenagers in the house,' I say.

'Indeed! We had those demanding creatures in the house too.' Elias laughs. I can't resist the opportunity to find out more about his family.

'We? Your family?'

'Yes. My wife, two boys, one of whom now runs the business, and our Persian called Fluffy, who we picked up from a rescue. Fluffy was a gorgeous little thing. The boys named him. They were all best pals when they were young.'

'Cats are such good company.'

'They are. Fluffy will be keeping my wife company up there now, no doubt.' Elias points to the sky, and we both look up.

'Oh, I'm so sorry. It's hard enough losing our pets, but losing your wife too. Oh, no. I don't know what to say…'

'It's been three years now. You get used to living without them. That's one of the reasons I love being out here. I feel close to her in some ways. It was always our dream to retire and sail around the Med one day. Of course, we didn't know that we weren't to have the luxury of time on our side.'

'Well, thank goodness you got this job then. How did it come about?'

'Oh, well, umm. Yeah. One of the boys knew someone who needed a skipper, and I had a few qualifications that I'd done in my spare time, and you know… It kind of all fell into place.'

Elias turns away from me and no longer looks me in the eye. Perhaps he doesn't want to talk about this time in his life.

'Great. Well, that was some consolation, I suppose.'

'Yeah, anyway. Let's get this boat back into the harbour, hey? You have some writing to do, and I've got some work on the yacht I have to finish.'

'Oh, of course. I really don't want to keep you when you're supposed to be working.'

After we safely get back into the port, Elias drives me to the apartment. There has been no further mention of dinner, so I begin to wonder if I put my foot in it, and perhaps he realises it is a mistake to go for a meal with another woman when he is still grieving for his wife. I decide not to remind him of our earlier agreement. So, as I leave him to drive back to his yacht, I thank him for the lovely day he has given me.

'I still can't believe we saw dolphins. It was very special. You've been so lovely to me since I arrived in Monaco, and I truly appreciate it, thank you. So, I'll be seeing you then.'

'What about tomorrow night? Didn't I say I have to take you for dinner? Surely, you're not going to welch on a bet, are you?' Elias removes his sunglasses and looks at me with a naughty glint in his eye.

'Oh, umm, yes. Of course. If you're sure that's okay?'

'Absolutely! I'll book a table somewhere I know. It's nothing fancy. No need to dress up or anything.'

'Well, that sounds perfect. I'll look forward to it.'

'Me too,' says Elias.

As he drives off, I notice Paulo coming up the road in his big Mercedes. I wave to him, but he ignores me. Maybe he doesn't recognise me without my friends. He drives into the car park, and I wait for him to show up at the door. But I don't see him again, so I assume he must stay in the block somewhere. If anyone is a man of mystery, it's Paulo.

I spend the evening catching up with Carol and Soraya who have landed back into a very wet Bristol airport before making their way home. I tell them all about my day with Elias. Carol is positively seething and wishes she had stayed on, but she has appointments for a full head of highlights and some OAP perms booked for the morning, so she didn't have much choice.

I still haven't replied to Michael and consider blocking him for the duration of my trip. Then I think better of it in case the girls can't get hold of me, and there is some huge emergency that is so bad it could only happen in my imagination.

Maybe it is the thought of how nice Elias is that makes me respond, but I finally answer Michael's message.

> Michael, this is nothing to do with you.
> Elias is a very nice man from Manchester.
> He's not a scammer. You need to calm
> down.

There. I've stood up to him!

Almost instantly, Michael replies.

> Elias? That's his name? He's made it up. I
> bet that's not his name. That doesn't
> sound like some geezer from Manchester.
> He should be called John, Pete, or Steve,
> or something... I don't think you should
> have any further contact with the man.
> Please stay safe, the girls need their mam.

I throw my phone down on the sofa. The cheek of this man telling me not to have contact with Elias! Then I start seething, pick it back up and type:

Don't you dare tell me what to do. You've no idea about him. He's a much better man than you'll ever be!!!!

I press send, and the ticks show he has read it. Immediately, I can see he is typing, so I decide that for one night, surely I can block him without there being some kind of emergency in this family. With a simple block, he is no longer typing.

After all, this is a break for relaxation, inspiration, dolphin watching and eating croissants. This is not a holiday where I will allow any drama from my ex-husband into my life.

Chapter Thirteen

I am fast asleep in my lavish four-poster in the midst of the most delicious dream about Elias. We are on the yacht, all cuddled up on that round bed of his, when he leans over and hands me an adorable little kitten with the most enormous blue eyes looking up at me. I am about to kiss Elias in my dreamy haze when there is the biggest bang, followed by shouting in French.

Now, normally, in the morning, I have to open one eye first — always the left one — and this slowly follows with the right eye. However, this morning, I am forced to abruptly open two eyes, and I quickly pull the duvet up around me to protect myself from the screaming woman standing at the foot of the bed.

'*Sortez, sortez!*' she screams. I remember seeing a sign saying something like that on an aircraft once, and I'm sure it must have meant exit. I think she wants me to leave, and I am afraid she is going to drag me out of bed hair first by the wild look in her eyes. I put my hands up in the air as if to say *I surrender* and climb out of bed searching for my kimono to wrap around me. What if Gianni hasn't told his wife that someone is staying here, and she thinks I am having an affair with her husband? I try not to panic. Surely, she will understand that I have a perfectly reasonable explanation for sleeping in their marital bed. The more my eyes focus, the more I realise that the woman looks like one of the big portraits that hang on the living room wall.

'Speak English?' I ask meekly.

'I thought you were from Poland?' she says gruffly. Okay. I am so confused.

'No, Wales. You know, *Pays de Galles*.' I am suddenly thankful for learning where I am from, along with *merci* from some old language cassettes I had years ago.

'I don't care where you from. You should not be sleeping in my bed!' Her voice is still a few octaves too high for my liking, so I quickly apologise. I now wish I had stayed in my old room when Soraya left. Perhaps they didn't expect their visitors to use the master bedroom. My heart is racing, my mouth is dry, and I would do anything to have the girls here for backup.

'Yes, I'm so sorry. I'll get my things out of here as quickly as possible.'

The woman stamps up and down, grabs some of my clothes that are left on the white leather loveseat near the bed and throws them at me.

'Out!' she shouts.

I stumble about and grab all my bits as the woman reverts to screaming in French once again. I didn't realise Gianni's wife would be this feisty, but I suppose she did find a strange woman in her bed.

Once I have all my bits from her room, a moisturiser bottle that I had left in the en suite comes flying towards my head. I duck and find myself apologising for her attempted assault.

'Why the agency send me such stupid people?' she shouts.

'The agency?'

I look towards the front door, feeling that I may need to make a sharp exit from here and notice a whole stack of designer luggage has been left by the doorway. I am guessing the lady of the house is back from her trip. Maybe she has left Gianni in Dubai alone. If only she would calm down a bit, I might be able to explain what I am doing here.

'You're fired,' she screams.

'Fired? I don't work for you.'

'Listen to me.' Her face is getting menacingly scary now. 'You work for me. Not the other way around. Now, I have to clean bed! How dare you sleep there!'

'I don't know what you mean. Look, I'm very, very sorry.'

'Get out. You're the worst housekeeper the agency ever sent me. I will make a big complaint with the company.'

'Housekeeper? I'm not a housekeeper.'

'I can see you're no housekeeper! Now take your *merde* and get out!'

I desperately grab the clothes that are falling all over the place as the lady gets closer and closer, then pushes me towards the door. I may have packed quickly for last-minute holiday offers over the years, but nothing like this. Luckily, I spot my phone on the top of the table by the door and snatch it before she slams the apartment door on me. I stand in the corridor, dazed. What on earth just happened? One minute, I was in a deep sleep, dreaming nice things about Elias, and the next, I'm thrown out of my holiday accommodation.

On my hands and knees, at a safe distance from the apartment, I put everything I managed to grab into my little suitcase. I comb through my hair with my fingertips and try to compose myself as I walk downstairs through the posh reception area. I look like someone doing the walk of shame. I am so confused and slightly panicked. How on earth could this happen? By the time I'm out on the street, I burst into tears.

I search for the nearest cafe so that I can calm my thoughts and consider what I should do next. I suppose the first thing to do is try to get on the next flight home. I could never afford accommodation here.

With my head in my hands, I manage to order a coffee, and then I hear my phone. At least my day can't get too much worse, as Michael is still blocked. I see it is a voice note from Soraya, who I need to talk to more than anyone right now. I press play to listen to what she has to say.

'The weirdest thing has happened. Andrew had a message from Gianni, right. He messaged Paulo to let him know you were staying at the apartment a bit longer... And this is really weird, but Paulo said that none of us ever turned up. He said he was at the airport that night, and we didn't come off the flight. He didn't think to let Gianni know. He assumed the plans had changed and Gianni was too busy to tell him we weren't coming. Where are you now?' I stare at the phone open-mouthed and pick up my phone to ring Soraya.

'Funny you should ask that. I'm on a streetside cafe, feeling a bit homeless as I've just been kicked out of the apartment by a furious French lady who I presume is Gianni's wife.'

'But Gianni is gay.'

'Well, there was a portrait of the woman on the wall in the lounge. Remember?'

'Yeah, well, I assumed that was his mam or something. Maybe it's his mam, then? Give me five minutes, and I'll ask Andrew to clear all of this up. I have no clue what's happening. Try not to panic. I'm sure there is a very easy way to solve all of this, and you'll be back in there in no time.'

I drink my latte and bite on the little macaroon that came with it. I have a feeling this is all the breakfast I am going to be having today, thanks to my new status as a vagrant.

Ten minutes later, Soraya calls me back. She clears her throat three times before she speaks, which I know means she doesn't want to say out loud what she is about to.

'So… Andrew spoke to Gianni. Oh my god. I feel like I'm to blame for everything. It's all my fault. I was a bit… let's say… sozzled when we landed, and I think we got in the wrong car with the wrong driver and stayed in the wrong apartment. It's not Gianni's. He doesn't know where we stayed, and to be honest, neither do I. When he paid for the restaurant, he assumed we were staying in his apartment, but it's only now he's spoken to Paulo and found out we didn't show up there. I did think it was a bit strange, as Gianni is such a perfectionist. I can't imagine he'd leave his place a bit upside down, and I did wonder where the big engine coffee table he bought from us was. I assumed he'd shipped it to one of his other homes. I'm mortified. The problem is, Gianni doesn't have anyone there with the keys for his place now, as Paulo's gone to visit his sick mother in a small village somewhere. So I can't get you access. I'm so sorry. This is all my fault. Please forgive me. Shall I try and book your flight home for you? It might be best if you come home right away.'

'I think that's a good idea. What time's the next flight?'

'I'll check and see what I can do and look for flights now. Stay where you are.'

'Well, I've got nowhere else to go now, have I?' I laugh, despite not seeing the funny side of this at all.

I drain the last of my coffee and wait for Soraya to call me back. I am supposed to be going for dinner with Elias this evening and feel disappointed that I will have to let him down, although that's the least of my concerns in the grand scheme of things.

But then I realise something even worse. My laptop isn't with me. It's still inside the apartment, and I can't possibly leave without it.

How on earth can I convince the screaming French lady to give it back? I can't afford to leave it there. I feel sick and realise that staying on alone was the worst possible thing I could ever have done. I might have known that fancy, glamorous trips were never meant for me. I attempted to fit myself into a world where I never belonged, and this was the result.

Chapter Fourteen

By the time Soraya finds a flight leaving at lunchtime, I decide that I can't possibly go home without my laptop. I don't have much choice but to somehow explain my predicament to the owner of the apartment. Could she possibly calm down enough for me to explain that there has been this horrendous misunderstanding? Something tells me she won't, but I have to give it a shot. Everything is on that laptop, including my emails and my social media; even worse, I need it to write my book. I had planned on spending the day writing after being so inspired by my wonderful day at sea with Elias. How can it be that the moment I am finally brimming with inspiration, I lose my laptop? What a twist of fate!

To make matters worse, a message comes through from Elias thanking me for my company yesterday and telling me how much he enjoyed our time together. He is looking forward to this evening. I am going to have to tell him that dinner is cancelled, and since I could really do with a friend right now, I pick up the phone to call him. I need to hear his caring, friendly voice.

'Hi, how nice of you to pick up the phone. People never seem to do that any more,' he says.

'Oh, I know. My daughters never phone anyone. It's always got to be messages. Anyway, I just thought it'd be easier to pick up the phone than message you because my trip just became very complicated.'

'Really? How come?'

'I have to leave. You won't believe this, but the girls and I have been staying in the wrong apartment. I honestly couldn't make it up. A screaming woman came back from a trip to find a strange woman in her bed – me, but she thought I was the housekeeper, and let's just say she was not best pleased.'

'How on earth could that happen? Weren't you picked up at the airport?'

'I know. Only Soraya could have so much champagne that she dragged us into a car with the wrong chauffeur who didn't speak English, and not one of us was any the wiser.'

'Oh, no. Well, that's a story for your book, then.'

'Yeah, except my laptop is now being held hostage in the lady's apartment.'

'She took it from you?'

I explain how I left it behind in my rush to leave, and once again, my Mysterious Mancunian of Monaco is eager to save the day.

'Look, my French isn't too shabby. We'll go together. I'll explain you need your laptop back and say how sorry we are for the confusion. We'll get your laptop back, so don't worry.'

When Elias says it like that, so calm and confident, I start to believe him. I don't think I can face the lady on my own, that's for certain.

'Would you mind? I'm so sorry about this.'

'Of course, I don't mind. You're my favourite damsel in distress. I'll meet you at the apartment block in twenty minutes.'

Is that what he thinks of me? A damsel in distress? I feel pathetic for the situations he has found me in since we met.

Twenty minutes later, I stand outside the apartment block and watch Elias as he comes bounding along towards me with a big smile on his face. I could burst into tears again with the relief of seeing the only friend I have here. As always, he is calm and kind; with no faffing about, he puts our plan straight into action.

'Right, we'll obviously have to speak to security first and ask if we can get upstairs. You're lucky you came in with the driver to get access when you first arrived. Hopefully he'll recognise you.'

Elias chats in French with the security guard and explains that he needs to speak to the lady of the apartment. I gasp as the security guard points at me and waves his finger around.

'Non, non, non!' he says.

Elias places both hands on my shoulders and talks quietly.

'I'm so sorry, but he says you're banned from the building. She's given him strict orders that you're not to come anywhere near here. She says if you do, she's instructed him to call the police.'

'Oh no. What am I going to do?' I try not to cry in front of Elias, but I am truly panicking that I may never see my laptop ever again.

'I've explained the situation to the guard, and *I'm* not banned. I'm going to see if I can speak with her and try to get the laptop back. Look, I'm sure she isn't going to want it hanging around. Security's calling her to ask if I can go and pick it up. We just need to give them a minute, but you'll have to wait outside the building, I'm afraid.'

'Yes, of course. I don't want them calling the police.'

'No, indeed. I won't be long, okay?'

I do as I am told and stand outside. Time seems to stand still as I wait for Elias, and I keep checking my phone in case he has any updates. I watch as convertible sports cars and Italian mopeds whizz by me whilst I stand on the pavement like some kind of fugitive.

Ten minutes later, Elias walks out of the building clutching my laptop in one hand and a pair of flesh-coloured pop socks that I use for my ballet flats in the other. Mortified!

'She said you left those too.' I blush as Elias hands over the pop socks and quickly smuggle them into my pocket. Then he hands over the laptop to me.

'You, Elias, are an absolute superstar, you know that? How on earth did you manage to convince her?' Instinctively, I throw my arms around him and give him the biggest hug. For a moment, it feels as though neither of us want to be the first to let go. Then, finally, he speaks.

'Ah, I smiled charmingly, gave her my best French and explained what a terrible mistake this has all been.'

'That easy? I don't believe you!'

'Well, no. She did have a bit of a rant. She explained that her chauffeur, who was called Franco and not Paulo, was instructed to collect a new housekeeper from the airport. Now he's been questioned and admitted that three women ran over to him, and he picked them up, assuming his boss had asked for more staff and didn't think to question anything.'

'Oh no. Now she realises it wasn't just me staying at her place.'

'Yeah, I know. She went ballistic when she found out there were others. But she's checked everything and can see nothing's missing. But, anyway, the fact is you were in the wrong apartment, and Franco should never have let you in. He's been fired and is to blame for the fiasco. It seems the housekeeper who should have arrived never showed up for the flight, so she's also demanding compensation from the agency. I tried to appease her by telling her that you'd tried your best to keep the place looking nice. Unfortunately, you're all still banned from the apartment block though.'

'Oh no. I wish I could help Franco. Poor man. It was partly our fault, too, that we just went bounding over to him. I feel so awful. I wish I could explain.'

'I think you're best leaving things alone. She's dead set on the police if she sees you again. There are lots of chauffeur jobs. I'm sure he'll find something.'

'Oh, what a mess. Well, she won't have to see me again. Now I've got my laptop back, I can give Soraya the go-ahead to arrange the flight later today.'

'You're set on leaving?'

'Yes, I'll just get whatever flight comes next. I suppose I'll have to get over to Nice.'

I look at my watch. I can be home by dinnertime if I get a move on.

'Do you have to leave? It'd be a shame not to stay a bit longer and get some writing done in the sunshine.'

'Oh, Elias. That's a lovely thought but, I'll be honest, the hotels here are going to be *way* out of my price range. I'm only here because Soraya knew Gianni and we were supposedly staying at his apartment. It's better I head home now.'

'You could stay at mine?'

'Yours?'

'Well, when I say mine, I mean where I'm staying. It's not mine, obviously. But there are two rooms on the yacht. I have one and you can have the other.'

'Goodness. I couldn't do that. What would your boss say?'

'It's fine. I'm allowed guests to stay. The boss is very easy-going, as I said before.'

'Oh.'

'Yeah, look, the Andalusia trip is seriously delayed. It's fine. Please, come and stay on the yacht. It'd be wonderful to have company. In fact, you'd be doing me a favour. I promise I'll be the perfect gentleman. There's even a lock on the door if you don't trust me.'

'No, of course I trust you, but I can't stay on someone's yacht. Especially after what's happened. Can I speak to the owner, perhaps, just to confirm it's okay?'

'I promise, it's fine. The owner is very busy. To be honest, they hate micromanaging everything and would be more annoyed if I checked every detail with them. They leave everything to my discretion, and I say you're welcome to stay.'

The sound of my phone ringing interrupts Elias as I see that Carol is calling. Soraya must have already shared the news with her. I can hardly even answer before I hear her practically screaming down the phone.

'I can't believe we stayed in the wrong place. Oh my god, we could have been arrested, and a hunky French policeman could have handcuffed us. No, seriously though, I can't get over the fact that we got in the wrong car.'

'I know. Imagine how shocked I was this morning.'

'Soraya told me all about it. You poor thing. You must've been terrified.'

'Yup, it wasn't the best start to the day.'

'So what you gonna do now? Are you on your way back?'

I look at Elias, who is standing close by.

'Well, you remember Elias? He's just kindly offered me a room on the yacht until I'm due for my flight, but yeah, Soraya's looking at flights for today.'

'Oh no she's not. I'm ringing her as soon as I put the phone down to tell her not to let you come back. You've got the offer of staying on that fabulous yacht and you want to get on a budget flight home? Are you completely bonkers?'

I look up at the blue skies, the sea in the distance and Elias's smile as he waits for me to get off the phone.

'Look, I have to go. Poor Elias is standing here waiting for me.'

'Oh my god. He's there with you now? Well, I'm not going off this phone unless you promise you're staying on that yacht tonight.'

'Carol!'

'Say it!'

'Okay. Okay. Right, I've got to go.'

'I'll let Soraya know the news, and don't do anything I wouldn't do.' I can hear Carol giggling down the phone as I put it down.

Elias has been so patient waiting for my reply, although I'm sure he must have heard every word. Carol always talks so loudly.

'Will we be moored at the marina? Or out in the middle of the sea?'

This makes all the difference since I would prefer that people aren't too far away if anything goes wrong in the middle of the night.

'At the marina,' says Elias.

'Okay then. Thank you. But it'll only be for a couple of nights. I promise I won't outstay my welcome.'

'I'm sure you'd never outstay any welcome.'

Elias looks at me, and something tells me that this is either going to be the best decision or the worst decision I ever make. I can't quite decide which. But I do realise that I need a bit of an adventure to write this book and inspire my writing, so I really want to do this. However, I unblock Michael's number just in case there is some kind of terrible emergency, and they were right after all.

Chapter Fifteen

As Elias opens the wardrobe doors for me to hang my clothes and shows me where everything goes in the master bedroom of the *Lady Jane*, I can't quite believe my luck. I've gone from being kicked out on the streets to staying on a yacht in just a few hours! Let's hope it doesn't end up as much of a disaster as the apartment did.

Elias leaves me to unpack, and I pop some of my bits in one of the drawers. As I am putting my things away, I open the last drawer and immediately find a photo in a frame. I can see it is Elias with a woman. I listen around for footsteps and realise that Elias is safely on another deck, so I pull out the wooden frame to take a closer look. The photo seems fairly recent, as he looks much as he does now. Elias is standing with his arm around a pretty, petite woman, who looks as though she is his age. Suddenly, I hear footsteps coming fast down the stairs and hurriedly shove the photo back in the drawer.

'Did you want a coffee?' asks Elias, poking his head around the door.

'Umm, yes, that'd be fab. Thanks.'

As I go upstairs for my coffee, I can't stop my thoughts running away with me. Is the woman in the photo his late wife? Or someone else? Perhaps he has a partner and has quickly hidden her photo in a drawer. So many scenarios go through my head, but then I wonder what I am worried about. It's not exactly like we are dating. He hasn't even hinted at anything like that. He is merely a friendly British face around Monaco who has been incredibly kind to me. As Elias sits closer to me and we sip our coffees on the big comfy sofa on deck, I try to remember this.

'By the way, don't mind me if you want your space to do any writing, or anything. I don't want to stifle your creativity.'

'No, you won't. You've helped inspire me more than anyone has in a long while.' I stop short from saying he is fast becoming my muse.

'My wife used to paint, so I know what it's like being around someone creative.'

'Oh? That's great.'

I think of Michael who would come in shouting and asking what was for tea when I was in the middle of trying to write a short story all those years ago. How nice that she had such a supportive partner.

'Some of her artwork is here. See that one?'

I look straight ahead at the painting of a yacht sailing on a brilliant blue sea.

'It's magnificent. She was obviously very talented.'

'She was. Yes.'

'That's incredibly kind of your boss to hang her work. Although it is a wonderful piece of art.'

'Yes, I was proud of her. She had a lot of potential.'

Elias looks a little lost and so I quickly turn to thanking him again for letting me stay.

'I'm so grateful you let me stay on this beautiful yacht.'

'You're so welcome. I'm relishing the company, and it's so lovely to…'

Before he can say anything further, Elias's phone starts ringing on the table. He taps my knee as he gets up to answer the call.

'Sorry, just got to take this.'

I watch him wait to answer the call until he has left the room. Then I hear him say hello to someone. I try to listen in. I don't know why I do that. I suppose I can't help myself. Maybe it's the inquisitive writer in me, but I wonder if it's someone from Monaco on the phone, or someone in Manchester? What if it's his boss and someone has told them that there is a stranger on board? I start to panic after what happened at the apartment.

'Yes, I've got all the stuff. It'll be with you any day now. I've just got to take care of some business out here first.'

Some business? Does he mean me, or some big deal I know nothing about? I am intrigued and listen in closer, but he isn't giving much away. It serves as another reminder that I really don't know him.

–

That evening, as Elias knocks on my bedroom door to take me for that dinner he promised, my eyes feel as though they will pop out of my head. I am reminded again what a handsome man he is. In a pair of cream chinos and one of his trademark polo shirts, he holds his arm out for me to join him.

However, instead of going out somewhere as we had originally planned, he has arranged for some food to be delivered on deck. I follow him upstairs, imagining a chicken curry from the nearest takeaway waiting for us. But I am stunned to find that he has transformed the dining table into something more fitting for the high-net-worth passengers of *Below Deck*. The table is set for two with silver placemats, glasses for water and wine, cutlery that is so highly polished the moonlight is almost reflecting off them and bright blue plates. The exact shade that Elias seems to love.

A silver ice bucket has a bottle of French wine, and Elias offers me a taste. I take a sip of the smooth, fine wine.

'It's delicious.'

Once I have sampled it, Elias pours me a generous glass as a candle flickers in the middle of the table. He quickly explains that they only have battery-operated candles on board to ensure there is no risk of a flame flying off errantly in the wind.

'Safety first, always.'

'The size of this glass of wine, I think you want me to fall overboard,' I tease.

'Ooh, I'd never want that, unless I could catch you in my arms.' Elias looks away, realising he shouldn't have said that. 'Umm, anyway, as I say, I take safety very seriously. And, on that note, I hope you don't have any allergies. I just realised that I went ahead and ordered a takeaway without checking with you. I'm not used to catering for people on board. That's not part of my job description.'

'No, it's fine. I'll eat anything. Except Mexican. I must be the only person on earth who isn't into enchiladas and fajitas. Soraya and Carol never understand it.'

'You're safe. It's not Mexican.'

'Then I'll eat anything.'

'Fabulous. Give me two seconds to get everything from the galley then.'

'Will you let me help?'

'No, have you ever seen the mess I leave in the galley? I'm a better skipper than I am deck crew.'

'Well, I'd say you've done a pretty good job with this,' I say, admiring the table set up.

As Elias rushes off to get the food, I enjoy my wine. I smile to myself as I think how luxurious the wine glass is, compared to the hand-painted one I use at home that Jasmine made for me at school. Both are equally as special, though.

With the stars shining down on the sea around us, I look around in disbelief. What am I doing sat on a yacht in Monaco with a mysterious but very handsome skipper? I can hardly believe my luck. I am beginning to think that leaving my purse back in the apartment that first morning was the best thing I have ever done, when I hear Elias's voice behind me.

'Penny for them.'

'Huh? Oh… I was just thinking how beautiful all of this is.'

'Yeah, it's not a bad place to work,' says Elias, holding out a big silver tray full of shellfish.

'Maybe I should apply to become your deck crew.'

'Now wouldn't that be fun! You and I together all day.'

He places the food down on the table, and I look at the buffet he has spread out in front of us. I have never seen anything so lavish for a takeaway. There are no poppadoms or prawn crackers, only mussels, oysters and scallops, slices of lemon and piping hot crusty bread. My mouth waters looking at it all.

'I do hope you like seafood?' says Elias.

'Like it? I love it. It's my favourite.'

'That's great. There's this really nice place I order from. That's one of the perks when you're close to the sea, you get all the fresh catches.'

I don't even know where to begin with the feast in front of me, but decide on the scallops, which have been poached in a white wine and garlic sauce.

'Oh, this is divine,' I say, whilst trying to avoid dripping any of the sauce down Soraya's beautiful kaftan that I have changed into for tonight. Who'd have thought? Me wearing this, eating the finest seafood onboard a yacht. I feel as though I died and came back as Soraya!

'I'm glad you're enjoying it.'

As I wrangle with an oyster, I can't help looking across to Elias. Such a fine man, yet I still get the feeling he is hiding something – that there is something I don't know. Call it a hunch, or perhaps it is the words of my family back home that keep echoing in my head, but something isn't quite adding up. Even the way his late wife's artwork is on board his boss's yacht seems a bit incongruous. But I try to quell the feeling. Perhaps it is my mind wanting to sabotage the moment because I don't feel worthy of such luxury.

'I have dessert if you'd like some,' says Elias.

'That sounds lovely, but I don't think I could manage another thing.'

'No, me neither. Maybe we can save it for tomorrow. I know I said we'd stay in the marina but what would you think of taking the boat out for a few days? Maybe take a tour around the coast? We could sail down to Saint-Tropez, Cannes… What do you reckon?'

Whilst I had insisted to myself that I wanted to stay docked up safely where people were around me, the wine and my new-found sense of adventure is making me want to agree.

'Wow, seriously?'

'Yeah, the yacht could do with a bit of a spin out. Keep the engines going. You know what they say: if you don't use it, you lose it. A bit like my dodgy knee.'

'Your knee doesn't look dodgy to me,' I say, as I think of him in his shorts.

'Hah, well, being up and down ladders all the time will do that. One of the reasons I needed a change of career. Although, this isn't much better for that. Anyway, enough about the knee injury, how about we go and sit on the top deck, relax with our drinks and plan out the next few days? Will you join me and my dodgy knee for a nightcap?'

'I'd love to.'

We sit on the deck, with a view that overlooks the whole of the marina. The temperature has started to drop for the evening, but it's still warm enough to sit out without feeling a chill. A shooting star darts across the sky in front of us.

'Wow, did you see that?'

'Yeah, you get lots of them out here. The sky's so clear. Look up there.' Elias points up towards a T-shaped group of stars.

'What is it? I'm useless with stars, unless it's horoscopes.'

'That's the constellation of Cygnus. It's Latin for swan.'

'It doesn't look like a swan.'

'No, I suppose it doesn't. That one over there, that's Delphinus, and that's Latin for… Can you guess?'

'Dolphin?'

'Exactly. You're practically fluent in Latin now.'

We laugh together, and once again, Elias has impressed me with his knowledge.

'See, that's what I love about being here. Dolphins, shooting stars, my goodness. You don't get that in a city.'

'You didn't mention the fine company,' says Elias.

'Well, that goes without saying, doesn't it?'

I grin at him, and he smiles back, and then there is quiet. Under the moonlight and shooting stars, I lean over and kiss him. His lips are soft and send shockwaves all through my body. I am taken aback by my action, yet I feel so happy and free that it feels like the most natural thing in the world to have done.

Elias puts his arm around me, and we lean into each other. I can feel his heart beating fast and strong right beside mine. Two hearts beating side by side. I place my hand on his chest and feel its rhythm. Elias kisses me again and we cannot get close enough to each other's bodies. Until now, I couldn't be certain that he felt the chemistry I could when we teased each other, but there is no denying how we both feel now. There is no doubt left in my mind as we hold each other, kissing and cuddling on the deck all night until the sun starts to rise, after we have fallen asleep in each other's arms.

Chapter Sixteen

When I wake up on deck, the first thing I notice is the blanket draped over me. It takes me a minute to remember what happened last night. Elias! Did that really occur, or was it the best dream ever? As I focus on my surroundings, I realise that it was most definitely not some kind of fabulous dream, as Elias stands above me with a coffee in his hand and a beaming smile on his face.

I feel my hair sticking up and pat it down quickly. Was I sleeping with my mouth open as I often do? The girls took a terribly unflattering photo of me on a train once when I had dozed off, and I swore I would never sleep in public again. I hope I didn't look like that when Elias put a blanket over me at some point in the early hours.

'Good morning, beautiful,' he says.

I am relieved by the positive adjective; surely he wouldn't have said that had my mouth been open all night?

'Good morning, gorgeous,' I reply. I hope that didn't sound too cheesy. It was all so much easier when I was drinking wine. Now in the light of day, I am feeling a lot more nervous around him, especially since everything has changed.

'Here, just as you like it. Milk, no sugar,' says Elias, handing me the mug.

'You even know how I take my coffee. A man who listens and remembers things. I like it.'

'You'd be surprised what you learn when you actually sit back and listen to people, instead of doing all the talking.'

'Yeah. I guess I talk a lot. I should try listening a bit more.'

'I suppose it comes from cleaning windows; I'm quite observant. You notice the curtains that never open, the warring couple who you can hear while you clean the windows, and you just know it isn't going to last.'

'Hmm... Does that mean you're nosy?'

Elias laughs. 'No. Definitely not nosy. Just observant.'

As he smiles, I feel the urge to stroke his cheek. He takes my hand and kisses it.

'Right, mademoiselle, fancy some fresh juice? From your favourite supermarket.'

'Wow, you really are observant! This is like a five-star hotel.'

'I aim to give good service,' he winks.

'Well, if you were on Tripadvisor, you'd be getting a rave review. Good food, superb facilities, excellent ambience.'

Elias puts his hand on my leg.

'Hmm, go on...'

'And very attentive service,' I say cheekily.

'Is that so? I can get more attentive.'

'Oh, can you now? In that case, who needs refreshments?'

I put my glass down as Elias leads me downstairs to his cabin and we make love on the opulent round cabin bed. I trace my hand all the way along the scar that leads down his chest, but I decide not to ask him about it. I noticed it when we went swimming, too, but now I can see it close up in the morning light. I figure if he wants to tell me about it, then he will.

We snuggle on the bed for over an hour. I smile to myself as I think of the contrast between Elias and Michael. If we ever made love, he'd be back up after five minutes checking his phone. With Elias, everything is so much more passionate and tender. We lie for ages looking at the sunshine through the skylight in the bedroom. Finally, he suggests we should get back to breakfast and begin our day of sailing. I try to stop myself from grinning. I can't remember ever feeling so free, or as thrilled, as when I look at Elias in front of me.

When he leaves me to go to the upper deck, I get myself together for breakfast once again and check my phone.

There are ten frantic messages waiting for me.

Three from Jasmine, four from Poppy, and three from Michael. They all indicate the same thing. They think I have been kidnapped, scammed or thrown overboard and demand I reply immediately.

I start typing a message to Poppy first since she has sent the most messages.

> I'm absolutely fine. Having the time of my life, actually. I'm off to Antibes, Saint-Tropez and Cannes probably. Not quite sure where exactly, but I'll keep you updated when I can.

Then I copy and paste it to Jasmine and send a photo of the yacht to Michael with no words. That will shut him up. He has always loved yachts and fast cars. I have only just pressed send when he starts typing.

> What are you sending me this photo for when the girls are worried sick about you? Do you know how much they're panicking that something will happen to you? Do you care how your poor daughters even feel? Have some consideration.

Did he have consideration when he went off on hot dates during our marriage? I don't think so. He winds me up so much that I find an emoji of the middle finger and consider sending it. However, I decide that I am not going to send that to my girls' dad, much as I would love to at this moment in time. I tell myself I am better than that.

Instead, I remind him that I am a grown woman, and we are now divorced. I have reassured the girls that I am completely fine and that if I want to go off with a skipper exploring the French Riviera then I shall. Although, as I type it, I can hardly believe what I am saying. I think back to all those days I sobbed my heart out and could hardly get out of bed, when I was utterly devastated that the man I had trusted had been having an affair whilst I looked after everyone else's needs, including his.

'You ready to set sail?' says Elias, interrupting my memories of a terrible time in my life.

'Absolutely.'

'Brilliant. I've managed to secure us a berth at a gorgeous port.'

'Sounds exciting. Ahoy, shipmate!' As I say it, I remember that I am not very well-versed with this terminology, and it's probably best I stay quiet.

I join Elias on the bridge and watch as he organises everything to sail away. I would end up overboard if I tried to lean over the way he does. I really can't imagine it is doing his knee too much good either, having to do all these manual tasks to get the boat out of the marina. He seems to be in his element, though.

As we sail away, we slowly pass yachts heading into the port, no doubt eager to take up our mooring. Even since the past day or so, it seems to be getting busier here.

The views of Monaco Old Town and the Rock of Monaco become a blur as we sail further out and head towards Port de Beaulieu. Elias tells me it is only five nautical miles away, but I daren't ask how nautical miles work. I have never been very good with maths, so whatever he says will probably go over my head. Instead, I try to look intelligent and as though I understand.

I offer to make us a coffee, and as I head into the galley, I see what he means about being messy. At least it shows he is human. I was beginning to think he was too perfect. I tidy everything up, and finally, with everything spick and span, I head back onto the bridge with our coffee.

As the wind blows in my hair and the spray of the sea splashes against my skin, I can't help grinning at Elias. I am so happy that I almost forget about work but force myself to remember that I promised I would write up a chapter of the book before we reach our destination. So, I leave Elias with his coffee and take out my laptop as I sit astride a sun lounger on the lower deck.

I gaze into the sky as if I will find the words I need written up there, but I realise that the universe doesn't have to provide me with creativity. I have plenty of inspiration since meeting Elias, and I type so fast that before I even realise it, the boat has slowed down, and we have reached our first port of call.

I make sure to save all my work and rush up to Elias to see if I can do anything to help.

'Just keep an eye starboard if you will,' he says.

I rush to my left.

'Right,' laughs Elias.

'I'm so sorry. Clearly not cut out to be a shipmate.'

'Oh, I don't know. I'd say you're a very good shipmate,' says Elias with a grin.

My cheeks glow at his remark. I hope he isn't just referring to what we got up to this morning.

With the boat safely moored at Beaulieu-sur-Mer, Elias takes my hand as we stroll through the pretty marina, surrounded by imposing villas.

'What a beautiful place. So, who owns all these yachts?'

'It's mostly locals. They only have a handful of berths for visitors.'

'Wow, imagine living here. Like, this is your life… Some people are so lucky.'

'Yeah. It's one of my favourites. I've always loved this place. I never thought I'd be sailing a yacht into it one day, though.'

'You came here before you sailed?'

'Yeah, we used to bring the car and drive through the French Riviera every summer. We never stayed anywhere fancy, though. To be honest, there was a campsite, and we travelled from there.'

'Oh, I went camping once in France in the Eighties. It didn't stop raining. The fields were flooded, and the shower block filled with mud.'

'Yeah, I remember those days. Fortunately, campsites have improved over the years. Of course, you can't guarantee the weather, though. Although it's perfect today.'

I couldn't agree more as the sun is blazing down on us. Thankfully, the light breeze keeps it cool enough to walk around without it feeling uncomfortable.

'It really is the perfect day. It's like I can hear that Lou Reed song in my head.'

'Oh, I love that. One of my favourite songs,' says Elias, turning around to look at me.

'No way. Me too. We should have played that last night when we had our drinks outside.'

'We will. Let's make a list of tracks and get Alexa to play them.'

'Brilliant. Is there anything better than being sat on deck watching the world go by drinking a glass of wine with the best music?' I ask.

'And the best company,' says Elias, squeezing my hand.

As we walk along the seafront, I notice that Michael has been messaging again. I look at the screen in disbelief.

Elias... That can't be his real name.

I choose to ignore it. There is no way I am responding to him when I am having the most wonderful day. I will not let him ruin it.

However, as Elias and I walk along the front hand in hand, I find myself watching him and that sneaking doubt creeps in again. What if there is something he isn't telling me? What if his name isn't Elias? Is he too good to be true? Despite wanting to ignore Michael's message and being annoyed at myself for letting my ex-husband's doubts crawl into my head, I ask him about it.

'Elias is an unusual name. Where did it come from?'

'My dad was in the army back in the Sixties. He was based in Cyprus when my mum got pregnant. There was a church called Profitis Elias near where they lived. Her waters broke as she was walking up the stairs to it, apparently, so they called me Elias, after that church.'

'What a lovely story. I wish I had a romantic tale like that behind my name.'

There you go, Michael! I refuse to listen to him again. He is only trying to cause trouble because he doesn't want to see me happy.

'Yes, my parents were the salt of the earth, you know. Doing what was right for their country. Being good neighbours. They always tried their best. Love thy neighbour and all that.'

'Well, I can imagine that since their son is such a caring man, anyone can see that. Look how many times you've had to help me out of scrapes since I arrived here.' I am satisfied that Michael has got it all wrong.

When we finish our walk, we find a spot to sunbathe on the beach. We rub suntan lotion on each other, and I find myself relaxing as he massages it into my shoulders. I've always worried about what people think of me, and I realise that suddenly I don't care. Elias makes me feel so much less self-conscious.

I look at the scar on Elias's chest again as he lies there. He doesn't try to hide it, and neither should he. Poppy and Jasmine would probably say that he was in some rival drugs gang and got the injury in a violent fight, but I have a feeling it is something much more innocent. As I think of the girls, a message from Jasmine comes through on my mobile, checking that I am still alive and haven't given over any money yet.

> I was just thinking! Has he asked you for anything, Mam? Like, said he forgot his money was tied up in a trust fund and he just needs ten million for a couple of days?

I laugh out loud as I read it. Oh, Jasmine. Such an imagination!

'Something funny?' asks Elias.

How do I tell this man who has been so kind that my family don't trust him? 'Just my daughter. She's a bit over-imaginative sometimes.'

'Oh, my boys are the same. Danny and James are so over-protective of me since their mum died. They think they're helping, but…' Elias stops abruptly and doesn't seem to want to go on.

'Well, at least it shows they care,' I say.

'They do, I hope. Although sometimes I feel it's about what they can get out of me. That sounds terrible. It's just that, when my wife died, everything changed in more ways than one, and… oh, I don't know. I don't mean to complain.'

'Oh, no, I get you!' I thought I was the only parent who felt as though their children wanted something from them all the time.

'You know, sometimes, I'd love to run away and see how much they really do care. They probably wouldn't even notice I'm missing until they needed money,' says Elias.

'Oh, my word! Me too. Let's run away together then.' I laugh as I imagine two adults running off into the sunset. Of course, I couldn't ever do that to the girls, although it does sound appealing.

Elias leans over to kiss me and strokes my hair. Then he looks at me and does that thing where it feels as though he is staring right into my soul again.

'We could do it. The yacht is waiting. Where shall we go?' It is hard to tell whether he is joking or serious, and I feel a twinge of panic that he may have thought I meant it.

'Oh, yeah, I wish.' I roll my eyes to show I was just kidding.

'Well, you've got a skipper at your command. You just have to say the word.'

'Thanks, but the girls would find me and hunt me down and they'd probably bring my ex-husband too. Actually, can we change the subject now? That's one person I really don't want to talk about.'

When we finish sunbathing, we go for a final stroll around the charming little fishing village. I can see why it is one of Elias's favourites as we pass a palatial pink hotel with large wrought-iron gates and then some old-style buildings with Juliet balconies. Elias breaks my thoughts as I try to picture the sort of people who must live in these homes.

'Hey, I'm just thinking… Shall we sail to Cannes from here? It's not far.'

Of course, he doesn't have to ask me twice.

'Umm, yeah, absolutely. What an adventure!'

'Every day's an adventure with me, I promise you that,' says Elias.

As I look up at him, I feel as though I could fall head over heels in love with this man. Not because of his lifestyle but because of his kindness, his enthusiasm, and, most of all, his spirit of adventure.

Although a warning in my head reminds me that I have worked hard to build my new independent life to ensure that I never get hurt again. Besides, sometimes, adventures can lead to disaster, and you have to be careful what you wish for. I mean, how many times do the fearless get stuck on mountain expeditions? Or an intrepid explorer gets lost trekking in the outback? Being adventurous is not for the faint-hearted; forget what they say about fortune favouring the brave. There is always a risk with adventure, but I may need to ask myself if this is one adventure that is worth the risk.

Chapter Seventeen

By the time we arrive in Cannes in the early evening, the port is bustling with people, cars and breathtaking yachts. It is so much busier than Beaulieu-sur-Mer, and I am surprised we managed to secure a berth. I don't know how Elias pulled it off, and I can only assume his boss has good connections.

After we have moored and made our way out of the marina, I look up at the big Ferris wheel that watches over the port. Elias catches me looking up at it. It is so pretty in the dusk with its pink and blue hues.

'Fancy going up and checking out the views?' he asks.

I haven't been on a Ferris wheel since I was a kid. It's not overly huge like some of them, and it looks like a fun thing to do, so I am eager to check it out.

I insist on paying for the ride, much to the annoyance of Elias, and hand over the money to the attendant. We step inside the little cage, and I feel a buzz of excitement. As the Ferris wheel moves upwards into the sky with the views of Cannes beneath us, Elias puts his arm around me, and we huddle together. I don't think I could possibly be any happier than I am right now as we soar above the heights of Cannes. Bright lights flash as cars pass along the palm tree-lined road beneath us. The lights of the yachts illuminate the marina, where I spot a glimpse of *Lady Jane*. I can't quite get over the fact that I am looking at the yacht

I am staying on from up here on this Ferris wheel. I never dreamt my life could ever be this glamorous. It is so far removed from home.

I watch as the people below us get smaller as we reach the full height of the Ferris wheel, and the yachts in the moorings now only twinkle like little candle lights. This place couldn't possibly get any more heavenly, and it's the perfect place to admire the views.

When we finally come back down, Elias suggests we head to Le Suquet, which, he says, has pretty cobbled alleyways. We make our way there, passing delicatessens with displays of the most delectable French cheeses in their window and a patisserie selling gold leaf macarons. I have to stop for a moment to admire them. If it was a bit cheaper here, I might be tempted to take some back to the yacht to have with a cuppa! Although, it may not seem quite appropriate to have something like that with a good, strong brew. They should probably accompany some exotic leaf tea that has been picked from the highest mountains of Nepal – not the sort of tea you can find in the local Co-op.

The shops are so enticing with their handbags and jewellery displays that I could walk into all of them. The temptation of evening shopping becomes too much, and I pop into a little boutique that Soraya would love, even though the price tags may surprise even her. When we finish perusing the expensive stores, we decide to stop for a drink at one of the many bars and cafes that line the pretty cobbled pavements. We choose a bar with a bright red canopy and matching chairs. A water jug holds red roses, and Elias hands me one.

'*Pour mon amore,*' he grins cheesily.

I am tempted to seductively put the rose between my teeth but decide it might be best not to since I am most definitely the type of person to end up with a thorn stuck in my lip and need emergency treatment at a local hospital. This is why I have never been the adventurous type. Things can't go wrong if you always play safe. But this man brings out the playful side in me that I thought was long gone and a sense of freedom that I have never felt before.

Over our drinks, we talk more than we ever have before. Elias tells me about how lonely he was after his wife died, and I admit that even before my marriage ended, when I had my husband beside me, if I am truthful, I can see now that I was incredibly lonely in that relationship. I don't go as far as telling him about the time I bought a sleek new dress and walked into the bathroom as he was getting ready, hoping he would say something. Hoping he would actually notice me, but instead, he looked straight through me. I don't ever recall his eyes lighting up when he saw me, like Elias's do.

Elias picks up his drink and then puts it down again. He looks thoughtful.

'I know I joke about them, but I think the boys are still finding it incredibly difficult to move on after their mum passed.'

'I'm sure. It must have been awful to see her ill.'

'It was, but I don't know how healthy it is that they want me to keep the house like a shrine. It's lovely, of course, that she's remembered. But they won't let me change anything because their mum chose this or put that in a certain place. I'm not saying we should all forget her, but it's difficult to move forward when there are so many reminders. Another reason I like being out on the yacht, I suppose.'

'Yes, it's hard at this age when circumstances change. We don't ever expect it.'

'Definitely not. But all we can do is try and get on with it. Dear me, this isn't a very happy conversation. I think we need to change the subject pronto! So, how do you like Cannes?'

'I absolutely love it. I love everything so far. Monaco, Cannes, what a place this is. I can't believe I almost didn't come on this trip.'

'Really?'

I contemplate telling Elias how I didn't want to accept Soraya's generosity but decide not to.

'Yeah, it's complicated. But never mind about that, I'm here now.'

'And I'm glad you are,' says Elias.

He stretches his hand across to touch mine, and a tingle runs through me. As we look into each other's eyes, I feel that Elias is not a man to let someone down. We might still be learning about each other, but the more time we spend together, the more I feel that my family is wrong about him. They are just being dramatic. I'm sure I can trust him.

–

After another glass of wine, we head back to the yacht, where Alexa provides the music. We dance to love songs in each other's arms on the top deck and curl up together when we need a sit-down. It is one of those pinch-me moments, and I begin to think I should have been more adventurous a long time ago. Maybe I should have said *yes* to more things over the years. Perhaps that has been my mistake in life.

In the morning, Elias manages to book us on a sight-seeing tour in a vintage French van. For two hours, we weave through the streets, stopping at Le Suquet once again and then at the Palais des Festivals et des Congrès of Cannes, where I have never felt more movie-star-esque as I stand in the place where the red carpet is rolled out during the Film Festival. The guide tells us that we have only just missed the event, which is a shame. Then, we walk along the Avenue of Stars and admire the handprints on the sidewalk. I spot Cameron Diaz's name and excitedly tell Elias how much I loved her in *There's Something About Mary*. However, he is more impressed by Sylvester Stallone's name and tells me how he watched every single *Rocky* film.

'You never know, when your book takes off, you might be asked to do one of these,' says Elias.

'I love how you say *when* my book takes off, not *if*?'

'I bet it will end up a bestseller.'

'Oh, well, I'm not thinking that far ahead. I'd just love to see my name on the cover of a book. It's been my dream since primary school.'

'You will. I have every belief in you.'

I give Elias's hand a squeeze in appreciation before we set off for our next bit of sightseeing at Palm Beach.

For five whole days we enjoy the best sights of Cannes, with its bars, beaches and *boulangeries*, and relish each other's company. Our physical relationship develops, and my body feels truly awakened by him. My fondness for Elias grows so much that I can't ever imagine him not being beside me, meandering around the streets of Cannes. I notice with some shock that this has begun to feel like daily life! Everything feels so normal with Elias beside me.

In between our trips out and our time together, Elias supports me in making sure that I have space to write. Sometimes on board the *Lady Jane*, feeling the gentle movement of the boat beneath me, and sometimes in cafes or bars on shore, taking inspiration from the people and scenes around me.

After a blissful week, though, it is time to head back to Monaco and try to get our berth back. Elias explains that this bit might prove tricky since the resorts are getting busier every day as the influx of tourists starts to arrive.

When we finally head out of the port, we both wave goodbye to the shore at Cannes. It has been the most wonderful time, and no matter what happens in the future, it has been an unforgettable trip. A holiday romance with a ship's captain, flitting around beguiling ports, following in the footsteps of the rich and famous, is something I won't forget in a hurry. I give Elias a kiss and wrap my arms around him as I thank him for letting me join him.

But then, as we are relaxed and bobbing about on the evening waves back in the direction of Monaco, we notice a boat heading towards us.

'That's weird,' says Elias.

I stare ahead, wondering if it is one of those optical illusions where it seems closer than it is, because it certainly appears as though it is getting nearer and nearer all the time. I search for the binoculars for a more precise view and feel slightly frantic as I realise the yacht is definitely on course to hit us if it continues at this pace.

'What can we do, Elias?'

'I'll warn him, don't worry.' He looks at me reassuringly.

I admire the way Elias remains calm under pressure despite the great big yacht hurtling towards us, because I am starting to panic. He sounds the boat's horn, but it doesn't seem to make any difference.

Elias turns *Lady Jane* sharply to try and steer away from the yacht's path, but we're out of time. Everything is happening too fast to move out of its way. The skipper on the out-of-control yacht is so close we can see him turning the wheel, but there is only one place he is going, no matter how much he tries to detour.

All the glamour and luxury of the past few days flash in front of my eyes in a blur as the other yacht jolts us sideways. The crunch of fibreglass against fibreglass is noisier than I ever imagined and will stay with me forever.

Elias quickly switches his radio over to the emergency band. We hear the skipper from the other boat shouting, '*Mayday, mayday.*' I may not know much about emergency procedures on board yachts, but I have no problem understanding that terminology.

After that, it doesn't take long for *Lady Jane* to start taking on water.

Elias throws me a life jacket. He then puts one on himself.

'We're going to have to abandon ship. Can you give me a hand with the tender?' says Elias, still calm but firm and focussed, as my adrenaline starts pumping.

I run around, not knowing what I am doing, but try to follow his instructions.

'It'll be okay. We just have to stay calm. Let me make sure you're safe first.'

Elias helps me as I scramble onboard the tender, which sways back and forth with the current. Then, he gives the yacht one last glance before joining me. We move away as quickly as we can from the yacht. The other people have already evacuated and are in a similar tender to the other side of us. I feel a wave of gratitude that we all managed to get off and nobody is injured. The sickening possibilities of what might have happened fill my head and make my stomach churn. Thank goodness Elias kept calm in a crisis and we are all safe.

'You okay?' asks Elias.

'Just about. My shoulder hurts where I stumbled when the yacht jolted. But it's nothing really.' Elias rubs at my shoulder gently.

'I'm so sorry. Nothing like this has ever happened before.'

How quickly things can go wrong when you're on a yacht. Elias was so safety conscious, yet someone still managed to crash into us. I still can't get over how fast things can unfold. We were left with no time to avoid it.

'I just can't believe it.'

I repeat the same thing most of the way to the shore of Monaco.

'Let's look on the bright side. It saves us from trying to find a parking spot, I suppose,' says Elias. He tries to sound positive, but I can hear the tremor in his voice. We are both shaken up.

The coastguard is soon with us and pulls up alongside our raft to check that we're okay and lead us into shore.

When we finally reach firm ground and are taken ashore, I am so relieved that I don't pay much attention to the fact that everyone is staring at us in shock at the whole incident. I suppose it isn't every day you witness such a collision. I look over to what they can see, and the black smoke from the other yacht is now camouflaging everything.

The police are waiting on the beach and ask if we need an ambulance. I notice there is one on standby and thank our lucky stars that we are both unscathed apart from what could be just a bruised shoulder.

'I think we're both okay, aren't we?' says Elias.

'Yes, absolutely. Thank goodness. We're not sure about the other boat, though. I think they all got out safely.'

'Don't worry about them. My colleague's taken care of it. If it's okay, I'll just take some details from you.' The police officer twiddles his pen in his hand and gets ready to make some notes.

'Okay. Sir, what's the name of the boat?'

'*Lady Jane*.'

'The owner's name?'

Elias shifts around on his feet and then looks across to me. 'Umm.'

'Sir, the name of the owner of the boat?'

Elias refuses to answer.

I look at him as if to hurry him up and tell the police about his boss.

'Elias, just tell them your boss's name.'

'Yes, name of owner, sir!' says the police officer. He looks as though he is starting to get annoyed.

'Um, it's a bit awkward… Um…'

'Is this boat stolen, sir?'

Elias looks at me again, and I stare at him with my mouth wide open.

'Look, I can explain. Umm…'

Elias is hiding something; what if the police officer has hit the nail right on the head? As if the shock of a collision wasn't bad enough, the thought that I could be on board a stolen boat had never occurred to me. Either Elias is concussed, or something is very wrong. Since he has been coherent since we abandoned ship, I can only fear the worst.

Chapter Eighteen

I watch Elias carefully as he paces about.

'Elias Norman Badington,' he says.

'Your name, sir? It's Elias Norman Badington, yes? You are the owner, am I correct?'

Elias looks at me and nods. What on earth is going on? It's not stolen if he owns the boat, but why in the world would someone with an impressive yacht deny owning it? Why all the stuff about his boss?

'I don't get any of this,' I say to Elias.

'I promise I'll explain later. Let's just deal with this first.'

My mind conjures up scenarios as to why Elias would pretend just to be the skipper. Is he on the run? What if he killed his wife? Maybe he made up a story about her being ill. He could have even thrown her overboard for all I know. Sometimes, I do wish I didn't have that over-active author's imagination. I feel sick as the cold realisation dawns that my family was right all along. I really knew nothing about him.

I hang around waiting for Elias to finish with the police, listening to every word he says as he retells his account of what has just happened. The police don't cart him away, so maybe him being wanted isn't anything I need to worry about.

When he is finally done, I look at him, my hands on my hips, and wait for his explanation.

'Not here. Look, we're going to need to check into a hotel. The only saving grace is that my wallet's in my pocket, and I've got all my cards with me.'

I think of the laptop that I've left onboard, not to mention all my stuff for the holiday. How could I have such a mishap with my laptop twice on the same break? I am beginning to wonder if this book is meant to be written. I've now lost everything, including Elias. He is obviously some kind of fraudster that I can't trust. However, as much as I don't want to get a hotel room with him, I don't know anybody here and have no money. I am not sure what choice I have. I decide that I will go with him so that I can shower and dry myself off and then I suppose I'll have to admit to my friends and family that I was wrong about Elias.

We look scruffy and out of place as we check into a posh hotel, and I notice a customer look me up and down. I have to bite my tongue to stop myself from telling her that she would look like this, too, if she had just been shipwrecked!

Elias tries to talk to me as we head upstairs to our room, but I have nothing to say to him at this point. I want to shower and dry off before I hear why he would lie about who he is. I rush straight into the bathroom and lock the door in fear of who the real person is on the other side.

As I close my eyes to the warm water that soothes my skin and washes away the tightness of the salty seawater, I have a flashback of the boat heading towards us. One thing I know is that, from now on, I am staying well clear of boats.

I dry myself off and prepare to face Elias. He has made me a coffee from the kettle in the room and it is waiting for me by the time I walk out wearing one of the hotel's luxurious white bathrobes.

'I'm sorry it's been such a tough day for you. You've had a few nasty surprises.'

'I'm not sure what's worse. Crashing the yacht or finding out you've been lying to me.'

'I have very good reason. I promise. I hope you'll forgive me.'

'You'd better start talking then.'

Elias sits on the edge of the bed and bites at his cheek.

'It's going to sound awful because it's not you that I did this for. I didn't know you'd be a lovely, genuine woman...'

'What are you on about? Tell me what you want to say!'

'Okay. I'll tell you everything right from the start.'

'Please do. I need to know everything if I am to ever speak to you again. Why would you pretend the boat wasn't yours? This is just so shifty. Are you smuggling fine arts? Some kind of drug dealer? An arms dealer on the run? Just tell me.'

'I won the lottery.'

'What?'

'Yeah, it was a rollover. Just over nine million.'

'Well, why on earth would you say you're a skipper and that it isn't your yacht?'

'Because money does strange things to people. Do you know how many people you can trust when you win money like that? Not many.'

'Well, I've certainly had my fair share of surprises today. I don't know what to say to you. I mean... Wow... is that really the truth about why you lied? The whole truth?'

I shake my head in disbelief.

'Yes, of course it is. I should've been straight with you from the start.'

'So, is that why you had your wife's art on board? And how you have blue crockery, which seems to be your favourite colour? What about all that business about checking with your boss to see if we could go on the yacht?'

'Yup. I know. It looks bad, but I'm not a flashy man. I almost feel embarrassed about the win. I know that seems strange to someone who went out and bought a yacht with some of the money, but look, my wife had cancer. I had a heart attack and a huge operation... You probably noticed the scar when we were... well...'

I nod my head.

'My wife knew I needed to take things easy. I always used to say, "If I win the lottery, I'll buy us a yacht and sail around the Med." She dreamt of painting landscapes of the ocean, and we had this dream that one day she'd paint on board, and we'd sail away into the sunset. But life doesn't always go to plan. As we saw today...'

'No, I understand that bit, for sure.'

'So, the thing is, my wife was a very kind woman. She always thought of everyone else, even when she was dying. She was more worried about the boys, how I'd manage and organising her own funeral to save us from doing it.'

'She sounds very special. What a selfless woman.'

'She was. And we did the lottery numbers for years. Even when she was dying, she'd remind me to do them so I could dream of retirement. And then they came up. She died a fortnight later, and it felt like the universe was telling us that you can't have everything.'

'Oh my gosh. I'm so sorry.'

'It was the most bittersweet moment of my life. Before she left us, she made me promise to buy a yacht and sail around the Med. Of course, the first thing I did was buy *Lady Jane*. She happened to be advertised in a sailing magazine I subscribe to, and I knew she was the one.'

'And your wife's name? Was it Jane, by any chance?'

'Exactly.'

Elias starts to cry, and I realise it has been an incredibly emotional day for both of us in different ways. Yet, I'm still hurt that he may have considered me a gold digger all this time. Why did he not feel he could tell me the truth earlier?

'Look, it was all supposed to be a dream. Win the lottery, become the happiest man on earth, and sail around the world. It just didn't work out like that. My wife died and I was all alone. When cousins I hadn't seen for years heard rumours about the lottery win, they all came out of the woodwork. The only thing people seemed interested in was what I could give them. Anyone who knew started treating me differently. I wanted to be the old me again. I loved the way you treated me as a normal guy who worked for a living. I didn't want to spoil that, and so I didn't want to tell you the truth. I thought once you found out then you might treat me differently. I didn't want that to end.'

There's so much I want to say, but it doesn't feel appropriate to interrupt, so I let him continue.

'Money doesn't buy happiness. I worked hard all my life. I come from a family of grafters. I'm not used to a champagne and caviar lifestyle. I'd rather have fish and chips and mushy peas with a pint of lager, to be honest. Although I am coming round to all these French wines.'

I smile at his confession. 'Hah. You and me both, but swap the lager for a Pinot. Soraya loves all that stuff, but I much prefer the local chippy. I want you to know that I'd never have treated you differently if I'd known the truth.'

'I know. I could see you and I were cut from the same cloth. But people judge you differently when they think you have money. I don't mean this to be a sob story, but they take advantage of you, even my boys do. Not that I'm saying you'd ever do that. This makes me sound terrible. I just mean that I wanted to be the old me. Those evenings on deck with no preconceptions, just the two of us relaxed in each other's arms, will always be a beautiful memory.'

'Yeah, I know.'

'So, that's why I lied. I've been lying the whole time, and I hated having to do that. But I won't need to any more because my beloved boat is gone, and now you know the truth about me.'

Elias smiles and moves his hand through my hair, which is still wet.

'What a day.'

'Well, I'm just glad I know the truth because I really don't like lies.'

'I know. I can't apologise enough. It's just that once I started, I couldn't find the right time to tell you the truth. I'm so, so sorry.'

Elias looks drained and tired after the unexpected events we have encountered. I begin to accept his apology as I think of all the nice things he has done for me since we met, although I still have my guard up.

'The police said they'd call this evening once they've got the other boat's statement together. I've given them the name of this place, seeing as I don't even have my phone with me. All that stuff we had to leave on board. What a nightmare.'

'I know. Even my laptop is on there. Hey, why don't I run you a nice bath and you relax for a bit while we wait for the police to call for an update?'

'That sounds very nice. Thank you.'

'Don't mention it. We're a team, you and I. You've helped me out of my scrapes, and now it's my turn to help you. It's your turn to be the damsel in distress.'

Elias laughs, and I kiss his cheek, closing the bathroom door behind him as I think about one of the craziest days I have ever had in my life. If only I had my laptop, there would be no shortage of inspiration for the book today.

Chapter Nineteen

We are almost falling asleep for the night when the hotel phone rings. We both jump up, startled by the old-fashioned chime.

Elias answers it, and by his tone, I immediately know it is the police. I try to make out his expression as he listens to what they say.

'Uh-huh. Right, okay… Oh, well, that's great news.' Elias gives me a thumbs up, and I wonder what this fortuitous news is.

'Yeah, sure. Okay. I'll be down in the morning. Thank you for all your help.'

He seems a lot more upbeat than earlier as he puts the phone down.

'So, it seems that the steering mechanism failed on the other yacht. It was a complete accident, and they take full responsibility for all the damage.'

'Oh, that's a relief then. It doesn't change what happened, but at least they're not fighting about who's to blame.'

'No, exactly. But the good news is that they've towed *Lady Jane* out of the water and are going to see what can be salvaged. They're hoping we might even be able to save some of our things.'

'That would be brilliant. I hope I can get my laptop back and my phone... And your late wife's artwork, of course.'

'Let's not get our hopes up too high. We'll see in the morning, hey?'

'Oh, yes, of course. The main thing is we're in one piece.'

–

As soon as we wake up, we head down to the marina, where the boat has been taken out of the water as promised. It's in a sorry state, with a big chunk missing from the side, as if a shark took a massive bite into it. It stands on a trailer, looking neglected.

A different police officer from yesterday meets up with us and points to a ladder where we can climb up and get on board to find some of our things. I decide to stay on the ground and wait where it's safer. It looks so tall and as though it could topple over and, after yesterday, I can't face going back on there. We agree that Elias will throw anything he can find down to me.

I wait around until he shouts that he's found my laptop, and it's not water damaged. It is an absolute miracle. Maybe this book does want to be written, after all. He checks what else he can find, and then I meet him halfway up the ladder to get my luggage, which Elias has quickly managed to pack with any belongings he found.

'Your phone's here too.'

It is down to one per cent battery, and there are messages from Michael, the girls, and Soraya, who is checking on how I am getting on. If only she knew.

I open a frantic message from Michael.

You've not been online for hours. He's kidnapped you, hasn't he? Well, tell him I can't afford a ransom right now. Come on, where on earth are you? We're all getting worried now, Looloo.

He hasn't called me Looloo since we first met. He must be worried. Before I can put him out of his misery, the screen goes blank. I hope Elias has managed to find my charger in there.

When I next see Elias, he is smiling and coming back down the steps with a bag of some of his things.

'The artwork was saved. I'll arrange to get it shipped back.'

'Oh, that's the best news. I'm so pleased. But perhaps you should send it by air and not ship, hey?'

Elias shakes his head, smiling, as even I begin to see the funny side of our mishap at sea.

We head back to the hotel with all our essentials, feeling a huge sense of relief, and chat about what we should do for the next two days. My flight was already booked for Thursday, and my time on the French Riviera is almost up. I don't know what Elias will do. I suppose he still has a lot to sort out with the boat.

'I know a fabulous place we could spend the next two nights. I only booked this place for last night, so we need to check out by eleven a.m. How about you let me take you somewhere special?'

Even though I forgive Elias for lying about who he was, given his tragic tale, I still wonder when – or if – he would have come clean with me. How long would he have kept his story up for?

'I don't know, but whatever we do, I insist on paying my way.'

'No. It's my treat to thank you for coming into my life and cheering me up. You have no idea how lonely I was feeling when I bumped into you. I want to give you a gift and an apology for not being straight with you from the start.'

'Look, I should be thanking you for all the meals out and the yacht trip.'

'Not at all. Please, let's not talk about money. Look, I know this chateau, and I think you'll love it. Let me make it up to you for not telling you the truth about who I was and… Well, I can't apologise enough. I'm so embarrassed about it. I also wish you hadn't been on board with me when *Lady Jane* crashed. I feel so bad that I could not keep you safe.'

'It's fine – I know it wasn't your fault. Please, let's just start again.'

We check out of our Monaco hotel and jump into our new hire car, a bright red convertible Fiat 500. Elias is back to his cheery self now and grins at me as though he is a young lad who just received a Scalextric for Christmas.

'It's so cute,' I smile.

'Isn't it perfect? Let's take it for a spin to the Grande Corniche, there's some spectacular views out that way. We can take our time getting to the chateau.'

I remember the scenery from the taxi ride I had with Soraya and Carol, but in this little Fiat with Elias beside me, it will be even better.

Once again, we weave through the winding roads as we head out on the coastal route. With *Club Tropicana* blasting out from the radio, I am in complete holiday mode and momentarily begin to forget about the book,

Michael, and things back home. I can feel the tension in my shoulders slipping away as we both sing along to the words of Wham! as the scent of the trees and flowers that line the mountains waft into the car.

'God, it's good to have company,' says Elias, glancing over at me as he drives.

'I know. It's lovely, isn't it?'

'Isn't it funny… People think winning the lottery will solve all their problems. Don't get me wrong, it changed my life, but not all of it was for the better.'

'I'm sure anyone struggling to pay their bills wouldn't agree with you, but I do understand what you're trying to say.'

'I'd have given it all back for my Jane to have not died. I'd rather have struggled with my bills, like we did when we were first married, than lose my wife of thirty years.' Elias sighs and then tries to raise a smile. 'Sorry. It's just that, for so long, I haven't been able to confide in anyone. Finally, I've met someone I can trust.'

'Well, I'm glad you trust me.'

'Just don't put my story into your book, will you?'

I laugh. As if I would. Although, I am going to ask him if I can sneak in the bit about the time we had sex on deck whilst listening to Rick Astley.

As I remember that moment, we pass a group of Ferraris driving along the coastal route.

'Is there a collective noun for that many Ferraris?' I ask.

'A flash of Ferraris?' says Elias.

'Hmm, how about a posse?'

'Nice one. What about a *bank* of Ferraris?' says Elias.

'A small appendage of Ferraris?' I suggest.

'Love it. Now, let me think. What else? Right, wait for it.'

We both giggle in anticipation.

'A flaunt of Ferraris.'

'Genius. You should have your own dictionary,' I tease.

We are still laughing together when we pass a huge pylon that is practically at the same height as us, making me realise just how high this sinuous road is.

'Wow, look at the pylon,' I say.

'Good job you don't mind heights,' says Elias.

'I know. I'm trying not to distract you. We don't want another accident... Although, we all know *Lady Jane* wasn't your fault,' I quickly add.

'Thanks for saying that. You know, it was on a road not too far from here that Princess Grace was killed in that tragic car accident.'

I think back to the cathedral where she happily celebrated her wedding.

'So sad. Sometimes it's better not to know what's in store for you. Can you imagine if you felt ill while driving with all those big drops below.' I shudder at the thought.

I am glad Elias is taking the bends slowly after realising this is the same road that the beautiful Princess Grace was on.

There aren't many places to stop for a look around, but Elias eventually spots a small layby. It is probably just as well that there aren't viewing points all along here, or people would be stopping every few minutes; it's so beautiful.

We pull up safely, and Elias stands behind me with his hands around my hips as we both look over at the spectacular views of the sea and the principality below.

'This is breathtaking, isn't it?' he says.

'It truly is. It's like a bird's eye view over Monaco. So different from how we saw everything down below. We really have had the best of both worlds.'

We drive a little further along and find ourselves in Eze, which I remember from the night out on Soraya's birthday. It is where she wanted to go if we had more time.

Soon, we pull up to an old stone chateau that teeters off the verge of a mountain with an incredibly dramatic view of the Mediterranean below. I thought I had seen some incredible sights on this break, but I realise that I haven't seen anything until now. My mouth hangs open as I look at the building in front of me. The stonework reminds me of Rapunzel's tower. Torch sconces hang from the medieval stone walls, and the pretty pink flowers all combine to make it look like a fairy-tale castle.

Inside, there is a grand open fireplace, chandeliers and portraits. This place really is like something from a fairy tale, although I dread to think how much it costs to stay here for the night.

When we reach our room, I feel like a real-life princess. I have never stayed anywhere like it. The huge four-poster bed has grand red curtains hanging down on four corners, and I look over to see a roll-top bath in the corner. It could be so easy to get carried away here, so I try to remind myself that this is only a holiday and not to get used to this lifestyle.

'Seriously, there's a bath in our bedroom?'

'We could always use it later,' Elias grins.

I run about like a child, not knowing where to look first. I open the French windows and walk out onto the patio with the most wonderful sea view.

'Is it my imagination, or does the sea look bluer than ever from here?'

'It's so clear up here, I guess.'

'I don't think I want to leave the room.'

'Well, we don't have to. Although, the food is supposed to be pretty good here. But I suppose we should make the most of our time at the hotel,' says Elias.

I take hold of him and kiss him, and then we both fall onto the four-poster bed.

'Oh, god. My knee. Hang on.' In my excitement, I forgot all about the dodgy knee.

'Oh, no, are you okay?'

He straightens out his leg and laughs, and then pulls me towards him. We spend the rest of the afternoon in our glorious four-poster bed, and Elias doesn't complain about his knee again.

Chapter Twenty

Our fingers are intertwined as though we never want to let go of each other, as we walk downstairs to the table that Elias has booked for dinner. We pass a big wine cellar as we find our table on the terrace outside. It is a good job we are not into fancy wines, as I would imagine some serious damage could be done with this selection.

We sit at the table we have been given, which looks directly onto the sea and the coastline below. I sit tight against the elegant black metal railings. It's so close to the drop below that if this railing gave way, I would be straight over the edge.

'I really can't get over this place, Elias. What a hidden treasure.'

'It's beautiful, isn't it? I always fancied staying here, but since having the money to come, I haven't had the company. It's not the same coming somewhere like this on your own.'

I hold my glass up to his and say cheers. 'To the meeting of two strangers.'

'Maybe it was meant to be,' says Elias.

'Well, I certainly never expected we'd end up like this when I met you at the supermarket, that's for sure. This was supposed to be a men-free holiday.'

'Well, I'm glad I managed to change your mind on that one, Lucy.'

I have goosebumps as I look at Elias and our surround-ings. I don't know if it is the emotions of being somewhere so beguiling or the slight chill in the air from being above sea level, but I wrap my pashmina around me that little bit tighter.

When the food arrives, it warms me up. The crab ravioli is to die for, and when dessert comes around, Elias's eyes light up at the waiter's suggestion of rice pudding.

'I bet it won't be as good as my mum's,' says Elias.

'Was she a good cook?'

'Oh, she was the best. I'd come home from school, and she'd always have something piping hot from the oven. She enjoyed her cooking, did my mum.'

'Yeah, my mother used to be a good cook. I hate to admit, but I definitely didn't follow in her footsteps. She used to try and show me stuff, but I was too young to be interested in cooking, really. I was more bothered about going out clubbing.'

I think of Poppy and Jasmine, who I am starting to miss. Maybe that's why I am so protective of them on their nights out. I still remember what Soraya, Carol and I used to get up to.

'So, were you a wild party boy when you were younger then?'

'No. Met Jane in school. We got engaged at eighteen. I took her out on her first date when she was fourteen. Only to an amusement arcade, mind you.'

'That's so sweet.'

'How about you? I can see someone annoys you on the phone from time to time. Your ex-husband, I'm guessing?'

Despite all our discussions, I have tried to keep Michael out of our conversations until now.

171

'Ha. Yeah. He's always annoying me. So Michael… Or Mickey, as he prefers to be known nowadays… wasn't a bad husband. I loved him. Met him when I worked in a retail store in town. He used to come in every Saturday looking for something to wear out on the town. He kept asking me for advice and then buying whatever I suggested. The girls in work always teased me that he fancied me. Eventually, I realised they were right when he asked me out one Saturday. I agreed, we went on a date to the cinema, some cheesy film, which I'm ashamed to admit I don't even remember now, and then we just hung around all the time. Then one day we realised we'd been dating for two years, and so we got engaged, married, had the girls and then… Well, he decided he wasn't getting any younger and, let's say, wanted to experience new things. Anyway, it's beautiful here, and that's enough about him.'

'Of course. I'm sorry to hear about what happened, though.'

'It's worse for you, losing the love of your life like that. I suppose Michael and I just plodded along. We fell into it all. It sounds like you and Jane knew from the start what you both wanted.'

'Yeah, we did. But sometimes you just do.'

I look away as Elias smiles at me. I gaze down at the flickering candle, anywhere but his eyes, which seem so sincere. It is all getting so intense.

'And now we crossed paths. If Michael hadn't had his midlife crisis, I wouldn't be sat here. I'd be watching TV back home in my dressing gown most probably.'

We both laugh as the waiter turns up with our bowls of rice pudding. They are a lot fancier than anything a normal mum would make, with the side of the dish decorated with pretty little lavender violas.

I take a spoonful of my creamy rice pudding. It has a tang that I can't quite place, but I expect it is a melange of so many different ingredients.

'What's the verdict then? How does it compare with your mum's?'

Elias looks around, leans in and whispers closely, 'It's nice. But not a patch on my mum's and a damn sight more expensive too.' Then he laughs and makes a face and we both start to get the giggles. The other diners, enjoying the candlelit romance of our surroundings, look at us in disgust as Elias's loud laugh reverberates throughout the terrace. It makes us laugh harder and louder until we can't stop, and I begin to realise that as fabulous as this place is, we probably don't fit in with the rest of the guests, who seem to think we are a bit beneath them.

'Old money,' winks Elias.

We manage to stop laughing before we get told off and finish the evening with a nightcap at the bar where Elias tells me about his heart attack.

'I have to confess, when we stayed on the boat, I was so worried about my scar. You're the first person to have seen it and the only woman since…'

'It doesn't bother me at all, Elias. I hope you realise that things like that mean nothing at all to me. I'm just glad the op saved your life and you're here with me now and okay.'

'That means a lot. My confidence took a bit of a hit after it. Of course, first of all I was paranoid about having another heart attack. But I was never in bad shape doing the window cleaning round, you know? It kept me fit, and suddenly, I realised I wasn't as fit as my body looked on the outside. Maybe it was the stress of the business side. Chasing payments and all that.'

'It's hard as we get older with health scares. You just have to try and do everything in moderation and look after yourself.'

'Yes, indeed. Time is limited. So, what do you want for the future?'

'A best-selling book? My friends seem to think I can do it! I guess that's every writer's dream, though.' I laugh to hide my embarrassment in case it sounds pretentious. 'Of course, that's probably never going to happen, and that's absolutely fine. I don't know that I'd even want that level of success. What do I really want though? I suppose to be healthy, live a quiet life and write. Like, can you imagine being in one of those villas we saw and going out onto your balcony with your laptop and just sitting there writing?'

'That sounds pretty good to me.'

'Definitely. So, what do you wish for, Elias?'

'Now that's a good question. I guess someone to share things with. Someone to take out for dinner. To share interests with and to wake up with every morning. Isn't that what everyone wants?'

'Yeah, unless you're completely introverted and prefer your own company.'

'Well, I can definitely see that could be appealing for some folk – no arguments over who's having which side of the bed or pulling the duvet off in the night.'

'Exactly.'

'You know, I'd let you have my duvet. Even if I had to shiver all night. You could have it,' says Elias.

'Such a gentleman.'

Elias gives me that intense look again, and I realise that I might be ready for a relationship in my life, after all. That's something I never considered when my trust was shattered after finding out about Michael's two-year affair. I didn't think I would trust anyone ever again. But as I look into Elias's clear blue eyes, I begin to wonder if I could trust this man.

But then I remember how all of this started and how it was based on a lie. What if Elias has other secrets, or skeletons in the cupboard? What if it's best I have fun on holiday and then end it all when I step on that plane? It certainly might save a lot of heartache down the line. Besides, we live nowhere near each other, and this is just a holiday romance.

Chapter Twenty-One

Tangled in our four-poster bed, we wake up the next morning with smiles on our faces and a reminder of how much we must have drunk from the flush emanating from our cheeks.

'This bed's so comfy. I could stay in here all day,' I say with my head on Elias's chest.

'We can if you like. Now that would be a good way to spend your last day,' says Elias.

I playfully tap his shoulder. 'You must be joking. Have you seen the breakfast menu here?'

'Fair point, we need some sustenance.'

I'm happy to see that I was not wrong about the breakfast. A basket full of croissants, pastries and fresh French bread awaits us on the terrace, where the aroma of frangipani from the garden melds with the fragrance of our freshly ground black coffee. Birds fly about in the sunshine above us as a waiter brings a plate of multicoloured fruit to accompany our pastries, with the brightest red strawberries, the bluest blueberries and vibrant kiwi.

'You do know I'm not going to want to go back to my usual life after this,' I tell Elias. The thought of returning to my soggy cereal with skimmed milk, looking out of the window into the rain, doesn't bear thinking about. I wish holidays could last forever.

'Well, you don't have to. That can very easily be arranged.' Elias winks at me and has a naughty grin on his face. I get the feeling that if I would allow it, he'd want to give me the best of everything. I quickly focus my attention on the freshly squeezed orange juice, not knowing how to respond.

'Yum. Have you tried the juice? It's gorgeous. And I thought the juice from the supermarket in Monaco was fresh!'

'It is indeed. Hey, I don't know about you, but I quite fancy a drive out to Saint-Tropez. It's a bit of a way, around an hour and a half, but I thought we could spend your last day there, if you'd like that, of course.'

'Saint-Tropez? I've always fancied going there. All that glamour and Brigitte Bardot fame. How fast can you drive? Just kidding, by the way. Please don't speed on those roads.'

'I promise I won't. Saint-Tropez it is, then. Your chauffeur awaits.'

Soraya is not going to believe that I'm on my way to Saint-Tropez, and so I message her after we set off to tell her.

> That's brilliant. So chuffed for you. Best thing you did was stay on.

I can see she is still typing, and another message soon follows.

> I don't know if I should tell you this, but Michael turned up at the workshop yesterday. Just as I was closing up.

What? I watch the dots as Soraya types.

> He's being a jerk. Was asking if I'd heard from you as you haven't responded to him. He said you're involved with a scammer and he's very worried about you.

I sigh out loud.

'Everything alright?' asks Elias.

'Yeah, yeah. Just stuff going on at home. The usual.'

'Okay. I can pull over if there's a problem.'

'No, keep going. I want to get to Saint-Tropez. Got to make the most of our last day together.' Now it is Elias's turn to sigh.

I return to my phone and message Soraya back.

> I hope you told him that the supposed scammer is gorgeous and I'm very happy.

> Ha. No, I didn't want to wind Michael up more than he already was. He told me how he's made the biggest mistake of his life cheating on you and how he misses you every day.

I lean back and take another sigh. Why now, Michael? Why now? We have been divorced for eighteen months, he had an affair for two years before that, and now that I am hanging around with someone else, he decides he made a mistake. I have only recently picked myself back up! I have to admire his timing.

I notice Soraya is typing again and worry about what else Michael has said.

> I'll warn you now. He says he's going to ask you for a second chance when you get back. He's apparently told the girls, and they're excited at the thought of their parents reuniting. His words… I shouldn't tell you while you're enjoying yourself, but I think you should be warned so it doesn't come as a shock when you get back.

'Oh, bloody hell,' I say out loud.

I imagine the girls listening to their beloved dad, hoping that the fractured family can get back together again. I think how much I would have wanted that at the start. I would have done anything to keep my family together. The girls were excitedly talking about their choices of uni when it all came to light. I wanted to protect them so badly from it all as they planned their future and their next steps into adulthood. They were absolutely devastated when we announced the split. The longer it's been, the harder I find it to forgive him for what he did to me and to the girls. He wasn't thinking of their best interests when he was in the throes of his affair, and that is something I can never forget. I am furious with him for speaking to the girls about this and giving them false hope when he hasn't even spoken to me. If I was mad with him before, I am even madder now! This is unbelievably manipulative of him.

'What's wrong?' asks Elias.

I think about telling him. I should be honest with him. But I don't want a discussion about Michael to spoil our perfect day trip. I tell him it's nothing, switch my phone off and am a little withdrawn for the rest of the journey to Saint-Tropez until Elias excitedly points out the panorama of the Maures mountains in front of us.

'Oh, that's magnificent. What a view. You're so know-ledgeable knowing the name of the mountains. I have to confess I would never have known that.' I smile, determ-ined not to think about Michael for a moment longer as we pass the best designer boutiques. My eyes are wide with excitement as I spot Louis Vuitton, Chanel and Gucci. Then, finally, we reach the famous Plage de Pampelonne, where we sunbathe and people-watch for most of the day. Soraya told me that this is where celebrities are supposed to hang out, although I haven't seen any recognisable faces as yet. Still, I watch bathers as they dip in and out of the sea in case I miss anyone.

Despite the fact there are gorgeous people everywhere, Elias keeps his eyes fixed on me. He must be the most attentive man I have ever met. If I was here with Michael, he would be ogling all these beautiful women that walk past us. With the hair of mermaids and thighs and biceps of steel, you couldn't blame anyone for doing that. Yet here I am in a bobbly old black swimsuit, my foot tangled up in seaweed as I go for a dip, and still Elias isn't taking his eyes off me. He simply helps untangle me from the seaweed like the gentleman he is. He certainly knows how to make a woman feel desirable and valued, no matter what state you're in.

When we eventually tear ourselves away from Saint-Tropez, the reality that it's our last few hours together seems to hit both of us. Neither of us says much all the way back to the hotel as we are both deep in thought. I wonder what Elias is thinking. I know what *I'm* thinking, and that is how much I don't want to leave him. I don't want to go back and face Michael either. I want to stay in the French Riviera, driving around in our little Fiat, sunbathing and hanging out at bistros with this gorgeous man I've just met. However, this isn't how life works.

We spend our last night together on the terrace of the chateau, dining on *moules et frites*, sipping on French wine and gazing into each other's eyes from time to time. The chemistry between us is off the scale, and before too long, we take what is left of our drinks back to the room and retire for the evening. Elias kisses me against the wall as we enter the room, and we giggle as we remove each other's clothes. I try not to think about the future and enjoy the moment in the here and now.

After we have been passionate with each other, I look out to the sea and wonder what the future will hold for us both as we return to the real world. Will things ever be the same with Elias in Manchester and me in Swansea? How can it possibly be?

–

I wish I hadn't booked a flight so early in the morning. We are both still half asleep as Elias drives me to the airport in Nice in the little Fiat 500. The ambience is so different to our usual drives along the winding roads. The music in the car is quieter, the roof is up, and the mood is subdued.

'How come two weeks ago I'd never met you, and now I can't imagine you not being here with me?' says Elias.

I have never been one for goodbyes or particularly sentimental – odd for an aspiring writer perhaps, but I can never find the words when it comes to my own life – and so I just shrug my shoulders and look out the window as I try to enjoy the last views of the French Riviera whizzing past.

'I'll be back in Manchester soon. Do you think I could come down to Swansea and see you?'

I think of the girls and Michael showing up without notice, and then remember this is *my* life. If this is what I want, then they can't stop me. It occurs to me that maybe on some level I've been using them as an excuse for not moving forward with my own new life. It feels safe being their much-needed Mammy. Elias has opened up a whole new world for me now, though, and I want to be brave enough to step into it. But what if he lets me down? The distance between us is a big problem for a start. Besides, surely our relationship could never be this magical when we are away from here with this beautiful scenery and the fancy venues. We will surely crash down to earth with a very big bang if we try to continue this back home.

'You're very quiet. Does that mean you don't want to see me back home?' says Elias.

'Yes, of course I do. It's just difficult, you know? The dynamics are so different back home. We've been free here to be whoever we want. Back home, well, I have the family and commitments.'

'I don't have to stay with you. I could get a hotel. I just don't want to think we'll never see each other again. But I don't want to put any pressure on you either.'

'No, of course not. It's not like that. I know I want to see you again. It's just I don't know if I'm coming or going and, oh, I'm a bit of a mess at the moment.'

'Well, you seem far from a mess to me.'

I smile at Elias and look at him. I take in the last sight of his fair hair, the stubble he has because he didn't have time to shave before my early morning flight. Why would I even consider sabotaging the chance of a relationship with someone like this? It doesn't make sense, yet I have never been more scared of taking the next steps in a relationship in my life.

'Sorry. I just didn't expect any of this. I came here to celebrate Soraya's birthday, get some inspiration for my book, maybe get a bit of a tan. I was staying well clear of anyone of the opposite sex, believe me.'

'If it's any consolation, the way I feel has taken me by surprise too.'

'Really? I'm pleased to hear that. But, oh, why does life have to be so weird sometimes?'

'From where I am standing, nothing seems weird. We're two single adults who enjoy each other's company, what's so strange about that?'

'You live in Manchester; I live in Swansea. I have a family that takes me for granted and want me at their beck and call… You have sons who still miss their mother. It's all so complicated.'

I omit the part about how scared I am that Elias could lie to me again or let me down, just like Michael did – the man I thought I knew. I had known Michael since I was in my twenties, and he caused great carnage. I may have only known this man for five minutes, but I don't think I can bear to be hurt again.

'The distance doesn't need to be a problem. I've got a car, there's trains. It needn't be an obstacle... Unless you want it to be, of course.'

Elias's tone changes as he says that last bit. He sounds disappointed.

'No, of course not. Let's just see how things pan out when I get back. I mean, you might feel differently when you get back to Manchester.'

I have to protect myself at all costs. Imagine if he lands back in the cold and decides this was just a holiday fling.

Elias looks disheartened but appears to accept my decision. He helps me with my bags at the check-in, and we prepare to say goodbye as my flight flashes up on the departure board. He holds me and kisses me, and when we finally let go of each other, we wave until we are both out of view.

I wander around duty-free in a daze as I pick up all the things the girls have asked me to get for them. The thought of seeing them again is the one thing I am looking forward to as my once-in-a-lifetime holiday comes to an end. Looking around for their bits makes me realise how everything I do is for them. Everything I did in my marriage was to keep Michael happy, but nobody ever thought about making me happy. No one ever thinks about what I may want now. I think back to my conversation with Elias at the chateau. What do I really want my future to look like? It is something I think about all the way home.

Chapter Twenty-Two

Arriving home late at night, I dump the duty-free gifts for the girls on top of the kitchen table. There are bowls with dried leftover pasta in the sink. My extra-sensitive nasal passages, an effect I believe is down to perimenopause, make me want to heave. The girls must have popped back while I was away and left their dishes for me to sort out. I love how they feel this is their home, but I am annoyed that they didn't bother clearing up. That's the problem when they have their own key and come and go as they please.

Once I have unpacked, I open the lid of the laundry basket to throw everything in, only to find that the girls have already managed to fill it. At least they didn't throw their dirty washing on the bathroom floor, I suppose. Sometimes you have to be grateful for small mercies.

I sigh as I walk into the living room. I would do anything to be back at that beautiful chateau right now instead of having to deal with the washing and messy kitchen.

After sticking the TV on to take my mind off all the chores that have welcomed me home, I message Elias to say thank you for the wonderful memories, but it doesn't go through.

One tick is all my phone will give me, and I become paranoid that I have already been blocked. I go to bed with no response from Elias, only messages from Poppy, Jasmine and Michael. Poppy and Jasmine ask how the holiday went and are pleased that they'll get to see me soon. They are so sweet that I forgive them for the pasta bowls. Then they ask if I could order tickets for a concert for them as they go on sale at nine a.m. tomorrow when they'll be in lectures. They promise to pay me back. We'll see about that.

Meanwhile, Michael says he needs to talk to me face-to-face urgently. If it wasn't for the fact that I know the girls are still alive and seeking favours the second I have touched down, then this would have freaked me out. Since I know they are completely fine, whatever he needs can wait. After what Soraya said in her messages, I know I am not up to dealing with him right now. Before falling asleep, I let the girls know that I'll make sure I'm online in the morning, check once again in case my message to Elias has finally gone through, and decide to ignore Michael.

Even though we are heading towards summer, the flat feels cold when I wake up. I guess I must have become acclimatised to the balmy French climate. I have to put the heating on, something I was hoping I could avoid at this time of year. I sigh as I remember waking up on the French Riviera with the sun shining through the windows and the warmth of Elias beside me. I switch my phone on, thinking my message will surely have gone through by now, and there will be a happy bleep letting me know that Elias has replied. However, there is nothing from him, and my imagination runs riot. I really thought I could trust him, but now I get that red flag again. After all, we did get off on shaky ground from the start. He could be anyone he wants to be in Manchester. His lottery win could be a lie, for all I know. What if I have chosen to ignore all the red flags that have been in my face all along? Perhaps

I should have prepared myself for this instead of trusting my instinct.

Once I have secured the concert tickets for the girls, following a stressful online ticket queue experience that I never want to repeat, I consider googling Elias. I fear the worst, yet still, I can't get him out of my head.

I open my laptop and type his name in, dreading what I might see. I almost want to close my eyes as it reveals the results. Will it help anything if I read something untoward about him? Maybe I should simply move on with fond memories and put it down to experience. Terrified, I look at the screen with bated breath. Thankfully, there is nothing, except a suggestion that I may have spelt the name wrong. Okay. That's good. Surely, it's a positive that he has no social media trail? It does strike me as a bit odd, though, as people who win the lottery are usually pictured in the papers opening a bottle of champagne and holding one of those gigantic cheques with a big smile on their face. Although, he will undoubtedly have opted for anonymity, which I certainly understand. He was still running the business when he won, and I expect he didn't want all his customers gossiping, either. Even now he's secretive about his win, so he's bound not to have allowed his photos all over the media. It still doesn't change the fact that there is no word from him yet, though.

Desperate for a distraction, I close the search engine page and open up the draft of my book. I should start writing while I still feel inspired by my trip, and concentrating on my book might help me take my thoughts off Elias.

I pour everything out onto the page. The words come thick and fast, and the writer's block I had the last time I sat in this living room is long gone. I am so engrossed in my work that time escapes me, and it is only when I pick up my phone again that I realise there are now two ticks on my message to Elias, showing it has been safely delivered. He didn't block me as my imagination feared! I punch the air and hope he picks it up soon. I put the laptop away as now I can't seem to concentrate on anything other than Elias.

I pace up and down, have a shower and put a load of washing on when, finally, there are three happy pings from my phone. Like buses, Elias's messages seem to all arrive at the same time.

> Lucy, hope you get back safely. Please message me once you get home. I miss you already xxx

> I'm just boarding my flight to Manchester. Time to say au revoir to Monaco. See you soon, hopefully xxx

> Lucy, I don't know if you've blocked me? My messages don't seem to be going through to you? I thought we both had a fabulous time together. Maybe I was wrong? xxx

I look at the last message in disbelief. We both thought the same thing about each other! As if I would ever block him.

I can hardly type back fast enough.

> Hi! All the messages are coming through in one go. Think you must have had problems with reception. I'm here! Hopefully my message has got through to you by now xxx

I notice as I press send that he has now read the message I sent last night and is typing. So I start typing, and our messages end up a jumbled, excited, heap of miscommunication as we interrupt each other. However, there is no confusion when it comes to how much we already miss each other.

Elias tells me he will give me a ring this evening once he is back home. He is at the luggage arrival, and his bags have just shown up on the carousel. I tell him how much I look forward to hearing his voice again tonight. But, by lunchtime, my plans of a cosy evening waiting for Elias to call and then watching the start of a new TV drama are shattered.

It seems that Poppy and Jasmine have a few days' study leave and are coming to stay. Poppy asks if I can get her favourite jeans that are in the wash pile ready for when she gets back. Like the dutiful mam I am, I throw them in the machine with the next load of washing.

When the girls turn up later on, I am surprised to see them carrying a takeaway. Usually, it's a case of, 'What's for food, Mam?' and then I have to think of something that could possibly appeal to their ever-changing tastebuds. I look at them impressed.

'Wow, what've you got there?'

'Chinese. From your favourite place.' Jasmine looks pleased as punch.

'Ooh, well that makes a nice change from having to cook tonight. I'm still shattered from the holiday. That's so thoughtful. Thanks, girls.'

Poppy stands in the hallway, and I ask her why she isn't coming in.

'Hang on a minute. Dad's on his way. He's parking the car downstairs,' she says.

'Dad's coming?'

'Yeah, it was his idea to get you the takeaway. He thought you might be too tired to cook tonight.'

I hear those footsteps that I'd recognise anywhere coming up the corridor.

'Alright, love,' says Michael, grinning, as he approaches us in a colourful, floral shirt that I have never seen before. What happened to those plain white shirts he used to wear? He looks as though he is off on a Caribbean cruise and not picking up a takeaway at the local Chinese.

'Umm, hi. I wasn't expecting you to turn up tonight.'

'No, well, I thought we could have a family meal, since the girls are home. They invited me, actually,' he says.

Oh, girls! Why would you do that to me? He's obviously brainwashed them with his ideas that I am most certainly not on board with.

As the girls and I unpack the takeaway, I notice my favourite dish. I look down at the stir-fried king prawns in a chilli and black bean sauce.

'Did you see Dad got your fave?' says Poppy.

'Yes, thank you. Lovely.' I let out a sigh. That's the thing when you have been married to someone for so long. They know all your likes and dislikes.

Michael looks over at me like a puppy wanting attention. 'See? I remembered.'

Does he want a Blue Peter badge for remembering my favourite food? I don't mean to be harsh, but he wasn't thinking of my favourite treats when he bedded some woman who lived round the corner. The bitterness and shock of that betrayal is difficult to move past, no matter how much he tries to make amends.

Poppy puts her arm around her dad.

'You try your best, don't you, Dad?'

Michael tops up my wine and smiles at me. 'Anyway, I wanted to treat you because you had us all very worried. Going off on a boat like that. What are you like?'

'I hope you can see that you were all overreacting. See, here I am. Safe back at home. Nothing bad happened. In fact, I had an amazing time, but I do appreciate your concern.'

I haven't told them about the boat crash, or they might envisage me being hauled up to a helicopter on some ladder, with my thighs desperately gripping on. Now that would not be the best of sights for anyone's imagination, and they would never let me forget it. It would be all the proof they needed to drill into me why I shouldn't have gone off on that boat.

'No, thankfully. I'm so glad. It made me realise that... Well...' Michael gives me that wistful look again. He used to make the same face when he wanted sex.

'Right. I'll clear up the plates then, shall I?' I say quickly.

'No, Mam. You leave it. We'll tidy up. You and Dad have a chat now,' says Jasmine.

Since when are the girls so keen to clean up? This is practically unheard of. Even when I was really sick with adult chickenpox, I still had to unload the dishwasher in our old home. I eye them suspiciously.

'Come on, Poppy.' I notice how Jasmine nudges Poppy with her elbow. This is something she always does when they have been plotting. The girls did the same when they wanted a stereo in their room when they were nine and ten, respectively, and again when Poppy was the first to want her ears pierced at thirteen.

'So, ahem. Yeah…' says Michael, looking at me intensely.

Thankfully, Poppy drops a plate into the sink, and it makes a big crashing noise, which means I can turn away from him.

'Watch my plates, please.'

'Sorry, Mam. Slipped out of my hand. We'll just leave you two alone a minute.'

Jasmine and Poppy walk out of the open kitchen and leave me looking at Michael as he clears his throat and starts giving me *that* look once again.

'What is it, Michael?' I realise it comes out rather snappily, but I can't possibly have him thinking that a takeaway container of stir-fried king prawns will be enough to wipe out the last few years and he'll have me running back to him.

'I don't know if Soraya said, but…'

'Yeah, she told me you swung by the workshop.'

'Yeah, so the thing is. The thought of you with some guy out on a yacht in the middle of nowhere… Well, it terrified me. You're my girls' mam. We need you. We need you here… Do you get what I'm saying?'

'You need me here. Yeah, I get it. To look after everyone, do the washing for the girls, that sort of thing, is it?'

'Now, come on. You know what I mean.'

I watch in horror as Michael's arm reaches closer towards mine and he strokes my wrist. I pull away sharply. He looks at me as if he has been wounded.

'Look, I'll just say it. I love you, Lucy. I was a fool. I don't know what I was thinking. It was a midlife crisis thing. I felt old and decrepit. I wondered if anyone would find me attractive ever again. Like if you died and I wanted to eventually move on… You know, after a long time, like. What if nobody fancied me? I'd passed my prime, and it scared me. Yeah. I was scared, Lucy.'

'I was scared when Jasmine had to have her appendix out after it ruptured. I was scared when I found out that my husband had some other woman, and she was posting it all over social media. Imagine how scary that was, waking up to see photos of my husband's car on another woman's driveway. But not once did I use that fear as an excuse to run off into the arms of another man,' I say.

'No, I know, and that's why I'm sorry. You wouldn't have done what I did. I've realised all the bad things I did to you. I've come to my senses, to be honest. You didn't deserve any of it.' Michael sounds genuinely sad as he says it and looks as though he wants to cry. I believe that he could well be sorry and has realised that the grass isn't greener, but still, it changes nothing.

'It's a bit late now, Michael. The divorce was finalised over a year ago. Why are you saying this now?' For once, I am firm with him and realise I probably should have been firmer during our marriage rather than going along with what he wanted half the time.

'I told you. Because when I thought you were off with the Tinder Swindler dude, my heart broke in two. I thought, what if he swindles you and what if I'd lost you forever? It was the wake-up call I needed.'

'Wake-up call? Because I'd met someone else?' My voice is rising higher and higher with every sentence Michael comes out with.

'And he is *not*, repeat *not*, a Tinder Swindler!' I still don't know that for certain, but I won't have Michael say that about Elias.

I jump when Jasmine and Poppy burst back into the room.

'Mam! Daddy's trying to be nice. He's trying to apologise. Don't be so mean to him,' shouts Poppy.

'Were you listening to everything? Now, me and your dad need to talk. This is private.' No matter what Michael does, he can do no wrong in their eyes. I protected them both from the days when I cried non-stop as I accepted our marriage was over. Now that he thinks I have met someone else, he decides his midlife crisis is over. Well, I can't forgive or forget that fast, even if the girls would do anything to have our family back together again.

'The thing is, babe, we've so many memories of us as a family, when the kids were young, when we went on holiday together and, oh my god, do you remember that time in Majorca, Poppy…' I look at him in shock as he brings Jasmine and Poppy into the conversation.

'Yeah! When I fell off the back of the tandem I was on with you, Dad. Oh, remember my knees?' says Poppy.

'Yeah, and we had to take you to the hotel to clean you up and—' says Michael as Jasmine interrupts him excitedly.

'I was fed up because I thought Poppy was trying to spoil the holiday deliberately. Remember, we were due to get me that massive unicorn rubber ring for the pool once we finished on the bikes? I thought she was jealous, and we had a big falling out.' Jasmine puts her arm around Poppy. 'Sorry, I know now that you were hurt and getting you patched up was more important.'

'Oh, that was a holiday. By dinner time you were the best of friends again. See, even the closest of family fall out with each other sometimes,' says Michael, looking at me.

I shake my head in disbelief that this has now turned into a family conversation.

'Great memories, weren't they, Lucy?' says Michael.

'Yes, they were.' *Shame you had to go and ruin it all*, I think to myself.

I watch Jasmine, Poppy and Michael as they laugh amongst themselves, chatting about their favourite family memories, and then I hear my phone ring.

'Excuse me,' I say, walking away from the dining table.

I pick up the phone, noting who is calling. I look back at the table where my family is smiling and laughing. I watch as Elias's name rings out.

'Is someone calling you, Mam?' asks Poppy.

'It's nothing. I can deal with it later,' I say, putting the phone back down.

Chapter Twenty-Three

Michael clearly doesn't want to leave as he continues to try and make amends. I am struggling to deal with him, and if the girls weren't here, I would insist he leave. However, they're enjoying us all being together for the first time in a long while, so I bite my tongue, despite being fit to burst. I try my best to ignore him, but I resolve that this is the last time he is coming round. I will make sure of it.

'Isn't that new ITV drama starting tonight?' says Jasmine.

'I know the one. I was going to watch that at home on my own. It'd be much nicer to watch it with my girls,' says Michael.

Jasmine takes charge of the remote control, switching the TV to the channel.

'Dad, do you want me to get you a beer?' says Poppy as she helps herself to the fridge.

She hasn't asked me if I want anything. I make a face and tell her I'll get my own drink. She smiles at her dad as she hands him one of the beers. At least he hasn't asked to share the bottle of wine he brought over.

'Ah, just like old times, isn't it?' says Michael.

'Yes, well, you do love a good drama, Michael,' I say with a hint of sarcasm.

'Don't spoil this lovely evening with one of your funny menopausal moods now, Mam,' says Poppy.

I squint my eyes at Poppy in a bid to warn her not to dare go down that road.

'Ooh, it's starting,' says Jasmine, turning the volume up on the remote.

I shake my head and take a big – make that *huge* – glug of wine. I take another as I see my phone is ringing. I don't need to look to know that it will be Elias trying again.

'This looks good, doesn't it?' says Michael. I note how he sinks further into the sofa snuggled between Poppy and Jasmine, making himself ever more comfortable.

'Isn't this lovely, Dad?' says Poppy, raising a glass to him.

I remind myself that this is their dad, who they love so much, as I look at the three of them in their element. Then I turn away and look at the TV in case I pop. I tell myself that it's just for a bit longer, and then I can get him out of here.

During the adverts, I take my phone to the toilet with me. Locking the door, I stand behind it, checking my phone. Elias has called three times, and there is a message.

> Tried calling a few times as agreed. Couldn't get a reply. Maybe we can talk in the morning? Sweet dreams, lovely xx

I quickly type back and plan a time for the morning and then return to the lounge, where Poppy has now opened some crisps and is sharing them around as they all noisily debate whether the main actress was from a soap they love or not. As I observe them debating and jokingly arguing between themselves, I start to feel guilty, as though I have been cheating on them. One minute I was enjoying being a free woman, and now it is as though I dreamed my trip to the French Riviera, where I felt so carefree. It's obvious that the girls feel I should give Michael a second chance, and after just one evening, I am starting to feel like I am cheating on them by messaging Elias. What is going *on*? This is ridiculous. Why did Michael have to decide he was sorry now? He wasn't sorry when we went through the divorce. He carried on thinking it gave him freedom to do whatever he chose. Now he is making me feel as though it is my fault that he finally realises the grass isn't greener out there. Somehow, after everything he has done, *I* will be the bad guy if I put an end to all this and the girls will blame me.

Poppy and Jasmine finally decide to head off to bed once the programme finishes, but Michael is still hanging around. It occurs to me that he has had a few beers in front of the telly and that he must be over the limit to drive home. I hope he is planning on a taxi and isn't going to suggest staying here. I start to clear all the glasses and crisp packets up as a hint that it is time to leave. My yawns get bigger, and still he won't take the hint, so I firmly tell him I am going to bed and he'll have to call a cab. I have given him far too much of my patience for one night.

'I thought I'd stay over if that's okay? The girls are here, it'd be like being a family again all waking up together,' says Michael.

'I've only got two bedrooms. Where did you expect to sleep?' I ask, coldly.

He gives me that face again.

'Don't even think about it.'

Since I am tired and want to get to bed, I eventually agree he can sleep on the sofa. I am mad with myself as I know I should make him leave, but the thought of the girls hearing that I made him go home when they so obviously wanted him here just takes the fight out of me. I tell myself it is just one night. But, still, it feels wrong having him here. This is my home, and he has never been a part of my life in this flat. This is the place I bought after he broke my heart, where I found refuge and worked hard to pick up the pieces after his devastating affair. Now he feels that he can walk back in, eat here, watch my telly and even sleep here. I am feeling very resentful towards him right now. How dare he do this to me!

I hurry to my room as he starts stripping off his shirt and trousers to sleep on the sofa in his underwear.

He laughs. 'Why are you rushing off? It's not like you haven't seen it all before.' Even though he is technically right, and we were married for so many years, it feels incredibly sleazy as he says it, and I am shocked that he doesn't seem to realise this.

I am glad to escape to bed where I read the goodnight message from Elias again. Then I scroll through the photos I took on the yacht, in restaurants, and of the scenery we enjoyed together. It is such a world away from Michael on the sofa in those stripy pants he insists on wearing that make him look like one of the Bananas in Pyjamas.

I look at Michael now and feel nothing. A year ago, I didn't believe I would ever feel happy again, and I realise just how special Elias made me feel. I don't need the yacht, the money, or the fancy locations, I just want to be back in his arms. I think of those muscles he has from all that manual work; his hands aren't smooth like Michael's, who works in an office, but they tell a story. Elias's hands will always show how hard he has worked during his lifetime, and whilst he got lucky winning such a huge amount on the lottery, he also lost his precious wife, who he would have swapped any amount of money for.

Conversely, Michael has always lived an easy life. He landed his job with a good pension straight from school, he is fifty-five with both parents still alive, unlike mine, both lost before I was forty. He has no idea what it feels like to lose someone he loves to cancer, or how hard it is to work outside in all weathers as he sits inside his warm office enjoying intermittent tea breaks and nibbling on Hobnobs. When I close my eyes there is only one person who is on my mind, and it is certainly not my ex-husband.

-

I forget that Michael has stayed over until I stumble into my living room half asleep and see those long, familiar legs hanging off the edge of the sofa.

I bang the kettle and run the water as loudly as I can in the hope that I wake him up. I figure the sooner he is up, the sooner I can get him out of here. Eventually, I see his head stick up above the sofa.

'Good morning, love.' Michael cricks his neck and stretches out his arms, giving a large groan. 'Would've been much comfier in the bed. Hardly slept a wink.'

'Oh, that's funny because you were snoring when I got up. Anyway, now you're awake, it's probably time to head home, hey?'

'There's no rush, is there? I thought we could take the girls down Mumbles for an ice cream. You know, like we used to when they were small.'

'They're grown up now. They don't need an ice cream.'

'Did someone say ice cream for breakfast?' says Poppy, walking out into the living room in her pyjamas with one eye open and rubbing the other.

'You heard right. You up for ice cream?'

'Oh yeah. I'd love that. Let me wake up a bit first though.'

'There's no rush. We've got all day, haven't we, Lucy?'

'Well, no. I have to work.'

'What? It's not like you've got a proper job any more, is it? Or do you mean writing stuff on that laptop of yours? Surely you can do that anytime.'

I glare at Michael. 'Well, I've given myself a deadline. I want to send it out to publishers soon, not keep it on my laptop forever. Anyhow, haven't you got to be at work?'

'Flexi-day.'

'And Poppy. I thought you two were supposed to be on study leave?'

'Yeah. Ice cream helps feed our brains, though.'

'Ah, I see.'

'Just like old times, hey, babe?' grins Michael.

I walk out of the room before I scream at him in front of the girls. Oh boy, if they weren't here now, he wouldn't know what had hit him. I always promised myself that I would hide any contempt for Michael in front of the girls to protect them. Now he is sat in my lounge, insisting we spend the day together as if he has never done anything wrong in his life, and this promise is proving harder to keep than I could ever have imagined.

Jasmine runs after me.

'Mam, I think Dad's really trying. He's learnt that he made a stupid mistake. He told us. Why don't you give him a chance? Let's just have a nice day with him.'

'You've all got to respect that I've work to do today. I have a lot on. I'll come for an ice cream with you – in my own car – and then I'm coming back to work.'

I am not playing happy families with Michael, not even for the sake of the girls. I figure if I agree to an ice cream with them all then it will get him out of my flat.

I turn on my heel and jump in the shower, letting the hot water run over me as I try to reclaim my patience with Michael. Then I sit on the bed in a towel and message Elias.

> Have a wonderful day. Hope to see you soon xx

He messages back immediately.

> I was thinking, there's plenty of trains from Manchester to Swansea. How about I come down and visit? Shall we plan something when we speak later? Xx

Although I had arranged a time when we could talk, it's not looking likely with everyone hanging around. I need to get Michael and the girls out of earshot. As for Elias coming to Swansea, as much as I would love that, I can't imagine the girls' response if Elias comes down in the middle of them plotting to get their parents back together.

So, instead of doing what I want, I go out for an ice cream and watch the clock as Michael reminisces about anything he can think of as we stand on the beach with our 99s. When a gust of wind blows in Michael's face, and he gets a mouthful of sand, it keeps him quiet for a moment. I try to look concerned as he splutters about. Looking at him being over-dramatic, I realise that any feelings between me and him are well and truly gone. He might think he can rekindle this relationship, but as I watch him with disdain, I realise that this ship has most certainly sailed.

Chapter Twenty-Four

I make my excuses and leave everyone on the beach so that I can call Elias. The sound of his voice almost makes me want to cry when I finally get the chance to speak to him. The kind tone he has and the way he says my name has me melting from the moment he picks up. We chat about his trip home and what he is planning to do now he is back in Manchester. He is waiting for the insurance payout on the yacht to arrive and then he is thinking of going away again.

'How do you fancy coming with me?' he asks.

'That sounds like a fabulous plan. I just need to…' I realise I was going to say that I need to run it past my family, but that would go down like a lead balloon. I remind myself that Michael let me down in the most awful way and that my life is now mine to do whatever I choose. Somehow, though, I know the girls won't accept that right now and will take some convincing. I don't want to hurt them.

I refrain from telling Elias that Michael stayed over when he asks me what I did last night, and it feels stupidly unfaithful. I feel as though I am going behind Elias's back, and that is the last thing I want to do. I want us to have a relationship that is out in the open. Free of any baggage as it should be, but now Michael and the girls have decided to play happy families as I finally take steps to create a new life.

A naughty thought crosses my mind of creating some kind of catfish account to trick Michael into messaging another woman. He has never been one to keep his concentration on anything for too long. It can be a sports car or a woman; if it gets his attention, then he will gladly turn his head. Just like a cat, he will go to whoever gives him the most, whether that's food or attention.

'Has everything been okay for you since you got back?' asks Elias. I fear he can sense how distracted I am with everything going on here.

'Yeah, yeah. Just miserable being back and remembering what a great time we had. Apart from that, it's all hunky dory.' *Hunky dory?*

'Great, so… I was thinking. *Carpe diem* and all that, how about I come and visit you this weekend? I checked the trains, and there's a fast one around lunchtime. I could drive, I suppose, but there's something about relaxing on a train. Getting a KitKat and a coffee and sitting back with a good book. Better than being stuck on the M5 on a Friday afternoon anyway.'

'Oh, yes. Indeed.'

'So, does that work for you if I get in around five-ish on Friday?' asks Elias.

I think of the girls. Since it's a study week, they will probably be here for the weekend, which means they'll want me to pick them up wherever they go on Saturday night. It is far too soon to introduce them to Elias, especially now that they have it in their heads there is a chance that Michael and I could reunite. I will need to handle this carefully.

'Umm, I'll have to check,' I say with a hint of regret, when all I want to say is how wonderful it would be to see him.

'Yes, of course. I didn't mean to spring it on you.'

'Oh, it's not that. It's just…'

'Have you changed your mind about us?' asks Elias.

'Oh, heavens. No, not at all. It's just that… Things aren't so easy since I've come back home.'

'What do you mean? Are you busy with the book? I totally understand, you know.'

'Yeah, the book… Look, how about you come next week instead. I'll work all weekend and take time off next week. You could come on Monday for a few days?'

'It means waiting a bit longer to see you, but as long as I can see you, that's all I care about.'

'Great. We'll do Monday then.'

'Monday it is. I'll look forward to it.'

–

I manage a few thousand words on the book before the girls return. I hear them chatting outside the door before they put the key in, and I can already detect Michael's voice among the chatter. I thought he would have at least dropped them off downstairs and finally gone home. I slam the lid of my laptop shut in despair.

'Hiya, love. We had a fab time, we went bowling after ice creams. Shame you couldn't have come with us,' says Michael.

'Yeah, Mam. Dad said how much he wished you were with us, didn't you?' says Jasmine.

'Yeah.' Michael does that downcast look as though he is a lost soul, but it doesn't wash with me. The thought of that catfish account is getting stronger by the second.

'Oh, well. There's always a next time. I was saying that maybe Friday night we could all go for dinner somewhere. We could go to the brasserie. I remember how you love the garlic mushrooms there,' says Michael.

'Oh, I won't be able to, besides, I've gone off garlic mushrooms.'

'Why can't you go? It's not like you to turn down the chance of a meal out. You're always moaning about having to cook.'

'It's been two years since we lived together. How do you know? A lot about me has changed,' I snap.

'Alright. No need to be like that. Calm down.'

'Anything on TV?' he says, looking around the room.

The longer Michael is here, the more I feel as though steam will start coming out of my ears. How did I even live with this man for so long?

With a documentary on octopuses playing in the background on the TV, I grab the remote control and switch it off. It is finally time to snap.

'That looked good.'

'Right, can I have a word, please?'

'Uh-oh, seems I am in trouble...' says Michael, rolling his eyes at Jasmine and Poppy.

I lead him outside to the hallway, out of earshot of the girls. I don't want to lambast their dad in front of them.

'What's wrong?' he asks.

'What's *wrong*? Right. I'm going to put this firmly so there's no mistaking what I'm about to say. You had an affair for two years behind my back. It came to light, and I realised we weren't the perfect little family I thought we were. I had to pick myself up and try and show a brave face whilst you swanned around with your mistress. Apparently, it hasn't worked out with her or anyone else, and so now you've come running back to me. On top of that, you then get the girls involved to try and convince me that we should all be back together as a family and play on their emotions. That's not on at all.'

'I didn't play on their emotions. They want us back together.'

'Yes, you did. You can't do that to them, and you can't waltz back in here just because you found out I met someone on holiday. Now suddenly you don't want anyone else to have me. Am I right?'

'No, I told you. It made me realise how much I loved you. The thought that you could've been kidnapped, or anything happening to you on that yacht, was awful. When you didn't reply to my messages, I was over-whelmed with sadness. There was so much I wanted to say to you.'

'But, you know, the one thing you've never said is sorry. Not once have you apologised for what you did to us.'

Michael looks at the floor and then picks at a bit of peeling paint from the wall of the corridor.

'Well, I'm sorry now. Alright.'

'It's too little too late.' I take a deep breath before I tell him about Elias.

'I've met someone else and I'm going to give it a go. It's early days, but he seems to appreciate me. He encourages me with my writing, and he understands that I have this dream. You never believed in me like that. I know you think me trying to write a book is a waste of time. I don't think you've ever understood my feelings about it.'

'Well, maybe we should have talked more and then I wouldn't have run off with another woman.'

'Don't even go there and try to blame me for this.' My voice is so loud that I realise people will hear us as the communal door downstairs slams shut. I try to lower my voice.

'I've said all I want to. Now please stop treating my apartment as your home. You've got your own place. We need boundaries.'

'Boundaries. Pfft. You sound like you've been seeing a therapist, have you?'

'What's going on, Mam, Dad? You've been out here ages,' interrupts Jasmine as she opens the apartment door and peeks around.

'Nothing. Dad's just leaving. Aren't you?'

'Yeah. Alright. Your mam seems to have made her mind up. I lost a good woman and it's all my fault.'

Unable to get around me, Michael says goodbye to the girls and makes his way to his car. Meanwhile, Jasmine and Poppy aren't amused that I have made their dad leave.

It seems I may have drawn the boundaries with their dad, but helping the girls understand that I have moved on from him is going to be much harder.

Chapter Twenty-Five

When the girls finally leave for uni, I get the flat ready for Elias's arrival. The thought of seeing him in this country makes me nervous. I know I'm desperate to see him, but what if it's all different without the sunshine, French wines and romantic settings that played such a big part in our whirlwind romance? Butterflies are playing havoc in my tummy by the time I set off to collect him from the station. I even manage to drop my keys as I try to lock the car.

But the moment I set eyes on him at the station, I know that I have nothing to worry about. He bounds towards me and lifts me into his arms.

'Oh, you're a sight for sore eyes,' he grins.

'You too,' I smile.

As we chat in the car on the way home, it dawns on me quite how much I have missed his wonderful company.

Back at the apartment, Elias is the perfect guest, removing his shoes without me saying anything. He is so considerate, and I force myself not to compare him with Michael in my head, not wanting to give that ex-husband of mine any more thought while I am with Elias. I make him a coffee, and we catch up for a while on what we have been doing since we returned, and I tell him of tonight's dinner plans.

Since Elias has already met Soraya and Carol, I have arranged for us all to go out for a drink this evening. I thought I had better do something in case I needed a bit of support if things were awkward seeing Elias again. I can already see that there was no need to worry, but it will be nice for him to meet Andrew, along with Carol's new friend, Duncan. She wasted no time once she was back from the holiday. Apparently, he came in to have a man weave, something that Carol specialises in at the salon. She says they got on incredibly well from the moment he sat down in front of her and confided in her about his vulnerabilities since his hair loss. It will be good to meet him – and check him out a bit, just in case there is more to it and he is only after a discount on his regular treatment. After all, those weaves don't come cheap.

Soraya and Andrew are already seated at the table by the time Elias and I arrive. They wave over to us, and I pray that Elias gets on well with Andrew. I am hoping that since they have both run their own businesses, albeit very different ones, they will hit it off. I introduce the two of them and they seem to get along. Soraya and I catch up, and just as I had hoped, Elias and Andrew discuss their relative businesses. It is amazing how much they have in common despite their different industries.

I notice someone walk into the pub and immediately know it is Duncan, even though I have never met him before. He has the most incredible hair I've ever seen on a sixty-year-old. Then Carol pops out from behind him, confirming I was right.

With everyone at the table, we order our drinks, and all enjoy each other's company. That is until Duncan announces that he works in the tax office. He has recently moved there, and I pray he isn't in the same department as Michael. I don't need him knowing about tonight.

By the end of the evening, Elias and Andrew have swapped numbers and become big buddies. On the way home, Elias tells me how much he liked Andrew.

'I noticed how well you seemed to get on,' I say.

'Yeah, we might even do some business together.'

'Oh, that's great.'

'Yeah, you never know. He's a nice guy.' Elias puts his arm around me in the back of the taxi, and I lean into him. I'm glad he gets on with my friends. That's always so important to me. I could never date someone who disliked my besties.

Back at the flat, it's just the two of us again. I had nothing to worry about as this is exactly like the nights we spent in each other's arms in France. As Elias lies beside me in bed, stroking my shoulder, I look into his eyes and tell him how glad I am to see him again. It's more wonderful than I ever imagined having him here. We definitely don't need fancy things around us to enjoy each other's company.

Waking up together to a brand-new day, I plan on taking him down to the Mumbles and showing him the lovely area I grew up in. But I should have known that my life is never straightforward. I have just thrown my kimono on to make us tea in bed when I hear a key in the door. Only Poppy and Jasmine have keys, so it must be one of them. I instinctively tighten my kimono around me as the door flies open.

'Poppy. I wasn't expecting you!'

'I'm not well. I did message you,' she says with a croaky voice.

She promptly tells me she has strep throat and has been sent off for the week despite having only just returned to uni. Her first thought was to come back here and have me look after her. I smile and tell her to go and sit down; my poor love looks pale.

While I am concerned for Poppy not being well, my heart is beating at a million miles an hour as I wonder how I can announce that there is a man in my bedroom, and it's not her dad. I can't exactly smuggle him out now that Poppy needs me.

'Why are you making two cups of tea?' says Poppy.

'One for you,' I smile. I lean against the kitchen island nonchalantly as I think on my feet. I am not going to be able to keep this up for long.

'Oh, thanks. Just what I need for my throat,' she croaks.

I notice her eyes as they turn towards the loafers that Elias left by the front door last night.

'Whose are those shoes? They're not Dad's.'

'What shoes?'

Poppy stands up and goes for a closer inspection.

'Whoever they belong to has got big feet. What's going on? Is there a man here?'

Right on cue, Elias walks out of the bedroom.

'Who the *hell* is this?'

'Now, Poppy. There's no need to be like that. This is Elias. You remember how I told you about the lovely man I met in Monaco?'

'You told me about a scammer who is probably after my inheritance,' she says.

'Poppy. Don't you dare be so rude. Elias is not a scammer. I really like him, love.'

'I don't care who he is. Dad told me you two are getting back together, so, what, now you're being unfaithful to my father?'

Elias's eyes open wide as he looks between the two of us. 'Umm, I'll get my things. I should probably go.'

213

'I'm not getting back with her dad,' I say, giving Elias a pleading look.

'Yes, you are. Why are you lying, Mam? Dad told us when we went bowling.'

'Look, I know what he might think, but I've put him straight since then, okay?'

I turn back to Elias. I feel as though I am caught in a crossfire.

'Look, please don't go because Poppy is here. Maybe the two of you can get to know each other.' Even as I say it, I realise what a futile hope this is. Poppy is never going to want to get to know anyone whilst being brainwashed by Michael that there is a chance of reconciliation.

'I think it's clear she doesn't want me here. I get that. And it sounds like you've things to sort out with, what's his name, Michael, was it?'

'Yes, Michael. My *dad*,' croaks Poppy.

I open my mouth and then shut it again. Anything I say now will only lead to a more heated argument. I know Elias has the wrong idea and I can also see that my girl is ill, confused and hurting. I feel frozen, torn in two directions and unsure what to do or say next.

Elias walks into the bedroom to get his stuff. I watch in regret as he removes his toothbrush from my toothbrush holder. It was nice seeing our toothbrushes side-by-side for that short time. It brought a sense of togetherness.

'I'm so incredibly sorry, Elias,' I say. 'Let's talk later.'

He doesn't answer but quietly packs his things away. His silence feels like the worst thing. What if he isn't open to talking it through with me and hearing what I have to say? What if this is over almost before it has begun? Elias throws everything in at great speed, and it's obvious that he can't get out of here quickly enough.

'If you're leaving, at least let me drive you to the train station.'

'It's fine. It didn't seem far when we drove over yesterday. I can manage.'

'Well, umm, see you soon?'

'Yeah, let's see, hey.' I can tell that it is one of those times when you say the words 'let's see' so that you can escape from a conversation. His face says it all. With his bag in his hand, he attempts to say goodbye to Poppy who is refusing to look at either of us, and he closes the door behind him.

It is obvious that he thinks I am getting back with Michael. That couldn't be further from the truth, but somehow, I need to convince Elias, and also Poppy.

Chapter Twenty-Six

Four days later, Poppy's antibiotics have kicked in and she feels so much better that she is heading back to Cardiff. Over the past few days, I have wanted to pick up the phone to Elias and speak to him, but with Poppy listening to every word and requiring soluble painkillers every four to six hours, it has been difficult to get the space and time to have any sort of honest discussion. It hasn't gone unnoticed that Elias hasn't tried calling me or messaging me either. I would like to think he is busy, but I know that is far from the truth. After what happened between us, it is me who needs to break the ice. How I want to so badly, but I also don't know where to begin. What if Elias won't take my calls? We had such a beautiful evening together and it's all ruined.

Poppy is still not in the best of moods with me by the time she sets off.

'You know that Dad realises what he did was wrong. Why won't you give him another chance?'

'Because too much has happened between us. He did things I never expected. It's taken me two years to get over the shock of it all. Now I'm finally at peace, and he's putting ideas into your heads. He can't just decide he wants us to be a family unit again.'

'But we were a good family. We were all so close. I know he messed up, but we all make mistakes.'

'Yes, we do, but some are bigger than others.'

'I know. He has been stupid, but…'

'Exactly. He has, and now it's too late.'

'But I always dreamed my mam and dad would be one of those couples I'd tell my friends in uni about. How they'd been together forever, and then one day, you'd be celebrating your fiftieth wedding anniversary. I never wanted my parents to be divorced. Imagine my wedding day. Where will you both be sitting? It's all gone awkward now.'

'Oh, love. I'm so, so sorry. I never wanted any of this either. It's happened now, though, and we have to get on with it.'

'Well, it's not too late to change your mind, Mam.'

I give Poppy a hug, and we both get a little emotional as we say our goodbyes.

Then, as soon I can compose myself, I decide to sort this mess out once and for all with a phone call to Michael.

'Hi, Michael. Are you free to chat?'

'Go ahead. I've got a very interesting tax form in front of me, but go on because I need a word with you too…'

By the tone of his voice, I can guess that Poppy has got to him first.

'Sounds riveting. Well, I won't keep you. I need you to explain to the girls that we're not getting back together. You've got to stop getting their hopes up.'

'Oh, and why is that? Would that be because of that Tinder Scammer that has been staying with you?'

'Right. First of all, it was one night, and yes, Poppy did accidentally meet Elias, as it seems you already know. Then secondly, we didn't meet online nor is he a scammer. How many times do I have to tell you? Do I interfere with whoever you're seeing? Since when are you so interested in my life?'

'Well, I mean, there's no need to go around flaunting this man about the place. People know me in Swansea. It doesn't look good. Imagine how I felt when one of the new guys in the office said he'd been for dinner with my ex-wife and her friends.'

'Duncan?'

'Yes. I'm horrified.'

'May I remind you, yet again, that we're divorced and it's all your fault that we are even in this mess.'

'That's why I want to make amends. Let's give it another shot. Lucy, we've so much history between us. We have the girls who I cherish more than anything. I made a big mistake, and now I'm paying the price. You're the only one for me. Let's try again. For the sake of the girls. We can be a family once more, just like we were. We'll have a new start. It'd make the girls so happy.'

'Do you know how much I used to wish we could have a conversation like this? I did everything I could to keep my little family happy, but it was never enough for you. You took me for granted for years. Whatever the latest thing was, it would always turn your head. Well, now I've got myself together and realise that my future is whatever I choose it to be, and you are part of my past. We'll always have our history, that won't go away, but it's time for a new start now.'

Michael is quiet for a moment and then snaps back at me. 'If you don't accept my apology and get back together with me now, then I won't ask again. It's your final chance.'

Any sympathy I had for him during this conversation has gone. He never did take rejection well.

'That's fine. It was over for me the day we signed the divorce papers. Now you go and do whatever it is you want to do with your life, and I'll do what I want. But just make sure the girls know that it's not Elias's fault we're not getting back together.'

'Fine. I was only trying to get back with you because I pitied you being on your own and for the girls' sake, anyway.' Michael's voice has turned meaner and more spiteful.

'Goodbye, Michael. Have a nice life.'

I put the phone down and pour myself a coffee to calm myself before I make the next important phone call. This one is much more nerve-racking because I realise how much it means to me. I rub at the back of my neck, take a sip of coffee and press in the number. It rings and rings, and I pray for it to answer, to hear that voice on the other side, but I don't. Instead, it goes to a generic voicemail from the phone provider. Do I really want to leave a message? I put the phone down, trying to keep a tiny glimmer of hope that he may call back. Twenty minutes later, there is no phone call from Elias as I had hoped and so I ring again. Still, there is no response, and it goes onto the voicemail. This time I decide that leaving a message might be the only way he will hear what I have to say.

'Hi, Elias. It's me. You know, Lucy. I'm calling to say sorry. I'm so sorry for what Poppy said. She didn't know what's been going on. You see, Michael did ask me to get back with him. I didn't tell you because it didn't feel important to tell you.'

I stop for a moment, thinking about what I can say next.

'So, it is true what she said, but…'

I am halfway through when I hear a recorded message down the phone.

'To record your message again, press one, or hang up if you've finished recording.'

I stare at it, not knowing what to do as I realise that my time is up. I've left an unfinished message telling him that it didn't seem important to tell him about getting back with Michael. *No, no, this has all gone wrong.*

I desperately ring back again, but the line is engaged. I start to panic as I imagine Elias's reaction as he listens to such a terrible message. Why did I not rehearse this before calling? I frantically ring again and again until I get through. When his number eventually rings out, I get that blasted recorded message again.

'Sorry, I got cut off in half. I'm going to speak super-fast this time. So, yes, he did ask me to get back with him, and I said absolutely not. That's why I felt it wasn't important to tell you. It didn't mean anything to me. Michael got this stupid idea into his head… Probably because he doesn't have anything better to do right now and thought we could get back together, but I was having none of it. I think it's because he realised that—'

'To record your message again, press one, or hang up if you've finished recording.'

I scream at the phone.

This time when I call back to continue with my final message, it isn't engaged. As soon as I hear the bleep, I start with what I really want to say.

'I think it's because he realised that I've met someone else. Someone I care for more than I ever thought possible. I never expected to meet someone again. I wasn't looking for love, but somehow I feel as though I have found something I didn't know I was looking for. I mean, I'm not falling in love… Of course, it's very early days, but what I'm saying is that if I was to fall in love, then it would definitely be with you. I hope you'll call me back so we can talk about what's happened. Please don't—'

'To record your message again, press one, or hang up if you've finished recording.'

I put the phone down and stare at it in frustration.

I consider calling back to finish the sentence but decide I'd best not spam his voicemail even more. So, I put my phone to one side and hope that he will eventually call back. In the meantime, I meet Soraya for a lunchtime glass of wine. Not something I make a habit of, but there is a lovely wine bar in the marina and, right now, I need Soraya to chat to and the wine to cheer me up.

As only a best friend can, Soraya tries to lift my spirits. She's sympathetic about my predicament and tells me how much she likes Elias.

'Andrew thought he was very nice too. Didn't they get on well?' she says.

'Yes, very well. But I don't need to hear that now, Soraya. Don't tell me how great he is when I might have lost him. How can I get him to speak to me?'

'He will. It's just a silly misunderstanding, and anyway, he lied to you about his money, so he can't exactly talk about hiding things.'

'No, I did think he might be a bit more understanding.'

'Well, maybe he's busy somewhere. Perhaps he's out buying a new yacht and so busy negotiating that he can't come to the phone.'

'Or avoiding me,' I say, taking a sip of my Sauvignon. 'Oh well, there's plenty more fish in the sea. Anyway, I never wanted another relationship after Michael, so I'm really not bothered. Who cares?'

'You clearly do,' smiles Soraya.

'I don't. Look, I'll switch my phone off so he can't call me even if he wants to.' As I grab my phone from my handbag, I see four missed calls.

'Oh my god. It's Elias, he's been trying to call!'

'You see. How glum you looked when you walked in, and now look at you. All smiles again. Just like you were when we were away. I fear he might mean more to you than you even realise, or want to admit to anyone.'

As the phone rings in my hand, I have to agree. All I want is to speak to Elias and hope that he will understand that there was nothing to this Michael business at all. The pessimist in me raises her annoying head to plant the fear that he might be calling to ask me to leave him alone and, for a moment, I look at the phone, scared of what he will say.

'Answer it, will you,' says Soraya.

I nod my head and quickly swipe to answer. 'Elias, hi.'

The line crackles and breaks up.

'Wait, Elias, let me go outside. I can't hear you.'

I look at Soraya, who gestures for me to hurry outside.

Looking towards the boats in the marina, I try to listen to what Elias is saying.

'I owe you an apology too. I ran out of there and didn't listen to what you had to say. I should have called you sooner. You listened to me when you deserved an explanation, and I should have done the same. I'm sorry. I guess this relationship business is harder than I imagined. My boys drilled it into me not to trust anyone. That everyone will be after my money, and...'

I consider how Poppy and Jasmine think the exact same way. If only they knew the truth that he definitely doesn't need my tiny flat when he has so much of his own. But I don't want to tell them the truth yet, either. Announcing that you're dating a lottery winner isn't the easiest thing to say. There are going to be so many preconceptions. Now I understand why Elias keeps it quiet. They may think he is some guy who spends all his money on women, boozing and bidding on football clubs.

'I'm scared, I suppose. I can feel myself getting closer to you. How fond I am of you, and I just think that I don't want to get hurt. Do you know what I mean?' says Elias.

'I totally know what you mean. The thought of getting hurt again terrifies me. That's why I wasn't looking for another relationship. Who wants to get hurt? It's the worst feeling in the world.'

'That much is true, Lucy. Look, we need to sit down together. I know it's difficult with the distance between us, but we can work something out.'

'Yes, absolutely.'

'I have an idea. This might sound a little too much too soon, but I have to get back to France in a couple of weeks. How do you fancy joining me?'

'I don't think I can. I've got a lot of work on the book that I want to do and, well…' I don't want him thinking I'm a freeloader. I know if I tell him I can't afford it, he will offer to pay for me, and I don't feel right about that.

'Let's see. Why don't you come back down to Swansea instead? The girls are definitely back in uni and not coming home at the weekend. We can try again. Or I can come up to Manchester?'

'I'd love to come back down,' he says.

'Great, this weekend?'

'It's a date.'

We end the call, and I have a big smile on my face, but as I sit back down with Soraya and finish my wine, something troubles me.

'All sorted now?' asks Soraya.

'Yeah, he's coming back down to see me again.'

'That's fab. It's not your turn to go to Manchester, then?'

'No, I did think that. He's happy to come here, but if I mention anything in passing about going up to see him, he doesn't really acknowledge it.'

'Hmm, that's weird. He's not hiding anything, is he?'

'I don't know. That's what's beginning to worry me. He said his boys live with him, so that might be what's wrong, but I'd happily stay in a hotel nearby. I don't have to go to his house. I didn't call him the Mysterious Mancunian of Manchester for nothing. He doesn't give much away.'

'Well, he seems quite deep from what I've noticed. He's just one of those guys who doesn't really show his feelings and keeps his cards close to his chest. I'm sure it's nothing.'

'I don't know.'

However, as I finish my glass of wine, I can't shake off the feeling that there's another reason he didn't want me to go up to Manchester.

Chapter Twenty-Seven

When the weekend approaches, I decide that I am going to ask Elias more about his home life. He has visited me in my apartment, yet I don't even know where he lives in Manchester. Is it Bolton? Is it Altrincham or Stockport? When I googled a map of Manchester, it looked huge. Soraya was right in saying that he keeps his cards close to his chest. This time, however, I am determined that he is going to tell me more.

The moment Elias arrives at Swansea train station for the second time, it is like a new start. I feel warm and fuzzy as I see his cute grin as he walks through the station. I'm immensely proud that it is me he is coming to see as a few women take a second glance at him. I feel like wearing a T-shirt with an arrow pointing towards him saying, 'I know, he's gorgeous, isn't he!'

Elias embraces me at the station and there is no mistaking that he's missed me. He doesn't notice the admiring glances he is getting; his eyes are purely focused on me, as they always are.

Back at the flat, he apologises again for not being sure what to believe about Michael and me. I realise that we are both treading in unchartered territory and neither of us are quite sure how to navigate this blossoming and unexpected relationship. So, I start by tiptoeing very carefully.

'How were Danny and James when you got back?' I ask over the ice-cold Sauvignon I picked up for his arrival.

'Yeah, they were okay. James is at uni, so he's been back and forth. Danny, as I mentioned before, took over the business. He was about to move out when Jane died, actually. After that, he decided I needed someone to stay with me, and so he let the flat that he'd planned to move into fall through, and that's how it's been ever since.'

'That was kind of him.'

'Yeah, he's a good lad. His heart's in the right place. Although I do tease him that he's doing it to save money on renting somewhere,' jokes Elias.

I want to ask if that is why he is so reticent about me going to Manchester, but I tread carefully.

'Would the boys be okay about you seeing someone?'

'Ah. Well, no, quite honestly. Of course, they think their mum is irreplaceable, which is understandable, but more than that, they think every woman who speaks to me is a gold digger. I'm like, umm, can a woman not like me for my sparkling personality and not be after my wallet?' Elias laughs.

'Well, that's definitely an attraction. I mean, your personality. Not your wallet! But, no, I'm sure they have to look out for you after your win. That's only natural.'

'Yeah, it's hard enough trying to tell them I'm ready to move on with my life after their mum. It's doubly hard when they think every woman is after my money.'

'Yeah, I can sympathise. When did the tables turn and we get told what to do by our kids?'

'When we got too soft, I think.'

'Too true. I've never been able to say no to the girls, and now I'm definitely paying the price. They get away with everything.'

'You and I should run away together like you suggested before. That'll teach them,' says Elias.

As he smiles, something in his eyes tells me he is serious. He is really thinking about my off-the-cuff remark in France.

I sit back and look at him curiously. 'Can you imagine if we did?'

'Yes, I can, and it would be bloody marvellous!' He doesn't hesitate. 'We could rent one of those places near the sea. Just one summer, you and I.'

'Oh, don't tempt me.'

'I am *trying* to tempt you! In fact, forget that – I'm inviting you. It's not quite June yet. How about me and you together for the rest of summer? We can lie by the beach, drink cocktails in the evening and then, well, we can let the nights dictate how they'll end. What you reckon?'

'You are quite serious, aren't you?'

'I am. Look, since you live all the way down here and I live all the way up in Manchester, and since we seem to have dramas with our kids in this country, let's just run away. It'll be like the reverse, and we're the youngsters who are in love and disappear together.'

Did he just say *in love*? I get a bit flummoxed and carelessly spill some wine on the coffee table.

'Poppy and Jasmine would never forgive me,' I say as I mop up the mess.

'James and Danny wouldn't either.'

'Yeah, we have our commitments. Even though the kids are older, they still need us. They've all been through quite a lot for such a young age,' I say.

'Of course, I shouldn't have said that. I'd never want to come between you and your precious girls. I caused

227

enough trouble when poor Poppy caught me staying over. Sorry, I get carried away sometimes. I get excited by things and am far too spontaneous for my own good.'

'No, it's fine. It's such a lovely thought. Imagine, you and I waking up with the sea lapping against the shore. The smell of jasmine flowers or frangipani in the air, all that good food and snuggling up to you. I can't think of anything better. It's a lovely idea.'

'It'd be absolute bliss. I tell you what, how about we start with you visiting Manchester? I'd like the boys to meet you. If that isn't too fast for you? I want to take our relationship further – if you'd like that too – and if I'm to do that, then I think I need to tell the boys about you.'

I am thrilled. He has finally invited me to Manchester! I couldn't be happier.

'That would be wonderful. Would that be okay for James and Danny though?'

'It'll have to be. You know what they say, there's no time like the present. Why put it off any longer? I mean, it doesn't get much more serious than wishing I could run off with you to France. Why don't you come up next weekend? It'll give me all week to prepare them for your arrival.'

'Oh, I can't stay with you. It wouldn't be fair to the boys when they haven't met me before.'

'It's fine. They use the house like a hotel anyhow. They're always having someone stay over. I can put you in the spare room if you prefer.'

'Yeah, I think that might be best.'

'Right, it's a deal then. I'll take you to my favourite restaurant in Cheadle.'

I memorise the name of Cheadle and am content that I will finally see where Elias lives, who his friends are, and learn so much more about my gorgeous Mancunian.

'Okay, but that means I have to take you to my favourite restaurant in Swansea this evening. Deal?'

'Sounds good to me, but first…'

Elias draws me to him, and we forget all about food for a while.

–

When we do finally walk up to the front of the restaurant, Elias tries to pronounce the very Welsh name. I laugh and tell him that I was born here and even I can't pronounce it. Looking at this place, you would think it was somewhere serving hearty Welsh grub. I can't wait until Elias realises what is on the menu.

The staff are attentive, and Elias is impressed with the service, but he still has no idea what is to come. Our little wooden table, decorated with freshly picked tulips, is tucked away in a corner near the window. Elias insists I have the pretty view of the restaurant gardens outside as he pulls his chair around to face me.

'So, what do you usually have here? Any recommendations?' he asks as we wait for the menu.

'Chips?' I tease.

'Sounds good. I'll have whatever you suggest.'

When the waitress brings over the menu in Welsh, English and French, Elias gives me a big smirk.

'*Moules marinière, soupe à l'oignon, canard?*'

'I thought we should get used to the cuisine… Just in case we do decide to run off to France.'

'I love it! Who'd have thought this Welsh restaurant would have such a fabulous French menu?'

'It's a hidden treasure.'

'Just like you. Where have you been hiding all this time?' says Elias.

'Ha. In my apartment watching the latest TV dramas, probably, instead of living my life.'

'Well, I hope that'll all change now.'

'So do I.'

Elias looks across the table at me with that irresistible smile of his, and I can't help grinning. This man makes me feel so incredibly happy. When our *moules* arrive, it is just like being back in Monaco and all the happy memories flood back.

We wash the *moules* down with a bottle of French white wine, and when we walk back to the marina, Elias takes my hand.

'What is it between us, hey? Sometimes you just connect with someone. It's like I knew you in a past life.'

'Well, I don't really go for that sort of thing, I'm not even superstitious.' I quickly let go of his hand and run under some scaffolding we pass to prove my point.

'You see? I don't believe in anything we can't explain. But I definitely can't deny we have a huge connection.'

Elias takes my hand again and kisses it as goosebumps enshrine my entire body. I have never met anyone who makes me feel like he does, and if I wasn't so sensible, I'd think he had put some sort of spell on me.

When we get back to the apartment, we kiss from the moment we walk through the door, then stumble over the corner of the sofa and into the doorframe of the bedroom as we are so desperate for each other. We tumble onto the bed, and I am engulfed with happiness as Elias pulls me to him and we make love.

We spend two wonderful days together without leaving the apartment, and I have never been so happy to stay confined in this small flat, chatting about our childhood memories, our family and how fond we are of each other so quickly. But when Elias has to leave to head back to Manchester, it becomes so hard to say goodbye. The last time he left was in very different circumstances. Having that miscommunication has brought us so much closer. Don't they say making up is the best bit? The past few days have certainly been pretty amazing.

If I could get past the barrier at the train station, it would probably be like a scene from *Brief Encounter* as I wave at Elias until his train is out of sight. However, this is modern-day Swansea, and I can't get past the barrier, or the station guard, who is standing at the turnstile making sure nobody is dodging the price of a ticket.

As I walk back to the car alone, I arrange to meet Soraya and Carol to cheer myself up. I don't feel like being alone, and thankfully, Carol's salon is closed today.

Within thirty minutes, the three of us are huddled around coffee and carrot cake at a cafe in the centre of town.

'Wow. Your skin's glowing. Are you using a new moisturiser?' says Soraya, as she steps back to look at me after kissing both cheeks.

'It'll be that man she's seeing,' says Carol.

'No, it's just…'

'Yeah, it's that gorgeous man you're seeing,' says Soraya.

'You don't need a man to have glowing skin, you know. Nivea works just as well,' I insist.

'Well, whatever it is, I want some,' says Carol.

'How's it going with your new man, Carol?'

'Oh, he was using me for hair weaves. He asked me if he had to pay next time. I said yes, you bloody well do, and, well, that was the last I saw of him. Blooming cheek.'

'Aww, I'm sorry to hear that. But probably best you find out now and not further down the line when he'd had a few freebies,' I say.

'Yeah, and besides, I think he was telling Michael everything about you as he was always asking about you and Elias.'

'Really? That's shocking. I bet Michael put him up to it.'

'Yeah, no doubt. Talking of which… I took a screenshot of this. I'm back on the dating sites now, and…' Carol removes her phone from her bag and flicks through her photos, then holds it up for both of us to see.

I look at the photo of Michael, wearing the same Hawaiian shirt he wore when he tried to get us back together. I read the bio he has written.

> Tom, 45, looking for good-looking, chill
> female, below 35…

Tom? Who's Tom? Chill female? Below thirty-five? What planet is that man from? I think his midlife crisis has found new depths. And he's taken ten years off. Although he's given his age away, calling himself Tom. I bet he's named himself after Tom Selleck. He was obsessed with him when we first met. He'll be growing a moustache next.

'Lucky escape there, Lucy,' says Soraya.

'To think that man broke my heart. Amazing, isn't it? He just looks such a fool and a liar now.'

'We don't always see it when we're with someone, unfortunately,' says Carol sympathetically.

'I just need Poppy and Jasmine to understand why it's so over between us now.'

'Maybe you should show them this,' says Carol.

'No, I've always tried to shield them from his behaviour. I'd be horrified if they found out what their dad is really like.'

'You're a good mam. I wouldn't have been able to resist telling them. Especially after they were trying to get you back together like that,' says Carol.

'It's not worth it. If they find out for themselves, then so be it. I can't protect them from that, but you know how much they idolise him and think I'm to blame for our breakdown because he's just let them think that.'

'That's so unfair though,' says Carol.

'It's fine. Anyway, it's behind me, and the girls have stopped trying to get us back together for now.'

'Good, I'm glad. So, how's the book going?' asks Soraya.

'I've just a couple of chapters left to write, and I'm very happy with it all so far. I'm so grateful to you for getting me out of that slump.'

'I'm so pleased for you. That was Michael stifling all the creativity out of you. You needed a change of scenery,' says Soraya.

'Thank you. I did, more than I realised. It's all thanks to you and Andrew for being the most generous friends I could ever have. I promise to pay you back one day.'

'We don't ever need paying back. That's what friends are for. You'd do the same for us. I know you would. Anyway, let's get back to more exciting matters. So, when will you be seeing Elias again?'

'Next weekend, and I can't wait. I'm going to Manchester to meet his sons.'

'Oh, that does sound serious.'

'Yes. I just hope it doesn't go as badly as it did when Elias met Poppy.'

'Oh, I'm sure they'll love you. Why would they not?' says Carol.

As I take the last bite of carrot cake, I consider James and Danny's reaction when they meet me. Will they like me, or could this be our biggest challenge yet?

Chapter Twenty-Eight

James isn't as I pictured him. He's studious, quiet and keeps himself to himself. He is studying marine biology and seems more interested in his books than getting into any form of conversation with me. I don't know what I imagined, but I suppose since Elias can be outgoing and rather gregarious, I assumed his sons would be similar. I thought James might be the life and soul of every student party.

Danny, meanwhile, is going to be the one I need to convince. From the moment I walk in through the front door, sheepishly hiding behind Elias, he looks at me suspiciously. He has dark brown eyes, like his dad. I smile and hold my hand out to greet him, but he turns on his heels.

'I'd better get going. Got to go around and collect for some bills that need paying.'

'Don't let Mr Henley hide behind the sofa this time,' teases Elias.

Danny doesn't smile.

'We've one customer, and every time I'd go round for money, he'd dart behind the door. I'd watch in disbelief as he'd crawl on his hands and knees to avoid paying. A real devil he was. He gets Danny every time. Maybe it's time to expand the business and get more staff in, preferably someone who can chase payments. I've been thinking for a while it should be more than a one-man band by now. What do you say, Dan? We could take on some big contracts for companies?'

But Danny is already gone. The front door slams shut. Elias doesn't acknowledge his absence, simply smiles, and insists he takes my bag upstairs. The house is big, but not something a lottery winner would live in. It's got five bedrooms and is the type of house someone with a successful business would own. I admire the pretty stained-glass window in the hallway with its kingfisher pattern, and Elias tells me that Jane designed it herself. Just as I thought, this was very much their family home. As we walk up the cream-carpeted staircase, I notice the paintings that lead up to the spare room. I can tell they are Jane's art since they all have a distinctive style and are all landscapes. There is no doubt she was talented.

The spare room is decorated with pink and white wallpaper, which is slightly dated. It could definitely do with a makeover. Parts of it are faded, and I remember what Elias said about the boys not wanting anything changed. Is it only the boys who don't want it changed though?

When Elias makes me tea in the kitchen, there is further evidence that Jane is all around us, with matching tea towels, oven gloves and a pink kettle. It feels a little unsettling, and I begin to wish we were back on the yacht, which had subtler signs of Jane.

'Jane seemed to like pink.' I smile.

'She certainly did. I should make it a bit more masculine in here really...'

'No, it's fine.' Although, with all the testosterone in here, it does appear incongruous.

'So, anyway, I thought perhaps we'd get a takeaway tonight and then I'll take you into Cheadle tomorrow if that's okay? I've told Danny to make sure he's back by six.

It'd be nice to all sit down, have dinner and get to know each other.'

'Yes, fabulous. Sounds lovely. I'll look forward to it.' But the truth is that I am not looking forward to it one bit. How on earth am I supposed to enjoy an onion bhaji when Danny is sat across from me, looking at me with those dark, suspicious eyes?

I was right to be sceptical, and, as I suspected, I can't enjoy my onion bhaji one bit because if I try to say anything, Danny shoots me down. I do understand that it is difficult for him, and I know how awkward the girls can be, too, so I try to remain polite, and no matter how much he unnerves me, I attempt not to show it.

'I hope Mr Henley paid you, did he?' I ask when nobody is talking around the table. I can't bear silences in awkward situations.

'Why? So, we've got more money?' says Danny.

'Danny! Lucy's only trying to be polite,' says Elias.

'Yeah, well. I suppose she knows about the *you know what*…'

'Yes, I've told her, but that's not why she's here.'

I notice how Danny scowls at me, and I try to move the conversation away from money.

'Your mum was a very talented artist, wasn't she?' I say, pointing to another of her paintings that hangs proudly in the dining room.

Danny ignores me and James crunches down on a poppadom, which drowns out any conversation I try to make.

'That one's a poppy field in France we visited. We were driving past, and she insisted I stop. She took photos and painted it when she got back,' says Elias.

'Wow, fantastic. Sounds like you had a beautiful trip.'

Danny suddenly grabs hold of his plate and the beer in front of him and storms off.

What on earth did I say?

'Danny, get back here,' shouts Elias.

'No, it's fine. Let him go,' I say.

'Think I'll take this up too,' says James, picking up his plate.

'Oh no. I'm sorry. I didn't want to cause any problems between you all. This is a disaster. I shouldn't have come.'

'Of course, you should. They'll come around. I promise.'

As Elias strokes my hand in a bid to reassure me, I don't have the same level of confidence. These boys might be in their twenties, but I can clearly see that they are still grieving the loss of their beloved mum.

Later, when I'm lying alone in Elias's spare room, I think about how much the boys are still hurting. You can tell what a close family they all were. Although I miss lying beside Elias, it wouldn't be at all appropriate to share the room he had with the boys' mother.

At breakfast the following morning, James just about nods his head at me, and Danny pushes past me. The atmosphere in the kitchen is colder than the milk on my cereal.

'So, I was thinking I could show you Cheadle today,' says Elias cheerily.

'Aren't you busy, Dad?' says Danny.

'Well, yes, I'm spending the day with Lucy. Showing her around.'

'I need help with a few of the invoices. I was hoping you could give me a hand,' says Danny.

'Of course. You want to sit down now?'

'No, well, I need to make a few call outs. Bang on a few doors. I thought we could go round together. The old customers would love to see you again.'

I get the feeling that Danny will make any excuse to ensure we don't spend the day together. I look at the kitchen clock. It's only ten a.m., and I already feel as though I have outstayed my welcome.

'You go, Elias. It's more important that you sort the business out. Get those invoices paid. We can do lunch another time.'

Elias looks at me and then Danny. I notice how smug Danny's expression is. It is as if he is trying to tell me that he has won the first round.

'No, you came all this way to visit... I...'

'It's absolutely fine. You know, in hindsight, I should probably get back home. I only have a few more chapters until I finish the book. I'm almost there. Why don't we both work this weekend. There's plenty of time to do something another time.'

'No, I won't hear of it,' says Elias.

'Dad, you know, Mrs Papadopulos would love to see you. She might even give you some of that olive oil she brings back from Corfu.'

Elias doesn't look convinced, but Danny is very persuasive.

'It's fine. Honestly, I'll leave. I forgot my laptop, so I can't get any work done, and I really need to get the book finished, so please don't worry about me. It probably wasn't the best timing. I'll head back.'

Elias tries to protest, but I won't hear of it. Danny is not going to be won round easily, and just like Elias felt when he visited me, I realise I am not welcome, and it is best I get home.

Elias can't apologise enough for the way Danny has treated me, but I remind him that even though they're grown up, our kids still just see us as the parents they grew up with, and they hate big changes – including the dynamics of a new relationship.

'You're so understanding, thank you,' says Elias, kissing me goodbye at Manchester train station.

'I'll see you again soon. We'll sort something out,' I say.

'I really don't want you to leave, but maybe I need this time to speak to Danny. I'm going to tell him how much you mean to me. Then I'm sure he'll come around.'

'That means a lot, thank you. I should probably speak to the girls too. Perhaps we need this time apart to sort out our family dynamics and, who knows, maybe one day our families can meet up.'

'Wouldn't it be lovely if we could be one big extended family,' says Elias.

'It would.'

'But, in the meantime, I still mean what I said about running off to France for the summer. If all else fails… Well, we may have to.'

Elias looks at me with the cheekiest look on his face, and I start to think that this might be the only option if we want to be together.

Chapter Twenty-Nine

I am disappointed to be on a train departing Manchester after only one night, so I can't help but daydream what it would be like to return to the French Riviera with Elias. I picture myself waking up with him every morning with the sun shining through the curtains and that lovely smile on his face. But my daydream is soon broken when I notice Poppy calling my mobile.

'Hello, love.'

'Mam, Mam… You're not going to believe this. Dad came up on a dating site I'm on. I was scrolling through the pages. You know how it is, swiping no, no, no… Then Daddy's face appeared, but it wasn't his name. I thought I was going to be sick!' says Poppy.

Oh no. She must have seen that awful photo and the lies.

'Oh dear.'

'Why don't you sound surprised? I was horrified. He's looking for someone younger than him. Can you believe it? I wanted to be sick. Jasmine said, maybe it's not really Dad, though? Someone might have used his photo because they obvs haven't used his name. Jasmine thought either someone's stolen his photo or it could be a prank by someone at work. Are they that bonkers in the office, do you think?'

It seems that Michael's true colours may have finally been revealed to the girls, although Jasmine is obviously refusing to believe it.

I want to say that he is indeed looking for someone younger and calling himself Tom, but I bite my tongue.

'Well, maybe you should ask him about it. I'm sure there'll be some kind of explanation.'

'Do you think it's because he's lonely? Because you haven't gone back with him yet? There might still be a chance for you both to get back together, you know.'

I stop Poppy right away.

'No. I'm sorry. I've told you that's never going to happen, and besides, I told you how I have met someone lovely, who you saw briefly at the flat.'

'Oh, Mam. I didn't like him. He looks well dodge. Why can't you get back with Dad instead?'

Elias is the least dodgy man I have ever met. Now, Michael, and the way he behaves nowadays, is what she would call dodgy if she knew all the facts.

'You just need to get to know him. You know, I've just met his sons. I'm on my way back from Manchester now. I'm sure you'd like them. One of the boys, James, is at uni studying marine biology. You like that sort of thing, don't you?'

'Oh, you remember my friend Emma? That's what she's doing up that way somewhere. I wonder if she knows this dodgy family. I'll have to ask her.'

'They're not dodgy! Don't be like that. He seemed very studious. A decent boy.'

'Yeah, right. Well, anyway, I don't want to talk about that dodgy bloke any more.'

I want to repeat that he's *not dodgy*! But I know there's no point right now. Once Poppy gets something into her mind, that's it. Like Danny, it looks like it will take a lot to win her round.

'Anyway, I've got to go. Just wanted to tell you about Dad, but I feel better now. I've got to get ready for the Student Union party tonight. I'm dressing up as a sausage.'

'A sausage? Well, you'll have to send me pics of that. Doesn't sound like your usual type of thing.'

'Yeah, it's a long story. I lost a bet with Jasmine,' she says sulkily.

'Oh dear.' The thought of Poppy, who is so image-conscious, walking around as a sausage all night almost cheers me up as I contemplate the thought of being back in my own bed alone. I smile to myself as I picture her outfit. I imagine she will be in the horrors all night.

On the train journey back, I am so mad with Michael that I send him a message.

> Just so you know, the girls have seen you on that dating app you're on, TOM.

Five minutes later, he replies.

> Huh? I don't know what you're talking about. Who's Tom? I don't need to be on a dating app. Haha.

He always adds in 'haha' whenever he gets nervous and has been caught out.

Stop lying. You've been spotted by more than just the girls and, by the way, you're a right catfish lying about your name and age like that.

Well, I don't want weirdos knowing my name, and I feel like I'm 45. I didn't lie.

Wow. You admit you're on there. Well, that's progress.

Since you're not interested any more, I moved on, and it's nobody else's business.

You've changed your tune. It is my business when Poppy calls me up disgusted, and I almost have to agree with her that someone put you on there for a prank! She was horrified you could be looking for someone practically her age!

Alright. I'll adjust the age setting then. Happy now?

He won't like that one bit, but that's what he gets for upsetting our girls.

-

It's early evening by the time I get back to Swansea, but it seems like the longest day. After having let Elias know that I arrived home safely as he made me promise I would, I ring Carol to see if she fancies a drink. I could really do with one, and besides, the thought of sitting in the flat alone is the last thing I want. Fortunately, Carol feels the same. I throw my bags down, freshen up and rush straight out to meet her.

At the wine bar, we order the two-for-one cocktails and have a good old catch-up. I broach the subject of Elias and tell her how the boys weren't very welcoming. I also tell her that Elias asked me to spend the summer in France with him.

'Are you for real? What are you doing still sat here?' she says, almost spitting out her pina colada.

'It's not so easy. I don't think either set of kids will accept us being together. Poppy sounds dead set on not liking Elias and you should have seen the looks Danny gave me.'

'Well, I suppose his boys have lost their mam and that's hard for them. It doesn't matter who you are, they're probably going to want to dislike you. I'm sure they won't when they find out how lovely you are though. I suppose it's the same with the girls. They never wanted you and

Michael to split up, and even now, they hatch plans to get you back together. It's never nice for anyone; any of this stuff.'

'No, that's the thing. Life was so much less complex in our twenties when we met someone. There are so many things to think about at this age.'

'I know. It's difficult. Maybe that's why you need to run off to France with him.'

'Hmm. That's what Elias thinks too. It's just that it all seems to be moving so fast. I wish he lived closer and we could start dating normally and build our relationship. With the distance between us and the hate we're getting from everyone, it's difficult to see things properly. I don't want to rush into something.'

'Well, I'd be rushing into something head first if I'd met someone like Elias. I think you're bonkers to even worry about anything. I know everyone will take time to come round to the idea, but you're being far too cautious. I mean, have you seen that man? Looks, personality and money! What more could you possibly ask for?'

'Well, that's the problem. I don't want anyone thinking I'm after him for the money. I don't want to be called a gold digger.'

'He knows you're not like that. I mean, you hung around with him when you thought he was a skipper. You didn't know he was a lottery winner.'

'I know and sometimes I wish I still didn't know.'

'You're overthinking. Say yes to France, spend more time with him and see how it goes. That's my advice and, if you don't go, then put in a good word for me. I mean, obvs, I'd never steal your boyfriend from under you, but I'm just saying... If you didn't want him, like...'

'Well, I'd be pretty gutted if he did go off with you,' I say. But I know she is only teasing. I ponder over Elias as I sip on my paper straw. 'It's just a bit tough when the people closest to you don't want you to be together… And that's from both sides. It almost feels doomed, and I don't want to get attached to him and get hurt.'

'Look, it's all early days. How can the boys not come around to you eventually? They just need time. Same with the girls. Once they meet Elias properly, they'll be okay about it all.'

'I wish I had your confidence. Poppy thinks he's "well dodge" at the moment.'

'You need to arrange something to get everyone together. Maybe on neutral territory. Who knows, the kids might even hit it off and all get along?'

'I think it'll take some time to get them all to agree to that, but it sounds like a good idea eventually.'

'Well, in the meantime, go off and spend the summer together. If you don't, then you'll never know what could have happened.'

I think about what Carol has said. Am I brave enough to take the plunge and spend the summer with a man I still don't know that well? The old me most certainly wouldn't dream of it. But where has staying close to home and letting my grown-up kids rule the roost got me so far? I am fifty, a grown woman who is letting my ex-husband and two daughters practically dictate my life. With a newfound confidence – or perhaps one too many pina coladas – I message Elias.

I hoped Elias would excitedly message me immediately, so I feel slightly forlorn when there is no response thirty minutes later. What if it was a flippant off-the-cuff remark? Perhaps he didn't mean what he said after all. Maybe it was one of those things like when you say, 'Let's go on a cruise one day', or years back when Michael dreamed of going on Concorde but only had the finances for a budget airline.

When I go to bed and there is still no response, I regret the text so badly that I decide to delete it. I am huddling under the duvet, regretting not accepting the offer earlier, when there is a knock on the door.

At first, I am nervous that someone is knocking so late, but I assume it's Michael having got drunk on his Saturday night out with the boys and without having successfully 'pulled' as the girls would say. He has probably come around here to have his last word about the dating site. I wouldn't normally answer at this hour, but the way Michael has been behaving recently, I suspect it's him.

'Michael, what do you want now?' I say as I open the door.

But when I look at the man standing there, I quickly realise that it is definitely not my ex-husband.

Chapter Thirty

I stare in shock as my eyes focus on Elias and the overnight bag at his feet.

'Were you expecting someone else?' he asks. He looks tired and not too amused that I thought he was Michael.

'I'm so sorry. I thought it was a drunk Michael. He can turn up sometimes... You know it's over between us, right? It's just he can be such a pain.'

I cringe as I make excuses about Michael. I am mortified at the greeting I have given him after he has travelled all this way.

'Did you get my text message?'

'No. In my haste to come here, I left my phone at home.'

'Ah, no problem, we can talk about it again.'

I awkwardly pull myself closer and hug him tightly. I have said completely the wrong thing and stumble as I try to make things better.

'Gosh, I wasn't expecting you. What a shock. A nice shock, but...'

'Yeah, I took the last train down and thought I'd surprise you. I hope it's not inconvenient.'

'Oh, my goodness. No. Of course it's not. It's amazing to see you. I just didn't expect to see you so soon.'

'Obviously,' he says. He sounds sarcastic, and the atmosphere feels tense.

'I mean. It's great, though. Really great. I'm so happy to see you. It's wonderful. Umm, absolutely wonderful.'

'Yeah, well, Danny was out. James was locked in his room gaming, and I thought, what am I doing here sat in the living room alone? I should be spending the weekend with you. Like a naughty schoolboy, I decided to bunk off and run away. Well, for the night, anyway. I've got to be back by tomorrow evening.'

'Wow, well… Thanks for coming down. It's the most wonderful surprise.'

Even though I was ready for bed, I soon perk up and make us both a drink. With my glass in hand, Elias pulls me closer to him on the sofa. The feeling of having my head on his shoulder is always one of great comfort. As we finish our drinks, Elias looks at me with a concerned expression and lowers his voice as if he is scared of my response.

'Tell me the truth, now, are you happy I showed up, or should I have checked first? I just grabbed a bag and jumped on the train. I didn't think you might be busy or in bed. Was I being a bit too presumptuous?'

'No, not at all. You've made me very happy.' I grin and then remove the empty brandy glass from Elias's hand.

For once, I decide to take charge of everything. I have never taken the lead in anything, I have always waited for others and followed like a sheep. But with Elias, something stirs within me, and I grab his hand and lead him into the bedroom. I remove the polo shirt he is wearing, pulling it over his head, and then move my fingers to the button of his jeans. Elias's face tells me that right now he wants this as much as I do and we sink into the depths of the double bed that I am so used to lying in alone. A summer spent like this would be the best decision in the world right now.

–

In the morning, Elias asks for my laptop and shows me a villa. It's in one of the villages we drove through in the little Fiat during our travels along the coast. I look at the pictures on the internet and can't help but contrast them with the rain lashing against the windows, despite the weather forecast having promised that a heatwave was on the way. I so want to spend the summer with Elias in this villa, with its white marble bathrooms and infinity swimming pool with views of the sea. Although, I am beginning to think that I would take a rat-infested budget hotel if it meant spending more time with Elias.

'Look, it's free from next Wednesday. Let's do it,' says Elias.

'Oh gosh, that soon? I don't know. I haven't even told the girls. I mean… And then there's Danny and James… What would they say?'

'Well, why don't you explain to the girls that you're taking a summer break? Use the book as an excuse if you don't think they'll like the fact that I'm there.'

'They'll be suspicious. They watch everything. I'd never get away with it. Besides, it's high time I told them the truth. That I want to spend every moment with you. They're big girls, and they need to know that their mam is one too. It's time for them to accept that I need a life outside this family, even if I will always be there for them.'

'If you're sure. I really don't want to come between you. Please know that's the last thing I'd want.'

'Same here with your boys. But I've put this off for far too long. I've always done what everyone expects of me, and I'm not getting any younger. It's high time I put my foot down and told them what I want. The next time they come home, I'm going to speak to them. I'm going to tell them how happy I am spending time with you.'

'Well, be careful. I don't want to upset them, but I'm glad to hear you're happy spending time with me,' says Elias.

'I am.' I kiss his cheek, and then he turns to face me.

'I can just see us splashing about in that pool,' says Elias, turning back to the computer.

'Oh, me too. Look, there's a barbecue area by the pool. Maybe we can use it. I miss not being able to have one here, living in an apartment.'

This summer is going to be the best one ever.

'If Madame would like a barbecue, then that's what she'll be having,' says Elias. As he grins, his eyes look so sincere. I think of Poppy's words about Elias being dodgy and can see that she couldn't be further from the truth. She just needs to get to know him, and so I decide to organise an impromptu lunch in Cardiff before Elias gets his connection to Manchester. Elias very much wants to put things right with her after their first disastrous meeting, although I don't warn the girls that he is with me.

I choose one of their favourite hang-outs because I know they'll do anything for a free lunch there.

Although, as Elias and I turn up to the loud music and funky student environment, I do wish I'd picked somewhere a little quieter. I also regret not warning them that I am with Elias. They both look horrified when I walk in and make disgusted faces at each other.

'Mam! I thought it was a girls' lunch,' says Jasmine.

'Be polite, please. This is my friend Elias. Poppy's already met him, and I wanted you to meet him too.'

Jasmine and Poppy grunt a hello, and Elias moves closer to shake their hands.

'Lovely to meet you. Your mum doesn't stop talking about you both and how well you're doing at uni.'

'We call her Mam, not Mum,' says Jasmine.

'Of course. Sorry, your mam. Anyway, this looks like a lovely place. One of your favourites, your mum says. Sorry, mam says.'

I can't look as Poppy rolls her eyes. I didn't bring them up to be so rude to a stranger. They're normally polite and helpful to people they don't know. But I suppose Elias isn't a stranger. He is someone making moves on their mother, and they are not happy about it.

'Yes, Elias. They love it here, don't you, girls?'

'Yeah,' grunts Poppy.

'Great. So, any recommendations on the food?' asks Elias.

'No, not really,' says Jasmine.

I cringe as I watch them both being difficult as Elias squirms. This is proving harder than I thought it would be.

With nothing to lose, I decide to tell them about the summer trip. After all, their reactions to us both can't get any worse and being in a public place might be the best way to break the news. At least they can't have a meltdown here.

I await their response when I finish telling them about the trip.

I was expecting some sort of tantrum, but instead, Poppy looks flabbergasted, and Jasmine looks like a goldfish as she goes to speak and then changes her mind a few times.

'You'd be welcome to visit us in France once uni is finished,' says Elias.

For the first time, both of them smile.

'Seriously?' says Jasmine.

'Yes, seriously. We've got a lovely place with a pool, two kilometres from the beach. Not far from Nice. Lots of good shops there. I'm sure you'd enjoy it,' says Elias.

Poppy and Jasmine no longer look miffed but instead seem impressed.

'We'd love that, actually, wouldn't we?' says Poppy.

'Yeah. We would,' agrees Jasmine.

'Right then. It's a deal. You give me the dates and I'll arrange the tickets.'

'It's not long until we finish term, is it?' says Poppy.

The thought of having lazy mornings with Elias flashes before me.

'Well, why don't you spend some time with Dad over the summer too? Then come out later on. Say, in August?'

'Are you trying to delay us coming out?' says Jasmine.

'No, not at all. I just… well… I mean, you'll need loads of spending money, and it's not cheap out there.'

'Well, we can sell some bits on Vinted,' says Jasmine.

'Yes, but a whole summer on the French Riviera isn't going to be cheap. How many three-pound skirts are you going to have to sell to have a summer like that?'

'She's got a point. Imagine if we have to stay in the villa all day because we can't afford to go anywhere,' says Poppy.

'Yeah, alright, two weeks then. I'll have to buy new clothes now,' says Jasmine.

'Yeah, and me,' says Poppy.

'What happened to selling clothes instead?' I laugh at the two of them as they already mentally spend anything they might make on Vinted and the rest.

As Elias touches my knee under the table, satisfied that he has won their seal of approval, Poppy and Jasmine excitedly chat about what else they want to buy. Bikinis are first on the shopping list.

Over their honey and feta parcels, they ask Elias questions about the villa.

'Does it have Wi-Fi? Is there a TV? How big is the pool?' asks Poppy.

'Yes, it does have Wi-Fi, TV… Ooh, I don't know how many metres, but you can do lengths in it.'

'Oh wow. We've not been swimming since we went to that stupid swim class you wanted to go on because you liked that lifeguard, remember? What was his name now?' says Poppy to Jasmine.

'Oh, him. Yeah, *do not* ever mention Jase. He took no notice of me when I pretended to drown. I could've died,' says Jasmine dramatically whilst rolling her eyes.

We laugh, and I am so pleased to see Jasmine and Poppy happy. It is the biggest relief that they have finally come to accept Elias, even though it might have been the persuasion of a free holiday that swung it.

Once we finish our lunch, Elias and I have to rush off, and so we leave the girls to order their desserts and pay the bill before we leave. The girls are polite to Elias as he says how nice it has been to meet them, and I am satisfied that, in the end, it has gone better than I could have ever expected.

In fact, as we go to leave, Poppy stops me and whispers, 'Maybe Elias isn't well dodge, Mam.'

From Poppy, that's the biggest compliment Elias could ever have.

Chapter Thirty-One

Michael would always leave all the holiday preparations to me. I'd have to check the passports, apply for new ones when necessary and get everyone packed and on their way. So, it is refreshing to find myself in a hire car on the way to a stunning villa near the beach knowing I haven't had to lift a finger. Except for packing, of course, which took ages, considering I am just here for the summer. I hadn't thought of the practical stuff like whether the property has a washing machine. As we pull into the driveway, I no longer care what utilities the kitchen has as the imposing double-storey creamy white villa looks like it has had no expense spared. It is huge! From the marble steps leading up to the front door to the huge columns and palm trees that hang over us, this villa is sheer paradise.

Two patches of lawn on either side of the villa have sprinklers keeping it lush and green. I dare not think how much the water bill must be for this place, between the lawns and the abundant bougainvillea, frangipani and jasmine plants.

Through into the spacious hallway, the villa is decorated with minimalist furniture and a deep blue velvet chaise longue that looks as though it is asking to be laid on. I can just imagine lying there reading a good book when the midday temperature gets up high.

'Oh, Elias. It's just beautiful.'

'I knew you'd like it. It's gorgeous, isn't it?'

'It's palatial, yet it feels homely too. I don't know how the owner managed that. Could you imagine living here?'

'Well, that's what we'll be doing for the next eight weeks, and I can't wait to spend every moment here with you,' says Elias, leaning over to kiss me.

I look at the villa and Elias, thanking the universe that I went to the supermarket that morning. Lady Luck was shining on me that day. My life has been transformed since meeting Elias in all the best ways possible.

'Come with me, I have something I want to show you,' he says.

I follow him to one of the rooms upstairs, which has a view of the sea that is not far away from the villa.

'I didn't show you this in the pictures as I wanted it to be a surprise, but I thought you could finish your book in here.'

I look around the study, which is so different to where I work at home, on the table with my laptop. A large Victorian mahogany wooden desk with a green leather pad faces the window. The huge matching leather chair looks comfy, and I run over to it, swinging around full circle from the view of the sea to face Elias. I feel like a director from one of those award-winning movies in Cannes.

'I couldn't think of a better place to finish the last chapter of the book. Oh, Elias, you're so thoughtful.'

'Come, let me show you the rest of it.'

The master bedroom is next to the study and so offers the same sea views. I look down at the swimming pool that can be clearly seen from the master bedroom and can't decide what I want to do first. Do I get changed and dive into the pool or have a sleep on the queen-sized bed that is stacked up with pillows and cushions? I remind myself that I have plenty of time to try it all, but I feel too excited to wait. I want to experience everything now.

Back downstairs, I am pleased to see a washing machine, although understanding the spaceship-like buttons might be a little tricky. The owner obviously opted for a top-of-the-range machine. Elias heads over to the super-duper coffee machine and starts making us a brew when his phone rings.

'I've got to take this,' he says apologetically. While he takes the call outside, I try to work the machine but don't want to break anything, and so I wait for Elias to return. However, he takes a while, and when he comes back, he seems upset.

'Everything okay?'

'Yeah, yeah. All fine.' The words he says don't match the expression on his face, and I am curious about who was on the phone. Whilst there might be some business dealings I am unaware of, my bet is that it was Danny.

Elias quickly changes the subject and suggests we have dinner out this evening. He says there are some places nearby where we can get a casual bite to eat. As he says it, his usual excitement about doing anything seems to be missing. I'm sure it has something to do with the phone call. I want to probe him further, but I'm aware that it might spoil the mood of our first night here. Although perhaps that is something that has already been ruined.

By the time we lock up the villa and head out that evening, Elias is still quiet, and it is only when we are sat sharing a bottle of wine at a streetside bistro that he admits it was Danny on the phone earlier.

'I'm so sorry, I'm going to have to fly back and see Danny. There's some trouble at home.'

I could see there was a problem, but I didn't expect that he would have to go home. I guess our holiday has ended before it began. My heart sinks. It's a reminder that when things seem too good to be true, they usually are. I should have known wonderful things like this don't happen to me.

'What sort of trouble?'

'Oh, it's the business. He's worried about a few things. I don't think he's got the confidence to run it himself. I suppose it's a big responsibility. As his sleeping partner, he turns to me for advice whenever he doubts himself.'

I suspect it's more likely that Danny thinks his dad is having too good a time with someone who isn't his beloved mother and could be a money-grabber. He has every right to be protective of his dad, and so I stop myself from getting annoyed. We were probably being far too optimistic to think this would work out.

'I'd better pack my things again then. I shouldn't have bothered unpacking,' I say.

'No, you don't have to leave just because I have to dash back. It won't be for long. I'll sort Danny out and be back as soon as I can. It'll be three days tops.'

'I can't stay here alone. I came with you. Maybe this was all a bad idea. Perhaps we were being a bit ambitious arranging a summer break together so soon, knowing how Danny feels and with things so complicated for you back home.'

'Oh, no. My goodness, no. It's just some contract with a chemical supplier I need to sort out. It's just unfortunate that it's happened now. It's not Danny's fault.'

'Well, can't they email you the documents you need? Surely you don't have to fly back?'

'If I don't go back and sort this out, then I'll never hear the end of it.'

I nod my head, trying to show Elias some understanding no matter how difficult this is for me. Blood is always thicker than water, and Danny needs him.

'So, yeah, just enjoy the pool, finish writing your book and relax. Then I'll be back, and we have the rest of the summer to enjoy.'

'Okay. I mean, it wasn't what I envisaged this morning, but I do understand that things come up. So when will you fly back?'

'Tomorrow.'

'Tomorrow? I thought perhaps we would have a day or two first. You've only just arrived.'

'Yeah, I know. Sorry. Danny's already arranged the flight for first thing.'

I rub my finger along the rim of the glass as I think of Danny possibly planning this all along. He may have even booked the flight before we had taken off.

'Okay, so I suppose we should make the most of this evening then,' I say.

Although, truthfully, Elias's news has turned the evening into one mighty damp squib.

Chapter Thirty-Two

As Elias leaves for the airport first thing, he promises he will be back as soon as possible. I watch sadly as the car he has only just hired reverses from the driveway. I try to smile as I wave goodbye, but, in all honesty, I am on the verge of tears. We were supposed to spend the summer together and now, after the first day, he has rushed off on urgent business. If I hadn't been to his home and seen how Danny struggles with the situation, I would definitely have trust issues at this point.

I close the door and walk around the villa, looking at the rooms as the morning light beams through the gaps in the shutters on the windows. I open them up and let the light cascade into the rooms, but still, despite the sunshine, I can't help feeling gloomy. I tell myself that I will finish writing the book by the time Elias returns and that we will have the rest of the summer to enjoy ourselves. What is the rush? But without him, this place feels enormous as my flip-flops echo on the marble floors. The warmth of the villa when I walked in with Elias yesterday appears to have vanished, and I shiver as I turn the air conditioning down.

Eventually, I tell myself not to be so silly. Why on earth am I complaining that I have been left alone in such a beautiful villa? I must make the most of it. So, I throw on my kimono and sit down at the desk. I feel like Barbara

Cartland as the creative flow pours out from me. Every now and then, as I type, I look up at the gorgeous views across the sea and smile. I might be here alone, but it is one of the most spectacular places to be by myself. Now that I am starting to get over the shock that Elias had to leave for a short while, I will be fine. In fact, I may even go for a wander around a little later if I can finish my work before it gets too dark.

I type away until the afternoon, when I realise I have been working for hours without a break. I need something to eat, but we only picked up a few bits in the supermarket on the way over here, as we were supposed to be dining out again tonight. I am about to see what I can find in the fridge when I spot an older lady walking up the driveway. It seems odd as I am not expecting anyone, and Elias certainly hadn't said anything about a visitor. I notice she is carrying a basket, so perhaps she is from the rental company that Elias used and is dropping something off.

'Bonsoir, madame,' she says.

'Bonsoir.'

'Parlez-vous français?'

'No, English. Sorry,' I say.

'Ah, no problems. The realtor said one English couple bought the villa.'

'Oh, no, we haven't bought it! We're just using it for a holiday.'

'Ah, okay. As you like. I'm Renee, your neighbour.'

Neighbour? I decide not to tell her once again that I'm only on holiday.

'I'm Lucy. So, you live near here, how lovely.'

Renee pulls at my arm and takes me outside as she points to her beautiful pink villa, which contrasts with our cream property. It has similar arched balconies and

263

white balustrades, but lemon trees grow bountifully in the grounds.

'Gosh, that's beautiful.'

'Merci, dear. It's nice around here. I brought you this,' she says, handing me the basket.

I look at the woven basket that reminds me of something I used in cookery lessons during secondary school. It's lined with red and white check linen, and inside is a selection of beautiful pastries.

'Oh, wow. That's so kind of you. Won't you come in? Please, let me make you a coffee.'

'That would be nice, thank you.'

I lead Renee to the kitchen and pray I can get the posh coffee machine to work in front of her. I used the ground stuff this morning as I couldn't get my head around how to work it once Elias left. I have never been very good with gadgets, so I ask if Renee would like tea or ground coffee instead. However, she points at the coffee machine and says she'd prefer one of those. I keep my back to her as I fluster around the machine, hoping she doesn't notice, but it's futile.

'Lucy, can I assist you?' she says.

'Oh, umm, would you mind? Sorry.'

'Oui, of course.' I watch as Renee effortlessly pops a coffee pod in, presses a few buttons and the machine kicks into life.

'Voilà. Would you like some too?'

'Oh, yes, please.' I feel terrible asking a guest to help, but she obviously knows her way around fancy machines better than I do.

We sit down at the kitchen island, which I notice is also marble-topped, like much of the villa, and I attempt to make small talk.

'So, did the villa sell recently? Maybe we're lucky to be the first ones to stay here.'

'Yes, to the English couple. Your husband, no?'

'No. I'm not married.'

'Ah, pardon. You are partners then, my mistake.'

Renee doesn't seem to be listening to a word I am saying. Do I tell her again that I am nothing to do with this villa? I wouldn't want her to be confused when the real owner shows up, so I tell her once more.

'I'm afraid I'm only here for a holiday. I don't live here.'

'Ah. Where's your partner? Maybe he knows where the owner is.'

'Hmm, indeed.' I think of how Elias booked the villa so quickly and then begin to worry. I am getting those doubts once again. What if it is someone else's villa, and Elias made an excuse to desert me, and the owner is suddenly going to turn up? After the misunderstanding in Monaco, I am not ready to take that chance.

I can hardly focus on the conversation as I wonder where he even got the keys from. I was tired after the journey and didn't think about it before but now that I do, we didn't meet anyone or go anywhere to pick up the keys. What if something fishy is going on?

'I belong to a bridge club, you're welcome to join me,' says Renee.

'Huh? Oh, yeah. That's very kind, but I've never played bridge before. But, thank you. If I change my mind, I'll let you know.'

As lovely and welcoming as Renee is, I can't wait to be alone so that I can call Elias and ask who owns this place. He will probably have landed back in Manchester by now, and I pray I can get hold of him right away. I am not staying here a minute longer with the ambiguity of whose villa it is. How can this happen to me twice in the same country? Maybe it is because both times I have let others make the holiday plans. Perhaps it was better when I was in control after all.

'So, it was very nice to meet you. I must go now for a yoga class. Do you like yoga?' says Renee finally.

'No, I'm not that bendy really. I'm a bit stiff.'

'Then you must join yoga. It'll help with this stiffness.'

'I'm afraid I'm more of a Zumba person. I couldn't possibly relax and do something that slow. I'd rather jump about. But thanks for the offer, anyway.'

I get up and lead Renee towards the door. I promise I will make up for being curt to her another time, but, right now, I have to speak to Elias. Every car that drives past and every noise I hear outside makes me jump as I consider that I could get thrown out of here at any moment. This time, if they think I'm trespassing, they may even call the police. I could get myself a record for breaking and entering posh homes at this rate.

As soon as I close the door on Renee, I rush over to my phone. The line makes a funny bleep, and then I hear the recording asking me to leave a message.

I throw down the phone in frustration. I need to get hold of Elias right away. I look out of the window as if I am a fugitive and become quite paranoid. I am not going to be able to relax until I speak to Elias.

I walk back and forth in the kitchen so many times that I fear I'll wear out the onyx marble. I tell myself to give Elias the benefit of the doubt. Perhaps this place belongs to a friend of his. That must be what it is. Rich people always have rich friends; look at Soraya. I bet Elias does, too, even though he insists he prefers hanging around with working-class folk.

By the time my phone rings and I see Elias's name come up on the screen, I am super relieved.

'Hi, how was your flight?' I ask.

'All fine. Sorry, once again. I should only be a couple of days.'

Since I am fighting with my intuition that something isn't quite right, I decide not to tell Elias about the next-door neighbour and what she said, as I don't want to put words in his mouth.

'It's okay. Don't worry. Like you say, you'll be back soon. I just wanted to ask something, though.'

'Yeah, what's up?'

'Well, I was curious. I was wondering whose house this is. I mean, I'm just here alone, and if anyone turned up, I wouldn't know what to say. Especially after what happened with Gianni's apartment and all that. Or, if there's a problem with, say, the electrics, who would I contact? So, yeah, I just wondered whose place it was.'

'The villa?'

'Yes, the villa.'

'It's just a rental. I don't know the owner. Someone French, I guess.'

'Well, how did you get the keys?'

'The keys?'

'Yes! The keys. We never met anyone to give them to us.'

Elias is quiet for a moment, and then, as if it has taken him time to think of an answer, he finally replies.

'Oh, they posted the keys to me.'

'They?'

'Yeah, the agent.'

'Okay, and who is the agent?'

'Um, I don't remember the exact name now, Lucy. I'll get back to you. I'm going to have to go. Danny's picking me up from the airport.'

'Yes, of course. Could you message me the name of the agent later, so I know who to call if there is an emergency.'

'There shouldn't be any emergencies.'

'No, I know, but just in case. Since I'm here all alone.'

'Sure. I'll speak to you a bit later. Okay.'

Before I can say goodbye, Elias has put the phone down, and I stand looking around the villa in disbelief that this has happened to me. I decide if Elias won't tell me then I will hunt for clues. I look at the kitchen appliances again. I remember that old TV show, *Through the Keyhole*, and in the voice of Loyd Grossman, the presenter, I start talking to myself as I walk around, trying to turn this potential nightmare into a game.

'This house belongs to a person who likes their gadgets.'

I look at the bright blue velvet chaise longue again. Someone likes blue.

'This house belongs to a person who likes comfort as well as luxury.'

Then I go outside by the pool. Apart from a lion fountain that spouts water into the pool, it doesn't give much away.

I go back inside and rummage through the kitchen drawers. Surely there must be some kind of post, a letter for someone in one of them. All I find is a canteen of designer cutlery and an electric tin opener. However, in another drawer, I find a few scrunched-up flyers for local bars and supermarkets. Why didn't the cleaners throw them out? I'm guessing whoever owns this house can be a bit untidy at times. I add that to my mental list of qualities for the owner.

Moving to the living room, I look at the white sofa, white rugs and white vases.

'This is a person who doesn't have young children.'

None of this stuff would last a day.

I gather all the visual evidence and think that this is someone who is either single or with grown-up kids. This points me in the only direction I can think of. And what I have suspected since I met Renee.

'Elias,' I say out loud.

Has he lied to me about this being a rental property? Has he bought this as a home, and he doesn't want me to know?

I rumble about in a bedside drawer, knowing that I shouldn't snoop, but also desperate for confirmation. There I find a utility bill with Elias's name clearly printed. It's the last bit of evidence I need; I am utterly devastated that Elias has lied to me once again. But why? The only answer I can think of is that he still doesn't trust me. Does he truly think that I am after his money, just as Danny does? I slump down on the kitchen bar stool as I realise that we don't have much of a future if we have continuous trust issues between us.

Chapter Thirty-Three

As I consider the fact that Elias has lied to me once again, I think about my journey these past few months when I arrived in the French Riviera. I came here believing that I would never trust any man again, and look what's happened. I have been proved right not to trust anyone.

Perhaps I just got carried away with the beauty of the region and the fondness that grew between Elias and me. This magical place spurred me on to believe a stranger's words and to write the love story that I always wanted to. As I finish off my book, I reflect on how it isn't about a knight on a white horse saving a damsel in distress, but about a man who helps a woman love herself again and find out what she really wants from life through deep conversations long into the night under the stars. Something that happened in real life with Elias. But now, as I am about to type in the final words of the book I have longed to write for many years, I hesitate. Is there really such a thing as an honest, loving man? I am beginning to have my doubts.

I should be celebrating this moment with Elias and not sat here alone with the realisation that he has lied to me yet again. I am glad I didn't confront him over the phone, as I think the frank discussion we need will be better done in person. So, I decide not to mention anything until he returns, when I imagine I will leave here and never see Elias again. I recognise that I made the mistake of letting my barriers down, and the lovely dream I had started to believe in has come crashing down around me. The disappointment is too much, and I burst into tears. It feels ironic, crying somewhere so beautiful, with so much luxury around me. If a stranger saw me in this villa, they'd think I have everything, but I have never felt so despondent and disillusioned.

As promised, three days after Elias flew out, a hire car pulls into the driveway. At least he kept his word about not staying away too long.

Elias is full of smiles as he walks in and wraps his hands around my waist. I kiss his cheek gently but can't reciprocate his enthusiasm at our reunion.

'Oh, I missed you. It's so good to be back.'

'Yeah… Me too. How were things with Danny? All sorted?'

'Yes. He kept saying there was more to help him with, even as I walked out the door. But I refused. I wanted to get back to the beautiful lady waiting in the sunshine for me.'

I manage a smile, although my head is full of questions.

'So, what have you been up to? Have you been swimming every day? Did you venture to the beach? Tell me all about your stay,' says Elias.

'Oh. I've been working the whole time. I managed to finish the book.'

'You did? Well, that means we must celebrate tonight. Why didn't you say anything on the phone when we spoke?'

'You were busy with Danny and, anyway, I only just finished…'

'Is everything okay? I thought you'd be over the moon that you finally finished the book. I thought this was your life-long dream. What's up?'

Elias has hardly put his bags down, and I am still making us a coffee. I can't plough into him right away, but neither can I stand not saying what is on my mind. I let out a big sigh.

'What is it?' asks Elias once again.

'It's just that… Well… I asked you who owned this villa.'

'Yeah, and?'

'Well, the next-door neighbour said it was someone from the UK.'

'And there are lots of people from the UK who buy places in France. I don't get what you're trying to say.'

'When I asked you who owned the villa, you specific-ally said it was someone French.'

'I may have said I thought it was, yes.'

'But I think it belongs to you and for some reason you won't admit it.'

'Why would I do that?'

'Because you don't trust me.'

Elias shrugs his shoulders. 'Don't be silly.'

'One minute. I want to show you something.'

I get up to leave the table and pull out the letter I have kept safe until Elias returned.

'Look, it's a bill for you with this address on. Utility bills aren't sent to people who are renting a holiday let.'

Elias looks at the letter and then at me. 'Where did you find this?'

Is there an easy way of saying I have been snooping about?

'I was looking for something that would tell me who the rental company was. I told you I was worried if I had a problem while you were away, I wouldn't know who to contact. So, I looked everywhere and found this.'

'Well, what can I say? I am so very sorry.' Elias avoids looking at me but instead gazes outside towards the pool.

'I really didn't think you'd lie to me again. You lied about owning the yacht, and now this. You obviously think I'm some money-grabber.' I am livid. I just want him to tell me why he does this. Why does he still not trust me?

'It's not like that. I told you. I don't want people knowing what I own. I've always been a private man. My dad was the same. How much money people earn or have is nobody's business except their own.'

'Well, maybe you shouldn't go out buying yachts and fancy villas then. It's bound to attract attention.'

'After working hard all my life, having an almost lethal heart attack, losing my beloved wife, and then having some luck on the lottery, don't you think I should be able to spoil myself a little?'

'Yes, of course, but everything we've had between us has all been based on lies and now there are more lies. How can I trust you when you lie to me? I already knew about the lottery win. You owning a fancy villa wouldn't have changed anything.'

'I know. I'm sorry. Nothing I say is going to sound acceptable. I understand that. But, look, I'm just not used to asking someone to come and stay in my pad in the French Riviera. It sounds so pretentious. I wanted to invite you here, but I didn't want to come off like some Lothario who invites women out here. I just felt it was easier if I didn't go into any of that. I messed up,' says

273

Elias. Then he pushes his coffee cup away and gets up to leave the room.

I know Elias isn't the confrontational type, but we need to talk about this. We have had conversations about how lonely he was after his wife died; we have talked about his sons and the issues they have struggled with since their mother died, but this is something we can't seem to get past. Maybe this lottery win is a curse, and it would be a lot easier if he didn't have the money. I want to love Elias for himself, not what he's got, but he doesn't seem to get it.

There is nothing left to do but pack my bags and head back home. Poppy and Jasmine will never forgive me for ruining their summer plans, but that's the least of my worries right now.

Chapter Thirty-Four

My kimono is still on the edge of the bed where I left it this morning, and I gather my things up as quickly as I can. I realise that I don't know the names of any taxi companies, nor do I know if there are any flights available, but I refuse to ask Elias if he can drop me off at the airport. In fact, as I start packing, I still don't know where I will go. I remember the lovely neighbour and decide to go to her. She will surely help me find a taxi.

I am sobbing and full of anger as I throw things into my bag loudly, secretly hoping Elias will stop me and ask me where I think I am going so that I can give him a big, dramatic response. But he doesn't. Elias has no idea I am packing my things as he has been standing by the pool, looking out to sea, since our fight in the kitchen.

From the study window, as I pack my laptop away, I can see Elias running his hand through his hair. He looks stressed, but I can't be to blame for that. He shouldn't have lied to me. He could have trusted me. It was Elias I was falling for and not his money. He knew how difficult it was for me to trust anyone again after what happened with Michael. Now I have someone who is faithful but tries to hide what he owns!

Looking around the study, I realise how new it all looks. According to the evidence, Elias has not long bought this villa. A thought crosses my mind that he designed this study especially for me as I notice a sleek silver dolphin statue that I hadn't spotted before. Did he buy that as a reminder of our day out on the boat? I think back to the excitement I felt that day when we spotted the dolphin and how I didn't stop going on about it. How I said that dolphins were so calm and joked that maybe I needed to keep one next to my laptop to stop me stressing. Surely, he couldn't have done this for me? I tell myself not to be such a romantic fool. It is probably because he is as fond of dolphins as I am. Nothing more than that. Besides, a little dolphin isn't going to charm me right now after finding out all these lies by accident.

With my laptop safe and the wardrobe emptied of a summer's worth of clothes, I close my case and drag it down the marble staircase. It bangs and clatters on every step, and I am secretly pleased that it alerts Elias, and he returns into the house to see what all the commotion is about. He catches me just as I am about to open the latch of the front door.

'Where are you going?'

'Umm, the airport. Where does it look like?'

'But why?'

'Because neither of us trust each other, that's why.'

'Oh, come on. Please, don't be like that.'

Even though I desperately want to change my mind and talk to him, it has gone too far for me to back down.

'No, I'm off. If you don't trust me, then how can you even have me stay here? I mean, I might run off with... I don't know... the little dolphin in the study.'

'Ah, you saw the dolphin. I bought that especially for you. Come on. Sit down. Let's talk about this.'

Elias closes the front door, which is now ajar, and takes the suitcase from my hand.

'We need to talk. Please, will you stay, at least until you hear what I've got to say? Then it's up to you to make your mind up about whether you want to go home or not. Just say that you'll listen to me first.'

'I don't know. I think I've heard enough. You obviously don't trust me. Do you even trust me to tell me the truth here?'

'Of course, I do. Honestly, I wish I'd never won that money sometimes. I'm all over the place. I'm sorry, but please listen to me, and then you can leave.'

Finally, I reluctantly agree to listen to him. I came all this way; I may as well see what else he has to say for himself.

'Why don't you go and sit by the pool, and I'll bring us some coffees out,' says Elias.

I wander outside and wait for Elias. I look up at the bedroom balcony where I like to sit and drink my coffee in the morning and to the window of the study that I love to work in. One thing is certain, Elias has very discerning taste. If I had to pick a dream home where money was no object, this would be the home I would choose.

Elias walks towards me, holding two mugs, and I look at his face. He looks older and tired. He smiles hesitantly as he approaches me. However, whilst I wanted this relationship to work out so badly, he would have to give me a pretty good reason to accept the fact that he keeps hiding the truth from me.

'So...' he says, putting down the coffee on the table beside my sunbed.

'So,' I say rather awkwardly.

'I suppose I need to explain myself properly. I never meant any of this. It's just that, like I said before, the money I won has been a blessing and a curse. I want people to like me for who I am, not what I've got.'

'I know, but we've been through this. I thought you knew that I adore you as a person. I don't care about the villa, the yacht, or anything else. It feels like the biggest insult to me that you pretended this was some kind of Airbnb and didn't trust me enough to tell me it was yours. I gave you the chance to come clean when I asked who owned the villa. You've had so many opportunities to tell me the truth. It's not about the money, it's about the lies. If there's one thing I despise, it's a liar.'

'I realise that now, but I don't like showing off. I mean, I'm still that window cleaner underneath all of this, and I don't want to come across like I'm trying to impress or show off. I didn't mean to lie. I hate liars too. Oh, I'm so, so sorry. I've made the biggest fool out of myself.'

'I just thought that we knew each other well enough now not to play games like this. When Renee from next door came and said that—'

'Renee?' says Elias.

'Yeah, the next-door neighbour. She came around to meet the new people who'd moved in. I felt such an idiot when I didn't know who owned it. That's when I started to get suspicious.'

'I'm so sorry I embarrassed you.'

'Yes, you have. You've not only made a fool of yourself but me too.'

'Oh, Lucy. Don't say that. You're far from a fool. You're the smartest, most gorgeous woman I am starting to fall for. I thought we had something special here, and I didn't want anything to spoil it. What if having all of this put you off me? Like I've said before, I just don't know how to deal with all of this without coming across as some kind of knobhead,' Elias smiles as he says this last bit. 'I promise I'm not a knobhead, even though I may seem like it right now.'

'Hmm, you do.'

'Look, will it help if I promise, promise, promise that I'll never do anything stupid like this again? I want to be transparent with you. Look, let me show you something...'

Elias fumbles in his pocket and pulls his phone out. He uses his fingerprint to open something and shows me the app for his bank account.

'Here...There's the balance. That's everything I've got.'

I look at the balance with all its zeros. 'You don't need to show me your bank account.'

'I do. If you think I'm hiding anything from you, let this show you that I'm genuine, and I'll never hide anything from you again. If I promise, Scout's honour, to never lie again, will you stick around with me and give me one last chance?'

I eye him suspiciously.

'Please stick around a bit longer and don't walk out on me, despite me being the biggest idiot ever. I'm sorry. The last thing I want to do is come across as some rich poser. I'm not very good at any of this – as you can see.'

'You just need to be truthful with me. Don't ever lie to me again. In return, I promise you can trust me. I like *you*, Elias, and definitely not your money.'

If we have any chance of this relationship working, we both need to be transparent with each other.

'No more fibs, okay?'

'Absolutely not. I'm so embarrassed about my behaviour. I can assure you that it'll never happen again.'

I move over to sit beside him on his sunbed and put my hand on his leg.

'Friends again then?'

'Friends.'

Elias looks at me with the biggest grin. 'So, you know how we said we would tell each other the truth?'

'Uh oh, what now?'

'Well, the truth is, all I want to do is jump into that pool with you. How quickly can you get out of those clothes?'

We both start laughing as I remove the summer dress I'm wearing and dive into the pool with Elias right behind me.

We make a big splash together as pool water sprays everywhere. Elias kisses me insatiably and holds me so close to him that I can feel that repaired heart of his beat against mine again. We may still have a few hurdles to climb, but during this intimate moment, I believe that everything may just work out after all.

Chapter Thirty-Five

For the next four weeks, when I am not re-visiting my book to get it ready to share with publishers and agents, I lie by the pool with Elias, drink cocktails in nearby bars and dine on seafood at the seaside restaurants. There have been no more lies, and I have stopped snooping around as the trust between us finally grows.

I am excited as we stand at the airport waiting for Jasmine and Poppy to arrive for their holiday, as I imagine them experiencing the villa and all the lovely things around the village. They are going to love it here. I just hope they keep the villa tidy.

Elias has swapped the little Fiat hire car for a bigger estate so that we can pick them up, and when I see the amount of luggage they have, I realise it was the right move.

'Mam,' shouts Jasmine when she sees me.

'You look amazing, Mam. Look at that tan you've got,' says Poppy.

'Aw, have I? It's surprising how much of a tan you get by walking about. Aww, come here you two. I've missed you,' I say, giving them both hugs.

'Yeah, we've really missed you, Mam. Seeing you on video chats isn't the same as popping around to the flat when I'm not well,' says Poppy.

'I know. That's the problem with me being over here. Anyway, it's only for a few more weeks and I'll be back.'

The thought of spending the winter in the flat alone, as Elias heads back to Manchester and we try to keep our long-distance relationship alive, is something I have tried to forget. For now, though, we are standing in this entrance hall, with the sun shining outside and it feels as though my whole world is complete as I look at Elias greeting my two girls. I have the most important people in my life in a place I have fallen in love with, and I'm going to make the most of every moment.

'I'm sure you've grown since I last saw you,' I tease Poppy.

'I think I've stopped growing, Mam. It's these wedges I picked up and my feet are bloody killing me.'

'Oi, language,' I say.

With the luggage packed up, Elias drives towards the villa with the girls in the back and laughs at their non-stop chattering. Apparently, one of the cabin crew was hot and Jasmine was disappointed that they ran out of bacon rolls on the plane. There are lots of exclamations from the back seat and everything we pass is either *lush*, *gorge*, or *totes amazing*.

When we reach the villa, all I hear is *Wow*.

Their jaws are hanging open as they look up towards the balconies at the front of the villa.

'Are you serious? This is where you've been staying?' says Jasmine.

'Yes. I didn't send you photos on purpose. I wanted it to be a surprise.'

'This is lush, and I mean *lush*,' says Jasmine.

'Imagine the Insta pics we can get here?' says Poppy. She is already pulling her phone out.

'Don't get me in that photo,' I warn.

They have only been here five minutes but already it feels so normal having them stay. Poppy and Jasmine are bickering about how they can get the best angle to take photos of the front of the villa. I leave them to it as Elias takes their bags upstairs.

'Mam, come quick,' says Jasmine.

I notice Poppy is outside, crouched down.

'Is she okay? What's happened?' At first, I wonder whether she is trying to get some fancy angled photo of the villa, but as I look down, her hand is reaching out into the bush at the front.

As I get closer, I hear an unmistakable noise.

'Look, Mam! Shh, come closer,' says Poppy.

Crouching down and looking into the bush, I see the most beautiful ginger kitten with big blue eyes looking up at me.

'Oh, my goodness. What a beauty. Quick, Jasmine, ask Elias for a bowl with some water. There might be a tin of tuna in the cupboard, but make sure it's the spring water one,' I say.

'Well, hello, my beauty. Aren't you gorgeous?' The pussy cat moves its teeny kitten paw towards me, and I feel the softness of newborn skin on the pad. I'll make sure we run to the shops for some cat food later.

'Shouldn't we give it milk, Mam?' says Jasmine as she finally returns.

'No, cats can be lactose intolerant. Water's better. I wonder where the mother is?'

While I put the water and tuna down, Jasmine and Poppy look around, but there is no sign of any of the rest of the litter or the mother. The kitten can't eat the tuna fast enough.

'What's this I hear about a kitten?' says Elias, crouching down to join me.

'Look.' I point at the kitten in the shade, and it seems to immediately take a shine to Elias and starts walking towards him.

'Do you have some sort of magic touch with kittens?' I tease.

The kitten comes out from under the bush and seems attracted by the lace on Elias's trainer. I notice how scrawny it is and vow to feed it up while I am here. When we make our way into the villa, the kitten carefully follows Elias.

'What should we do? I don't want to take it inside in case the mother comes looking for it. I mean, imagine if someone locked one of my babies in a villa and I couldn't get to them,' I say as I look towards my girls.

'This is different, Mam. I think it's been dumped,' says Poppy.

'Well, we'd better be careful. Let's make an area in the shade and leave the bowl there. We can keep an eye on it a bit longer and see if the mother returns.'

'I think that's the best idea. Anyway, come on, you want to see your rooms?' says Elias.

The girls can't believe their bedrooms as they look at the white gauzy curtains that sweep across the corners of their four-poster beds.

'This is like a fairy tale, Mam,' says Poppy.

As the girls settle in and unpack, quickly making themselves at home, Elias prepares us some lunch and I check on the little kitten again. It's now fast asleep in the shade after enjoying the food and water we gave it.

'He's still there, Elias.'

'Okay, well, let's see tomorrow what happens. In the meantime, I'll pop to the supermarket and see what I can find for it. Let's have lunch first though, yeah?'

Elias has prepared a salad with the rosiest red tomatoes and the freshest of ingredients that he found at the local market. I love how fresh the food is here. I arrange the table outside by the pool and call the girls down for lunch. I can't wait to see their faces when they investigate the pool.

As expected, they are quite dramatic when they see the outside. Poppy hangs onto Jasmine and pretends to faint.

'Oh… my… god… Seriously?' says Jasmine.

'I've died and gone to heaven,' says Poppy.

'I've got to post this *now*,' says Jasmine, taking photos immediately.

'Come on. You've got all day to take photos. Elias has prepared a gorgeous lunch for you both. Come and eat up.'

Jasmine breaks off a baguette, dropping crumbs everywhere around the pool.

'Where's your manners?'

'Sorry, Mam.'

I roll my eyes. They might be messy, but it's good to have them here, and I feel so content. It doesn't matter how old your children are, it's lovely to be under the same roof.

Elias tells the girls about what they can see around here. He talks about hiring a boat as he waits for his insurance payout. He wants to take them out to see the dolphins, but I manage to talk them out of that for now. After our mishap, I am still not ready to get on a boat with Elias, even though he wasn't to blame. Perhaps an organised tour would be better. As Elias chats to Jasmine and Poppy as though they have known each other forever, I enjoy watching them all get along.

'It's nice to see Mam looking so happy,' says Jasmine.

'Well, that's good to hear. I'm glad she looks happy,' says Elias. He looks at me and smiles.

'She's a very special woman, your mam is.'

'I know. She can be annoying, but she's alright, really,' says Poppy.

They all laugh as I pretend to scowl at them.

'So, Mam told us you bought the villa. It's so beautiful. You have good taste,' says Jasmine.

'Yes, you do. Fair play to you. I wish Dad had taste like this. He can be a bit chavvy at times, can't he?' says Poppy.

I stifle a laugh as I think of Michael back home getting up to goodness knows what.

Then I hear Poppy ask Elias something. 'Are your sons coming out soon?' she says.

'Oh, I'm not so sure. We haven't planned anything.'

Elias looks at me, and I see the hesitation in his eyes. Poppy and Jasmine have no idea that Danny still won't accept me. Meanwhile, James doesn't say anything negative or positive about me. He seems quite ambivalent.

'It would be great to meet them, wouldn't it?' says Poppy to Jasmine.

'Yeah, that'd be cool.'

Elias nods his head, and I look away. The last thing I want is a showdown with Danny in front of the girls. Once Jasmine and Poppy get an idea into their heads, though, they never let it drop.

'Why don't you invite them out? It's not like there aren't enough bedrooms. It'd be fun to hang around with people our age,' says Poppy.

'Yeah, I'll have to ask them,' says Elias.

'Call them now. Go on. See what they say.'

I begin to regret not having told them the truth about the situation. I want to make signals to tell them to stop, but instead, I sit there quietly, staring at them as they plead for Elias to pick up the phone right away.

'Umm, what do you think, Lucy? Shall I give them a ring?'

I can hardly say no, so I nod my head and think about how we will have to resolve this situation somehow if we are going to be together in the longer term. I suppose inviting the boys out is the best way to do it. Perhaps if they could see how fond we are of each other and they get along with the girls, Danny might come around. Or he might not.

Chapter Thirty-Six

I am surprised when Danny agrees to fly out with James two days later, especially since he is running the business. But as James has agreed, Danny has hopped straight on a flight too. I only hope that it's not because he's worried that I am getting too close to his dad, and I pray he will at least be civil to me in front of Jasmine and Poppy.

I can't help but feel nervous as Elias goes to the airport to pick up his sons, although the little kitten, Marmalade, consoles me. It was a collective decision to call him this because of his ginger colouring and the marmalade Renee from next door brings around. The name seems to suit him. He happily meows when he sees me, which I have a feeling might be a nicer greeting than I am going to get from Danny.

Jasmine and Poppy are sunbathing out by the pool, and I am petting and talking nonsense to Marmalade when I see Elias's car pull up. I hadn't planned on being on the doorstep when they arrived as I was pretty sure I would not be the first person Danny wanted to see. However, I wave and try to smile at Danny and James as they get out of the car.

'Hi there,' I shout across.

I think I hear a grunt from James, but Danny doesn't look at me.

'Guess what I picked up on the way to the airport?' says Elias with a big smile.

'Ooh, I don't know.'

He removes the boys' bags from the boot of the car and then pulls out a lovely blue cat bed, patterned with little black paw prints.

'You bought Marmalade a cat bed? It's perfect – I was just thinking we needed to get one for him.'

Yet again, we think alike. Now if only the boys can see how well suited we are. But, looking at Danny, who has walked straight past me and darted into the villa, I can't see how I am going to get around this. What hope do I have when he didn't even say hello to Marmalade!

For the rest of the day, I try to figure out how to handle him. If I try to be nice to him, it seems to aggravate him further. Sometimes, when the girls are in one of their funny moods, they are best left to their own devices, so that is what I do with Danny.

I promised myself I'd finally send my book out to my dream publishers and agents while the girls sunbathe, and I let the boys settle in. So, I figure I'll try to make small talk with him this evening at the barbecue we have planned. Hopefully, my happiness will be contagious as I celebrate sending my book out. I press send on the last submission on my list and blow the email a kiss for luck. I have a good feeling about this one.

I can see from the study window that James is by the pool sitting with Poppy. They seem to be getting along, and I watch Poppy as she playfully hits him over the head with a pool noodle. If only it were as easy as hitting Danny over the head with a noodle to bond with him, but I can see how hard it is for him to accept me. It is similar to how the girls struggled with Elias at the start and will no doubt take time.

I notice there is no sign of Danny or Jasmine. It is only when I am closing the laptop that I hear Jasmine's wedges banging against the tiles.

'Come in here,' she says to someone.

I listen to the male voice and realise it is Danny.

Oh, my goodness. She is taking Danny into her room? Please let it not be the worst imaginable scenario here. She hardly knows him!

I open the study door and leave it slightly ajar as I listen in. I promised I would stop snooping, but this involves Danny and my daughter. The rules are out of the window. I listen to their conversation, hardly breathing in case I miss something.

'How old was your mam?' says Jasmine.

I hear Danny tell her how she was only forty-nine.

'She'll never see her grandkids; she never saw James go to uni. It's not fair. She was so kind. She was a mum in a million. I can't get over it,' says Danny.

'No, that's awful. I can't imagine what it'd be like if I lost my mam. I'd never manage.'

'You do what you have to in order to cope. You take each day as it comes. There's no other choice.'

'Yeah, I suppose. How awful. I suppose it doesn't matter what you do, it's always on your mind.'

'Always. You know, when my dad won the lottery, it was amazing. For five minutes we were screaming and over the moon, but only for five minutes. When we calmed down and got over the shock, we quickly went back to thinking about Mum. The woman who should have been celebrating with us but was in her final days. All she ever wanted was for Dad to take it easy after his heart attack.

Before Mum got sick, we never thought that Dad would make a full recovery and she would end up dying before him.'

Poor Danny, it's not been easy for him. No wonder he can't accept me. Inside, he is hurting so much.

'I'm so sorry you've had such a tough time. But I'm sure your mother wouldn't want you to be sad. I know my mam wouldn't. She's the bestest mam you could ever have. All she wants is for me and Poppy to be happy and live our dreams. We don't always appreciate her, and I feel so bad now after what happened to your mum. She sounds amazing.'

Hearing how Jasmine talks about me leaves me feeling emotional. I never expected them to have such a deep conversation.

'Yeah, my mum was truly amazing. That's why I find it difficult to see Dad with someone else. He should be with Mum now enjoying their retirement.'

I step back and lean against the wall as I eavesdrop. Hearing him say this reiterates everything I thought. No wonder the poor lad has been so distant and hostile towards me.

'But it's not your dad's fault, or my mam's, that they're together. I'm sure, just like you, your mum would want your dad to be happy. Would she want him miserable being on his own all his life? It was hard for me to see my mam and dad separate. I even tried to get them back together, but then I realised Dad had been a jerk to Mam and she didn't deserve that.'

Since when did Jasmine become so sensible?

'No. You're right. I've been unfair. It's just that Dad could attract all sorts of gold diggers if they know what he's got. I can see your mother isn't like them. She wouldn't have raised such a nice daughter if she was.'

Tears spring to my eyes as I listen to the two of them talk about giving me a chance.

'I did notice she was very kind to that kitten outside. I wanted to stop and say something and have a look at it, but I didn't know what to say. I've been so mean to her that she might not forgive me.'

'Oh, she's very forgiving. I promise. My mam doesn't hold a grudge. Unless you manage to ruin her brand-new top. She doesn't forget things like that.'

They both laugh and I join them with a giggle.

'What was that?' asks Danny.

'What?'

'I thought I heard someone laugh outside. God, I hope no one's overheard our conversation.'

'No, everyone's down by the pool.'

'Are you sure?' Danny pops his head out of the room and sees me at the side of the door. Sheepishly I smile at him while cursing myself as I realise that I have been caught snooping about yet again. I just hope he doesn't tell his dad.

Chapter Thirty-Seven

Marmalade is purring in his cat basket in the kitchen as we take drinks out for the barbecue that Elias is preparing by the pool. He is quite a content little thing and quickly becoming a valued member of our household.

All the young ones hang around the pool in shorts and flip-flops whilst I float around in my strappy summer dress feeling like I belong here. I never thought I'd fit in somewhere like this, but Renee has welcomed me with open arms to the neighbourhood. She says she will introduce me to some of the other neighbours once both sets of offspring leave, and I have found myself quite looking forward to it.

I look across to Danny, who is drinking a bottle of beer. He glances over at me, and I smile. After he caught me sneaking around, I fear I may have damaged all the good that Jasmine did, but he lifts his beer bottle as if to say cheers and nods his head at me. That's certainly a more positive interaction than I have had so far with him. I decide to try my luck at a conversation and gingerly approach him since he is sitting with Poppy.

'Hi, you enjoying the place so far?' A bit of a lame question, but how do you thaw the ice with someone who has taken a dislike to you through no fault of your own and who then caught you eavesdropping?

'Yeah, great. I didn't know I'd have so much in common with Poppy here. She plays soccer at uni. I'd no idea.'

I am so relieved that he is finally willing to speak to me civilly.

'Yeah, she's very good too, aren't you? She has a whole language of her own. Like offside and flip flap, what on earth is that? I thought she was playing soccer in her flip-flops when she said that.'

'Oh, Mam, you're so embarrassing,' says Poppy, rolling her eyes.

'Dad's the same. Comes out with some right clangers,' says Danny.

'That's old people for you,' interrupts Poppy.

'Oi, excuse me,' I say.

I look across to the barbecue, where Elias has left James in charge for a moment as he heads over to join the three of us.

'What's going on here then? Am I missing anything exciting?'

'No, just talking about the stuff you come out with,' says Danny.

'All intellectual, I assume?' says Elias.

'Umm, no, quite the opposite, but never mind.' Poppy and Danny laugh, and Elias pretends to look offended. Then he takes my hand in front of Danny, and I worry he might find it difficult. I watch Danny as he notices, but then he looks at his dad and smiles. *Oh, Jasmine! You have worked wonders on him.*

'Did Danny tell you he's renting a space for artists to display their work, in memory of his mum?' says Elias.

'Oh, how fantastic. Well, if we can do anything at all to help, please let us know.'

'I will. Although Dad said that you've been writing a book.'

'Yeah, it's finally finished. The scary bit comes next – waiting to see what the publishers and agents think of it.'

'Well, if you ever fancy doing a reading at the new place, let me know. The venue I've rented is suitable for all kinds of creativity, not just paintings. We're going to hold poetry readings too, although that's more my girlfriend's sort of thing,' says Danny.

'Gosh, that's so kind of you. I'd love that. I'm not sure it'll get published. I mean, I hope it will, but it's not easy. But if it does and I build up a bit more confidence about public speaking, then that would be a great idea. Thank you.'

Danny smiles at me and this conciliatory gesture feels like an important moment between us all. I have finally been accepted.

As I watch Danny and Poppy chatting, Jasmine helping James with the barbecue and Elias walking into the kitchen to check on Marmalade, my life feels complete. There is nothing more I could possibly wish for.

Chapter Thirty-Eight

It is eerily quiet after our adult children finally leave France to return home. It takes a while to get used to the emptiness around the villa, although Marmalade fills any void with all his mischief. I don't dare tell Elias that I caught him climbing up the silk curtains in the living room yesterday. I must pick up more cat toys to keep him amused the next time I go shopping.

It's surprising how busy we have been, as Elias and I make the most of the last days of summer in this gorgeous villa. I will miss the neighbours I have coffee with and the marmalade that Renee still insists on dropping off, despite the cupboards bursting with it. I will miss the cocktails in the sunshine by the sea, and I will miss Elias more than anything. We haven't discussed how we will manage our long-distance relationship when we get home. We have simply made the most of these happy times and not tried to plan anything or look too far into the future, but now that the time to leave is drawing near and I need to organise a pet passport for Marmalade, it is a subject that can no longer be avoided.

During our walk home along the beachfront from our favourite local bar, I bring up the subject of Marmalade's passport.

'I think we'll need to book the vet as soon as possible. I need to organise Marmalade.'

'Ah, I wanted to speak to you about that,' says Elias.

I start to panic and kick at the sand beneath my feet. What if Elias wants to keep Marmalade with him in Manchester or, even worse, suggests that we don't take him home with us? Imagine if he is a monster who wants to find a new home for him.

I am almost afraid to hear what he is about to say.

'What's wrong?'

'Nothing's wrong. Quite the opposite. I wanted to ask you…'

My heart quickens as I look at the ocean in front of us as the waves lap back and forth onto the shore.

'It's just that, I thought…' Before Elias can finish, my mobile starts ringing.

'Oh no, what timing. I won't answer it.' I swipe at my phone to end the call but notice it is Soraya.

'You'd better answer it,' says Elias.

'Don't worry, I'll call her back.'

'But it's Wednesday. You always have your video chat with Soraya and Carol on a Wednesday night. You've never missed it.'

'It's okay. I'll call them back as soon as we get home. We'll only be a minute.'

I need to sort Marmalade out first, as this conversation is really troubling me.

'Well, in that case…'

Elias pulls me to him and strokes my hair.

'What was it you wanted to say about Marmalade?' I say, desperately.

'It's just that I think it would be a shame to send Marmalade to the UK.'

'What?' *No, Elias. Please do not burst my bubble.*

'So, I've been thinking. We have joint responsibilities here now. We can't really leave them to go back. How about you move in with me here permanently? It's time for a new chapter now. You, being a writer, will hopefully agree with that one.'

'A new chapter?'

'Yeah, let's not go home. The kids will be happy enough to visit us. I mean, look what a success it was having them all stay.'

'Yeah, Jasmine told me she speaks to Danny nearly every day, and James is going down to Cardiff next week to stay with them.'

'Exactly, and I was thinking... I know you miss your friends, but I'd like to invite Soraya and Andrew out to stay. Of course, Carol is welcome too. But I wanted to thank them all again. If it hadn't been for that birthday trip, I'd never have met you and my life would be far less exciting. What's the point in having money when you don't have anyone to do things with?'

'Well, I know they'd certainly love to come over.'

As we put the key in the front door of the villa, Marmalade comes out and pokes his sleepy head around. He stretches and does the cutest of yawns.

'How could I possibly leave this little one's home? Of course, I'll stay here with you.'

I bend down to stroke Marmalade, who lets out the biggest purr. If I was a cat, I would be purring right now too.

A Letter from Helga

For my sixth book, I wanted to take you on a journey to a glamorous setting with yachts, the rich and famous, and a foray into how the other half lives. However, in keeping with all my books, the main character is a regular Welsh woman who gets immersed into this fairy tale world and often feels uncomfortable in her surroundings.

This was such a fun story to write as I researched places such as the casinos of Monte Carlo and the streets of Saint-Tropez and hopefully you fantastic readers will enjoy this visit too. I hope that *Escape to the French Riviera* will whisk you away into a world where dreams come true, and love prevails.

I am always responsive on social media, so please feel free to contact me if you enjoy the story. You can contact me via:

www.twitter.com/HelgaJensenF
www.facebook.com/helgajensenfordeauthor
www.instagram.com/helgajensenauthor

Acknowledgements

Thank you to Keshini Naidoo at Hera Books and the rest of the team at Hera and Canelo for the wonderful opportunities I have had publishing my stories. These past few years working with you all has been truly amazing. As all my books will acknowledge, my editor, Jennie Ayres, is also truly amazing, and she is the person responsible for whipping this final story into shape. Her input is invaluable. Thank you also to Lindsey Harrad for a fabulous copy edit and Lynne Walker for yet another wonderful proofread. Diane of D Meacham Design has designed another stunning cover and I am so delighted. I have always wanted a pink-themed cover so this could be my favourite one of all!

Thank you to RYA-trained JK for listening to me plot out a yachting incident and to Mr B for being the best boy. My amazing friends, special people, and writing buddies, thank you for all your support. To my writing bestie, Jenny, I am so grateful for your words of wisdom in any crisis! Also, a huge thank you to my fellow PhD cohort, Sarah, for your invaluable advice about yachts. I will always remember you when I see a yacht and remind myself that they are made of fibreglass!

Finally, the biggest thank you to every reader who may pick this book up. I can't thank you enough for choosing to read my stories.

Happy reading X